A GORDIAN WEB

A GORDIAN WEB

BOOK TWO IN THE SPIDER TRILOGY

GUY BUTLER

POLKAJIG
PRESS

A GORDIAN WEB

Copyright © 2013 by Guy Butler.

Publishing Consultant, Flying Pig Media
Cover & Interior Design by VMC Art & Design, LLC

ISBN: 978-0-9848726-2-6

*"A Gordian Knot" is a metaphor for a problem
deemed insurmountable, yet easily solved
by thinking outside the box.*

*When the impossible problem involves
The Spider, it is better characterized
as "A Gordian Web."*

ACKNOWLEDGEMENTS

This novel is dedicated to the Butler and Wojcie-chowski families—especially my wife, Teri—and our children, Jadzia and Remy.

I am most grateful to several wonderful friends and acquaintances for their diligent comments after reading countless earlier drafts: Janna Buckley, Mark Estrin, Bill Fagan, Roman Yurkiewicz, Ted Robinson, Daniel Mikolaschek and Bryan Thomas.

In particular, very special thanks to Kristin Lindstrom and Victoria Colotta.

A
GORDIAN
WEB

PROLOGUE

From worse to worst

E uphoria should have abounded that spring, but there was none. In their hope-filled dreams, the sun shone, birds sang and the air was crisp and clean, but these dreams shattered against hard reality. At the very least, those Poles who survived the six-year Nazi scourge would rejoice in the freedom of self-government, but the situation deteriorated from worse to worst.

The brief interlude created by Germany's retreat from Poland and Russia's establishment as 'the new landlord,' allowed Polish Resistance, known as the Armia Krajowa (AK), to melt into obscurity. This nettlesome decision was predestined by Premier Joseph Stalin's massive Soviet forces taking a ringside seat during the Warsaw Uprising to watch the AK and German garrison decimate each other. Stalin, the self-proclaimed 'Man of Steel,' ordered his invading armies to adopt the role of passive observers, boasting he preferred to occupy a Poland unencumbered by annoying freedom fighters. The sixty-three days of genocide on the streets of Warsaw went a long way to accomplishing that mission. President Władysław Raczkiewicz and the Polish government-in-exile finally ordered all surviving Armia Krajowa freedom fighters to disband on January 20, 1945, in preference to certain death in a Gulag labor camp.

Stalin knew exactly what he was doing, as members of the Armia Krajowa were far from subservient during the years of oppressive Nazi occupation. In fact, they aggressively resisted giving up their country to Adolph Hitler. Gestapo tactics never quelled the AK in Poland or for that matter, the Partizani in Yugoslavia and those two brave groups worked to drain the resources of the Third Reich, eventually driving the Germans to distraction.

Throughout these intensely difficult times, hearts were uplifted by the exploits of a fearless Polish folk hero known as the Spider, or Pająk. The legend sprouted from the deeds of a young AK patriot called Czeslaw Orlowski, who claimed graphic responsibility for the mayhem he foisted upon the enemy. His infamous calling card depicted an oval surrounded by eight legs — a pająk. The fable mushroomed over time by the AK crediting every successful sabotage to the Spider and leaving his calling card at the scene.

The People's Commissariat for State Security, the dreaded NKGB, was painfully aware of the unifying effect this 'legend of the Spider' was having upon the proud Polish nation. If the spirit of this populace was to be crushed, they knew they had to eliminate the Spider very quickly and very publicly.

But first, they had to find him.

However, even the copious files of the NKGB had failed to note that their quarry had spent the past eighteen months on a series of secret missions for British Special Forces.

One of the most brazen took place right under the nose of Dr. Joseph Goebbels and his Nazi Ministry of Propaganda causing massive embarrassment to the Third Reich and a corresponding surge of patriotism in London. The Spider engineered the daring escape of one of Britain's favorite sons, international soccer icon Malcolm McClain from the high-security POW camp in Maribor and as a by-product, a strong bond of friendship developed between Orlowski and McClain.

But a subsequent mission trumped even that success when the Spider led a marauding band of Polish and Yugoslav guerillas on a seemingly suicidal mission to destroy the final testing of Germany's V-2 rocket program; a weapon of such technical sophistication it would assure dominance in the theatre of war. The scientist needed just a few final tweaks before presenting their Fuhrer with certain victory and an eternal place in history as the Emperor of Europe. However, the ants ate the elephant and the decline of the Third Reich was ensured.

The British wartime Prime Minister, grateful for the heroic exploits that had quantifiably saved millions from death or servitude, was persuaded that political asylum for the Spider would be both a justified and popular conclusion to these adventures. So the Brits also sought the elusive Pole, but for entirely different reasons than the Russians.

The NKGB, given its number one priority by Premier Stalin to find the Spider, used their disciplined, methodical practices to identify traditionally Polish-occupied regions in eastern Germany that might have high potential as his hiding place. Neither side was yet aware that after urging his Krakow division of the AK to retreat into obscurity, Czeslaw Orlowski married his sweetheart and settled down as a nondescript farmer in Żagań, a small bucolic town in Lower Silesia.

By unfortunate coincidence, Russian armies massed

rapidly in this area as Stalin planned to repatriate all lands east of the River Oder back into Poland, thereby laying claim by the Soviets to strategic access to the Baltic.

The noose was tightening and the Spider could feel it inching closer. Several weeks before, he had pleaded his predicament by letter to Malcolm McClain, his dear friend in England, and even managed to persuade a Red Cross delegation to attempt delivery.

Who knows if it made it past the keen eyes of Russian censors? It's this damn uncertainty without hope I could do without, Chez worried.

Malcolm, my dear friend.

I hope you are in good health and still playing for Blackpool. Jadwiga and I are happily married and live with her mother and four sisters on a small farm. I cannot reveal where because I'm afraid our days on this earth are numbered.

The many hours we spent together during the escape from Maribor were dangerous at the time but all I remember is the joy we shared when talking about our girls and the many

children we would have after the war.
I have dreamt about our future kids
growing up and playing together but
the Russian armies are hunting for me
with intensity you cannot imagine; the
soldier who kills me will be rewarded
well and I sense the end is very close.

If this letter reaches you, know you
are in my thoughts. When we last
parted on the runway in Semic, do you
remember promising that if I ever got
in trouble you would send a couple
of lads from Belfast to bail me out?
Well, a couple might not be enough,
I am a stalked animal with a price on
my head so we will probably never see
each other again.

I hope you have found bliss with your
beautiful Margery. Enjoy your love,
your family and your freedom. They
are the most precious things in this
life. Your prayers would mean a great
deal at this time; I am in desperate
need of a miracle.

Your friend forever.
Czeslaw.

PART ONE

CHAPTER ONE

1945 – Hidden in Plain Sight

He was puzzled, but couldn't quite put his finger on why. Long before the cock crowed he lay wide awake and restless, trying to reconcile an uneasy feeling coursing through him. It was a familiar sixth sense; one that had never let him down and saved his life on many occasions. What was it trying to warn him about? The peril could not be inside or outside the immediate farmhouse because his geese provided cacophonous security. No, this pressure in his temples had not yet manifested itself into anything recognizable so his tortured mind strained to filter the cause of his alarm. Perhaps it was an out-of-place sound somewhere in the distance. And then it all crystalized,—there were no sounds. The wild animals of the valley must have retreated behind the security of silence in the face of some intrusion into their world. The danger would surely head his way and he needed to be ready.

Although it was late February and bitterly cold in this part of Silesia, the young farmer had beads of sweat covering his forehead as he raised himself off the pillow. He decided to get up and walk around to clear his head, so he glanced over at his wife, Jadwiga, to make sure she was still asleep. Her large brown eyes popped open the moment she felt his gaze upon her. Now there could be absolutely no doubt that something was wrong,—but what?

"I feel it too, ukochanie, this will be the day they finally find us. Hug me close," Jadwiga whispered.

There was a thin film of ice all over the metal water jug in the bathroom. Czeslaw filled the white pottery basin and sluiced the cold water over his head and torso before drying himself rigorously with a rough towel. It brought a pink sheen to his skin, which he quickly captured with a fresh flannel shirt, tucking it into his work pants as he returned to the bedroom.

Jadwiga was now anxiously peering into the farmyard through a small gap in the curtains.

"Czeslaw, I can see one of our geese, she is sleeping but moved her head. At least for now, our yard is secure but you need to leave the farm immediately. I can buy you time by sending them on a false trail...."

"......I appreciate your love and your bravery—more than I can say—but that simply won't work, Jadzie. The Russian troops will hand you over to the NKGB and I could not live with the thought of what those bastards might do to you.

"Get your mother and sisters up, pack essentials and hide out at the railway station. I'm going to contact a couple of old friends who might be able to shed a little light. I'll meet you there as soon as I can—but if I'm not there by noon, catch the next train to Poznan and stay with your cousin, Franek. The Germans abandoned Poznan to the Soviets last month so there's still great confusion there, but your Russian will serve you well. I'll rendezvous as soon as I feel it's safe. Don't worry." He kissed her tenderly and left the room, pausing only to grab his dark blue woolen jacket.

The frozen ground crackled underfoot as he pushed his old Wul-Gum motorcycle from the shed to the edge of the farm before pounding all his weight onto the kick-starter. As he passed through the farm's five-bar gate he was planning to turn right towards the town, hoping to arouse Szymon Grabowski. Żagań's elderly postmaster was a proud man who still kept tabs on what was left of the Polish resistance in this area. The thought brought a grim smile to Czeslaw's cold lips.

"That old goat will be able to tell me if something is brewing."

Szymon lived above the Post Office and the young man could be there in less than five minutes. Then, for some unknown reason he stopped and stared into the night sky. His mouth pursed in determination and relying on instinct, he suddenly swerved left and accelerated towards Przemcow.

Since settling down on the farm, Czeslaw always rose at dawn to begin his chores; swilling pigs, planting or harvesting crops, lugging great pails of water to the house; backbreaking tasks small farmers perform in all corners of the world. When finished, he would sometimes unwind by cruising the thirty kilometers to Przemcow and assist Zenon Majewski at his small grocery store. Zenon had once helped Czeslaw out by lending the young stranger some of his murdered son's clothes to make him more presentable for a pending date with his future wife, Jadwiga. Czeslaw had never forgotten this act of kindness and the frequent visits with the old man allowed him to replace some of the load a missing son might have carried. In truth, Czeslaw also enjoyed Zenon as the father figure in his life and it never hurt if the old man filled the young farmer in on any unusual troop activity in the area.

On this occasion, there was no cruising. The Wul-Gum roared through the crisp night air at purposeful speed and the closer Czeslaw got to Przemcow, the stronger his intuition warned him about danger ahead. By the time he was within sight of the village, he had to pull over and take deep breaths to regain control of his heartbeat. As he carefully concealed the motorcycle within a thick copse of mature trees, his persona morphed into his alter ego, the Spider.

By now, birds were welcoming the new day and frosted dew tossed off sparkles from the light growing in the pink sky to the east. A tall, healthy pine tree allowed him to climb unobserved onto a high branch where he waited patiently for the sun. As daylight arrived, the perch gradually afforded him a clear view of Plac Wolnosci, the small square containing the Majewski Grocery Store. Nothing appeared amiss,— but the hair on the back of his neck seldom lied.

CHAPTER TWO

Przemcow

High in the pine tree, the Spider remained motionless and waited. After about ninety minutes, two Russian soldiers departed Majewski's Grocery Store, their body language transmitting a clear visual message. If they had merely been buying milk or bread, they would have strolled out casually; these two left with frenetic movement, their eyes darting furtively around as they jumped into their vehicle and headed north. Either they had stolen something—or they had been up to no good. Czeslaw was now certain his friend Zenon was in dire straits.

He shimmied back to the ground and dipped a rag into the gas tank of the Wul-Gum to scrub the pine tar from his hands. Then, using every piece of cover at his disposal, he stealthily approached the rear of the store. It took almost twenty minutes before he finally located himself under the windowsill of the rear room where he knew Zenon Majewski slept, cooked and eked out his lonely existence. He strained his ears for clues and suddenly tensed at the sound of metal on metal transmitting through the thin glass.

Could be my paranoid imagination but that sure sounded like a live round going into the chamber of a Kalashnikov, he thought.

To create enough distraction for a quick glimpse into the room, he scuttled around to the front door, knocked and called out, "Morning, Zenon," in a loud voice, then scurried back to beneath the window. As he cautiously raised his eyes above the sill, he saw the prone body of his friend on the floor and the broad backs of two Russian soldiers sighting their rifles onto the interior door.

So, a trap had been baited and the most likely prey was a Spider.

How could they possibly have traced me to Prezemcow? he pondered before a dark rage overtook him. Returning silently to the front door, he eased it open just a few inches, enough for him to reach up with his hand and mute the spring-loaded bell before sliding silently inside. He knew Majeweski's store well and vaulted softly onto the counter. The oak planks that served as a floor were known to squeak in protest against their nails but the counter was solid. Czeslaw moved like a ghost to the rear of the store and lodged himself above the frame of the interior door by supporting his entire weight from a giant meat hook that Majeweski used to hang the occasional large ham. The Spider took firm grasp of the hook with one hand and braced both feet against the wall, freeing him to reach down with his other hand to knock loudly on the door.

"Zenon, it's me, the Spider. How are you doing today?" An immediate volley of hot lead exploded through the door into the space where a normal person might be expected to stand. There was a silence of perhaps ten seconds as the soldiers in Zenon's back room listened for any sounds of life. Then they pushed the decimated door open wide and entered the store to claim their trophy.

"Chto za huy! Where the fuck is the body? If he isn't dead he must be mortally wounded—yet I don't even see any blood……"

Czeslaw watched and listened from above until that perfect moment arrived, then dropped down to wrap a strong arm around each man's neck, cracking their unsuspecting skulls together as they fell. All three collapsed in an ungainly heap on the floor of the store but the Spider was up in a crouched fighting position immediately, his sharp knife seeking a target. With the whistle of air over steel, the tracheas of both groggy Russians were sliced back to their spines.

He dragged the dead bodies behind the counter and quickly locked the front door before hurrying back to check on Zenon. The old man was still alive but Czeslaw knew he had to act fast; the noise of the volley might keep Plac Wolnosci deserted of locals but would certainly encourage a visit from any Russian troops within earshot. He cradled Zenon's head and stroked back the old man's hair as he whispered softly.

"Zenon, it's me, Czeslaw. How did this happen?"

Old Majeweski had stubbornly hung onto life for this very moment and, as he stared fondly at his young friend, he spluttered out some gasping last breaths.

"They...came here... looking for...the Spider. I knew it must...be you... because...they traced him... by a Wul-Gum." Czeslaw laid him back and ran into the store to get a cup of water whereupon the old man found the strength to continue. "I told them nothing... They got your bike's description... from someone in...Krakow. Get rid...of your bik..." And with that, he was gone. The young Pole gently closed Zenon's eyelids over the dead man's blank stare.

The Spider stood up and crossed himself. He had not been involved with an organized religion since he was four or five but it felt like the right thing to do for his friend. Then he spun around, returning to the front of the store livid with rage. He kicked the corpses of the dead soldiers repeatedly until emotion overcame him and he sank onto the floor, buried his head in his hands and cried.

As suddenly as the sensation had welled up, it disappeared and the cold grey eyes of the Spider stared at nothing as he re-assessed his situation. Then he sprang to his feet and left the store by Zenon's rear window without a backward glance.

I probably have a little time while they investigate the store, search the immediate area and interview every Pole in the district about sightings of a Wul-Gum motorcycle. His mind flashed to the obvious origination of this incriminating evidence, his old AK friends, Brunon and Filip in Krakow. Even though they would almost certainly have been tortured, he made a mental note to check them out when the occasion arose.

First things first, I have to get to Poznan and protect my family. On second thoughts, these bastards are bound and determined to hunt me to the ends of the Earth, even more so after they find those two bodies in the store. Should I head in the opposite direction to put as much distance as I can between me and Jadwiga?

He was well aware he had no safe transportation and no idea when the sand in the hourglass would run out.

No matter, either way I'm fucked!

The young Orlowski was now in full Spider-mode, nerves of steel showing no regard for his own safety but a nagging clinical analysis of his situation causing him to contemplate his options.

If the Ruskis are looking for a man on a Wul-Gum, that is what they're going to get, but I cannot lead them to my family. No, I'm damn sure whenever they catch and kill me, I have to be hundreds of kilometers away from Jadwiga to give her a chance to survive.

With this thought foremost in his mind, he returned to where he had hidden his bike, gunned it into life and roared noisily through the center of Przemcow on a beeline to Warsaw. Several Russian soldiers were surveying the carnage inside Majeweski's Grocery Store when they heard the motorcycle thunder through the square. Their captain ran outside in time to see a plume of dust headed east before excitedly yelling into a field telephone.

"This is Captain Voloshin reporting from Plac Wolnosci in Przemcow. The squad charged with interrogating the old man about the Spider must have hit the jackpot. Unfortunately, both Yakunin and Sheremetyev have been brutally murdered, along with the witness. The Spider now has the blood of two brave Russians and an elderly, innocent Pole on his hands and we almost caught him in the act. I personally just saw him speed out of here on a motorcycle and it looks like he's headed towards Leszno. It's only about forty miles away so get roadblocks set up immediately. Try to take him alive, this bastard is going to have a very public trial so this damn country can watch their hero die for brutally murdering one of his own countrymen.

"Oh, and tell Colonel Tarasov I wish to personally serve on the firing squad."

CHAPTER THREE

Concern in London

U nbeknownst to him, Czeslaw's desperate letter to Malcolm McClain was in the hands of the addressee. Red Cross Captain Laura Moore was never one to break a promise and almost the first thing she did upon returning to her base in Geneva was to hand the stained missive to her boss, General Carlo Santoro, requesting he ensure it left for London in the next diplomatic pouch. After the letter's arrival in England, it took several weeks before His Majesty's Post Office finally delivered it to Blackpool Football Club, the legendary home of 'the Seasiders' on the northwest coast of England.

McClain had left his native Belfast in the early

1930's to establish an enviable professional career with Blackpool, one of the top teams in the English First Division and as a stalwart defender for his country, Northern Ireland. Now a national treasure due to his exploits on and off the field, Malcolm read the message from Poland in shock. He had little knowledge of the Spider's many covert exploits but no doubts that the man had saved his life on several occasions during the escape from Maribor. In addition, he loved Chez Orlowski like a brother. Malcolm read the short plea for help repeatedly, his emotions welling at his apparent helplessness. The other players shied away at the unusual sight of the team's tough defensive player huddled in a corner of the locker room, head in hands, shoulders heaving from heavy sobbing. Somebody ran to the front office and as a result, the calm voice of manager Joe Smith brought McClain back to reality and the two talked privately for almost an hour.

"This has suddenly become the most important thing in my life, Joe. Because without this man, I would be dead. I'm going to do everything humanly possible to return the favor, even if it means going over there and fighting by his side to the end."

Joe Smith had known McClain for over a decade and they had developed a close friendship. "Malky, calm down, you might have more weapons at your disposal than you think. Let's make a couple of phone calls before that Belfast blood of yours rolls to a boil."

The sage Joe Smith was proved correct, as politically, the immensely popular Malcolm McClain could not be ignored; to do so would alienate any politician from an entire generation, both male and female. The phone calls made that day granted McClain a high-level meeting with Lord Acheson and Field Marshal Alexander at the War Office in London to discuss the situation. Wheels were set in motion to extricate the Spider and his family to the safety of the British Isles.

Whenever a meeting of this delicacy makes it onto the political calendar, Whitehall decides who 'needs to know' and subsequent briefings set ground rules that ensure the end result conforms to His Majesty's Government's position on the issue. As such, the day before McClain's scheduled meeting, Field Marshal, the Honorable Sir Harold Alexander, was invited to Number Ten for a private conversation with Winston Spencer Churchill.

The Prime Minister had recently returned from Yalta, a miserable resort in Southern Ukraine, where he attended a brutally exhausting summit conference with Roosevelt and Stalin to discuss carving up the post-war world. He was in animated conversation with Marion Holmes, one of his favorite secretaries, as the field marshal was shown into the White Drawing Room through four paneled doors, hinged back to create a ten foot by twelve-foot opening. The famous façade of Number Ten, official residence of every British Prime Minister since 1735, belies the size and opulence of the building beyond, no better example being this magnificent corner room with two, twelve-pane, Georgian sash windows on each of its two exterior walls. The Prime Minister was seated at an antique kidney shaped desk between two of those windows and absorbed with Ms. Holmes as they perused a pile of official communiques. Wary of inadvertently overhearing privileged conversation, Alexander stared upwards at the painted plaster relief ceiling and coughed politely.

"Ahem, Mr. Prime Minister, I can wait outside until you are finished?"

"Nonsense, Harry, Holmes and I were just discussing who received the most bed-bug bites at the Vorontsov Palace. Mind you, some bloody palace with one bathroom for every two dozen guests. Poor Holmes, most of our delegation resorted to finding a bush outside rather than wait. I think Stalin got quite a laugh out of the whole damn fiasco.

"Any way, Holmes, KBO, the Field Marshal and I need about thirty minutes of uninterrupted privacy."

"KBO, sir?" Alexander whispered with a puzzled look.

"Top secret code for Keep Buggering On," laughed the indefatigable septuagenarian. "Stalin had all our rooms bugged so we had quite a bit of fun feeding him nonsense to pass the time."

The ever-faithful Marian Holmes closed the hinged doors behind her and the two men were able to relax into an informal conversation more reflective of their long personal friendship.

"Well Harry, I understand you are meeting the great Malcolm McClain tomorrow?" Churchill grunted through a cloud of cigar smoke. Although it was the middle of a Sunday afternoon, the great man was wearing a red and gold dressing gown over his pajamas as he alternated attention between the cigar and a large snifter of brandy. "He is a remarkable man and his popularity in this country is quite amazing. You know he came to London yesterday, scored the Blackpool goal that sank Chelsea's title hopes—and the entire bloody crowd cheers him off the field! Chelsea, Harry, where the most impassioned football fans in London inhabit 'the shed' at Stamford Bridge. They have unrelentingly booed some of the greatest players in the world when they came to play against Chelsea. Yet McClain gets cheered off the bloody field!" Churchill then started to chuckle. "If Malcolm McClain ever decides to run for Parliament, I must make sure he is in my Conservative Party.

"Apart from all that, Harry, is McClain aware of everything Mr. Orlowski has pulled off for us over the past year? Tens of thousands of our citizens are alive today because of this Spider character and if there is anything we can do to help him in time of need—within reason—I think it should be done."

"I doubt he knows any details, Winston. The disruption of Hitler's V-2 rocket program is still very hush-hush—just in case the bastard manages to revive it yet again. The British people's morale is still slowly recovering from the pasting we took from the V-1 attacks. If they had any inkling that Hitler almost launched rockets ten times the strength, there would be certain panic. You will be able to tell all in your memoirs—after the war is over."

"Too bloody right Harry and let's keep it that way. Regardless, elevate the status of getting the Spider and his family safely out of western Germany—soon to be Poland thanks to Yalta. In fact, elevate it to high priority; it's the least we can do.

"Here we are, sitting outside the gates of Berlin at the behest of the Americans waiting for Joe bloody Stalin—or 'The Vozhd' as he now likes to call himself—to take his own sweet bloody time securing his Eastern Empire before he marches in for the coup de grace. Franklin is very seriously ill; a mere shadow of the man he used to be and Uncle Joe is taking full advantage of the situation. To the best of our knowledge, this Truman chappie has not even been apprised by Franklin's inner circle and is completely unprepared to take over should anything happen.

"Cigar?"

Sir Harold, an old friend, was well aware that this invitation was Churchill's patented crutch when he needed to buy time to think. There was a distinct ritual involved, requiring undivided attention by both men as they each pierced the end of their '*La Aroma de Cuba*' with a Swan match rather than using a cutter. Churchill twizzled the end of his cigar over the flame of a candle, waiting until the ash began to glow before he passed the candle to his friend. The ensuing silence lasted a full five minutes before the Prime Minister felt any need to continue their discussion.

"Allow me to explain the pickle, Harry. Two of my main objectives last week were to protect Greece and Poland from being completely mauled by the Russian Bear after this war. I negotiated some breathing room on the former but the post war boundaries for Poland will shift significantly to the west, ceding valuable land east of the Curzon Line to Russia in return for returning Silesia to Poland. The new boundary will most likely be along the Oder and Niesse rivers to gift the Russian Navy a warm-water port on the Baltic. Unfortunately for the Orlowskis, this decision most likely puts wherever they are hiding firmly under Russian control."

"Do we have time to extract these folks whilst they are still technically in Germany?" Alexander interjected.

"That, my old friend, is a technicality Uncle Joe will

vehemently object to. As far as he is concerned, what Russia occupies, Russia owns and they are massing for the Oder Offensive even as we speak. As if that is not enough, MI6 has picked up traffic indicating our friend, the Spider. is currently number one on the NKGB's most wanted list. This is going to be far from easy, Harry, if not impossible." Another perfect opportunity for both men to pull pensively on their Cubans was taken but Mr. Churchill still had the floor.

"I am fairly certain I can get King George to grant the Orlowski family political asylum and subsequent citizenship as I have brought the matter up with him a couple of times without apparent objection. Once that's been achieved, I would like to get them here as soon as possible. However, the Spider is a major thorn in Russia's side and they are hell-bent on exterminating him to destroy the legend as publically as they ca…"

He did not do it very often, but on this occasion, Field Marshal Alexander interrupted the Prime Minister as an amazing conundrum unfolded in his mind.

"…So if we accede to McClain's request and extricate the Orlowskis, Uncle Joe gets pissed—which might jeopardize the assault on Berlin and our relationship with America and Russia after the war. To make matters worse, the President seems to have orphaned us in recognition of Russia's strategic domination of

Eastern Europe. Can't really blame him for that in light of his failing health and a new page about to turn. What the bloody hell do we do, Winston?"

"It's what we cannot do, old chap. We cannot let the Russians or the Americans think for a second that we are working against the common good and ... we cannot, and will not, let the Spider down. So KBO as we say in the Crimea."

Keep buggering on with what? puzzled the veteran soldier as he rose to leave. The Prime Minister must have read his mind because he placed a comforting arm around his friend as they reached the chequered black and white tile floor adorning the entrance hall of the residence.

"This is a Gordian Knot, Harry. Do what your namesake, Alexander the Great did. Slice through it with your sword!"

After dissecting the seemingly insurmountable problem during a restless and sleepless night, the shrewd mind of Alexander knew exactly what he had to do.

Winnie is right—we need a sword—and I know exactly where I can find a bloody sharp one.

Before he and Lord Acheson met to placate Malcolm McClain the next morning, Sir Harold Alexander summoned Brigadier Bryan Zumwalt, commander of the elite Special Air Services to leave his southern Italian base in Brindisi by the next long flight to London.

Three days later found the two elite SAS officers in deep discussion over lunch at Boodle's, an exclusive, eighteenth century private club located at 28 St. James Street. An unspoken code was in effect and the Club ensured the two men were seated at a table served only by Bentworth, an employee whose security clearance had been vetted to the highest levels.

After enjoying morsels of delicious Scottish salmon, served with sour cream, finely chopped red onion and capers, Bentworth encouraged both veteran soldiers to try the Club's 21 year-old Aberfeldy single malt Scotch. The Grampian Mountains impart a light honey and almond nose to this whisky and it seemed an appropriate way to transition into the crux of the matter.

"Will that be all for now, my lord?" Bentworth enquired. "Shall I leave the 1924 Aberfeldy?"

"Yes, thank you on both counts, Bentworth but the Brigadier and I would like to relocate to the corner table, please."

This apparently random decision by Alexander was a further security precaution, thwarting any remote possibility that their important conversation might be compromised.

"Must be bloody important, Harry, if you can't trust Boodles."

A perceptible cone of silence fell over their two, winged, red leather chairs positioned across the small corner table as Sir Harold replied in a barely audible voice.

"Important doesn't even begin to describe what I am about to tell you, Bryan. Yesterday, at the P.M.'s request, Naval Intelligence gave me a briefing that scared me to the marrow. I am permitted to share certain critical pieces of information with you, starting with their conviction that a mole exists within the War Office. So we have to be bloody cautious. MI6 has intercepted radio traffic from Germany that contains baited information only the upper echelon of our government was privy to. We still do not know who the bastard is but Adolf Hitler might as well have an office in Whitehall at this point."

For a brief moment, Zumwalt wondered if he himself was being tested by this revelation, until Alexander noticed his unease.

"Don't be concerned, Bryan, I'm not trying to trap you. There is certain background you need to be aware of before I get to the main reason I ordered you all the way from Brindisi so let's get on with the business at hand—that is after I make a quick trip to the loo, if you'll excuse me."

Bryan Zumwalt welcomed the respite to glance around Boodle's dining room; it's luxurious mahogany paneling supporting framed original oil paintings of past heroes; Wellington, Nelson, Gordon of Khartoum.

He could not help thinking to himself, *My God, Boodle's has been here since the late 1760's and much of the history of the world has been directed from tables in this very room. God Bless Mother England!*

The field marshal then returned to his seat and broke this train of thought by immediately embarking on a precise recapitulation of his meeting with the Prime Minister. He finished with a very deliberate, "Bryan, it is absolutely critical to the P.M. that no overt incursion beyond the River Oder sour the war effort. I completely understand that your Major Paddy McBride and the Spider have developed a rather unique, mutual-admiration society but I cannot stress enough how disastrous it would be for Great Britain if a group of your men went gallivanting behind Russian lines to try and hot-extract their friend. You will advise your men in the sternest of terms of the ramifications—I trust Major McBride will obey your command?"

"Not one, single, fucking chance in hell, sir," replied the brigadier promptly.

Sir Harold said nothing and refilled their glasses.

They left the club together and a rueful smile could not help playing on Zumwalt's lips. Before they casually parted company at the rear door of Alexander's Bentley, the older man wound down his rear window to instill a final comment.

"Bryan, I can tell you are gravely concerned at the revelations we have discussed, especially about possible traitors amongst us. Remember, the Nazi ship is sinking fast and that is when the rats reveal themselves on deck.

"You might want to keep a close eye on that potential problem as it might pertain to our own organization. If any double agent is going to expose himself, it will be within the next three or four months."

CHAPTER FOUR

Ballymena, Northern Ireland

Although Zumwalt was under direct orders from his superior, the unspoken message was crystal clear: deniability would filter all the way down from the top but spare nothing to get the job done. If the British government and its army planned to disavow all knowledge of a hot extraction, so be it. It would not change the rules of engagement for the SAS—not for one second. His men would bring the Spider home or perish in the attempt.

In many ways, the 21st. Battalion, SAS Regiment needed a distraction. Colonel David Stirling and Lieutenant Jock Lewes had co-founded the commando group but Lewes had been killed in Libya and Stirling, recently captured behind enemy lines in Tunisia, was currently a guest of the Third Reich in Colditz Castle. Knowing this, the brigadier held a closed-door meeting at SAS headquarters in Ricksmanworth, Hertfordshire to formulate a basic strategy with the man in charge by default, Major Paddy McBride. As a result of the meeting, select individuals at various locations around the world, received sealed orders, were given immediate relief from current assignments and transported to a clandestine meeting scheduled for five days later in Northern Ireland.

God help any Russians or Germans who get in the way of what I'm about to unleash, prayed Brigadier Bryan Merfyn Zumwalt as he watched his plan develop an inexorable life of its own.

Located 28 miles north-west of Belfast, Ballymena is the home town of Major Patrick Samuel McBride of His Majesty's Special Raiding Squadron under the SAS.

McBride at six-foot-five, two hundred and thirty five pounds of solid muscle, is an intimidating human being in every sense of the word. He grew up in the small market town and before the war was declared, treated his community to nationwide dominance in any sport the large-boned athlete participated. His lack of fear and natural propensity to enjoy violence brought him the British heavyweight boxing title before his twenty-first birthday and worldwide notoriety as a member of the 1938 British Lions rugby team that toured South Africa. When asked by a local Pretoria reporter what position he would be playing, McBride famously replied, "Scrum."

Key to Zumwalt's plan was to have the major lead a clandestine squad of Special Forces to pluck the Spider and his immediate family from behind Russian lines and deliver them to the safety of the United Kingdom—without anybody being the wiser. Paddy had met Chez Orlowski shortly after the Polish freedom fighter had rescued Malcolm McClain from the Maribor P.O.W. camp and the three men cemented a friendship based upon mutual admiration. The brigadier knew the major would jump at the challenge—keeping it covert; that was another matter.

Under these circumstances, the most-famous son of this rural, County Antrim town was able to advise certain folk to stay—and certain folk to leave for a while, so a total lock-down was in effect. Security could not have been tighter as his elite, hand-chosen squad began to arrive. For reasons soon to become apparent, linguists and a couple of 'designated hitters' supplemented the regular hard men who accompanied McBride on his many hair-raising missions.

The SAS squad commandeered the entire Adair Arms Hotel on the Ballymoney Road for their headquarters. Located in the center of this bustling town, the 1846 building was easily defensible by local militia who needed to know nothing more than Big Paddy required a little privacy to cook up his next adventure.

The group arose at 6:00 a.m. every day, not by choice but by habit, then met in the breakfast room dressed in white shorts and light blue shirts, the training skip of local professional soccer team, Ballymena United. The 'Sky Blues' had been on hiatus since beating Glenavon 2-0 to win the 1940 Irish Cup, the last final played before the war suspended football. McBride felt if anybody saw a group of very fit men running around in these colors, they would naturally believe it was the new United squad, in training for the eagerly awaited league re-start after the war ended.

It was on one of those early morning jogs that the first designated hitter joined them in spectacular fashion. The squad was five miles into a run up Slemish Mountain, a 1,500 foot hill where legend had St. Patrick working as a teenage shepherd, when they heard the sound of a single-engine aircraft headed towards them. The highly trained squad immediately dived for the cover of rocks and hedgerows with weapons at the ready, just seconds before a bright yellow Sopwith Camel fluttered over the horizon. Paddy grinned, stood erect and waved his arms at the plane. The wind on Slemish is vicious and swirling, causing the pilot to crab in almost sideways before using his last fifty feet to turn into the wind and set the plane down right in front of the men. The landing was so precise, the plane had virtually no forward motion after its wheels touched down. It simply stopped like a bird landing on an overhead wire and the pilot closed down the prop. The squad applauded spontaneously in appreciation.

Paddy strolled over to the port wing to greet a rotund man with a handlebar moustache who was sporting a leather RAF flying jacket festooned with insignia. The man jumped to the ground to salute formally while announcing, "Squadron Leader William Wallace Fagan reporting as ordered, sir."

"Welcome aboard, Billy. And absolutely wonderful to see you again," replied Major McBride, giving the pilot an enormous bear hug.

Billy Fagan had met Paddy and the Spider when they expatriated him and his fellow POW's from Yugoslavia last year. McBride dismissed him as an overweight, affable fool but when Brigadier Zumwalt sent out surreptitious feelers around the Royal Air Force in search of a bush pilot, someone with the innate talent and ability to fly a plane under extreme conditions, Fagan's name surfaced regularly. Apparently, Billy

Fagan downplayed his considerable skills by masquerading as a gin-drinking bon vivant in an attempt to line his pockets with wagers against the unwary. His favorite, insane party trick was to bet an entire pub he could land his personal, yellow Sopwith Camel on the rear bed of a speeding truck. He always won this bet but there were a diminishing number of public houses around his base in Hampshire left to fleece.

McBride thought such a pilot might be a useful supplement to the team so Fagan received clandestine orders to fly to Ballymena.

The second designated hitter simply appeared one day as the team sat down for breakfast. Midway through the routinely jocular banter, Staff Sergeant Mike Johnston was pouring a cup of coffee when he noticed an extra, hooded anorak in the room. He frowned, then stared down Paddy McBride to gain his attention and reached for his side arm.

How the hell did this arsehole break through security? McBride took in the situation and showed Johnston an index finger against his pursed lips. Mike shrugged reluctantly.

"Welcome, Takeo," Paddy said barely loud enough for the room to hear, though all present sensed the tension. The rest of the elite squad started as they realized the danger they had been in. As he stood to flip back his hood and bow low from the waist, the stranger's movements were catlike, flowing with a grace that elicited appreciative whistles from the assembled. They slowly began to recognize him—either from a previous mission—or by legend. In addition to all of this, Captain Takeo Atobe owned a reputation as one with whom even Paddy McBride would not spar.

Atobe-san, the only non-ethnic Japanese in the world to have achieved fifth dan status in the three deadly martial arts of Shotokan Karate, Ninjutsu and Aikido, replied softly, "Domo arrigato, McBride-San, for the honor of inviting me to your little party."

"If you would, I'd like a word, Takeo? Let's go over to the corner." Once out of earshot of the group, Paddy lowered his voice even further.

"Takeo, I'm glad Zumwalt managed to get hold of you. Apart from this covert mission, I've been charged with assisting MI6 in a little skullduggery for which I could use your help. What do you know about the Soviet-Japanese Neutrality Pact?"

"I think it refers to some kind of peace treaty Japan signed with Russia just before I left Kyoto," was Takeo's guarded reply.

"Well, your former country does not know this,—obviously, but we think we can plant some false evidence on our upcoming mission that might cause Russia to renege on the treaty before the war with Germany concludes. America is prepared to offer all kinds of territorial concessions to the Ruskis if they pincer Japan from the north and west while they charge in from the Pacific.

"The brigadier has a file he wants me to review and I thought, as you've lived there, you could help me understand the subtleties. Top Secret, of course, and strictly between the two of us but I should receive the details as we pass through headquarters in Brindisi. It might even open up some opportunities for SAS to help America out on the Asian front. Of course, you'll need to ponder the danger your family will be in if the Japanese lose the protection of Russia."

There was a momentary flicker of surprise in Atobe's eyes, enough to tell Major McBride that this revelation had shocked the young captain but he quickly regained his stoic Asian composure.

"Sure Paddy, I will assist you any way I can. For the record, both my father and mother were murdered last year. After the war, I will be going back to my village to set things straight."

The newcomer could be mistaken for an Italian or Spaniard but had almond-shaped black eyes and his English was flavored with a distinctive Asian accent. As Paddy and Mike sat down with him, the rest of the men moved away but continued to stare at the threesome.

"I've heard of this guy," whispered Jacqueline

Siglar, the team's premier sniper. "Is he as big a bad-ass as they say? And, how the hell did Zumwalt get a Jap-Wop kung-fu expert to join our squad in the first place?"

Scotty Miller, who up until Atobe-san material-ized, had been the group's premier smiling assassin of unarmed combat, answered without his eyes leaving Takeo. His voice took on an eerie monotone as he responded to the group.

"After I was recruited into the SAS, I was trained for two years by that man right there. Before I joined, I was your typical cocky black belt and thought I was very, very good, even unbeatable; Takeo Atobe showed me I knew next to nothing.

"Common knowledge has it he's half Portu-guese, half Japanese. His parents met when his dad, a junior diplomat at Tokyo's Portuguese embassy, fell hopelessly in love with his interpreter. They married within days of meeting and, when a son came along, they dropped out of the society whirl and retreated from Tokyo gentility to rural Kyoto. Once there, they adopted the mother's maiden name of Atobe to better assimilate into the ancient society. The medi-eval Japanese capital is the mother's ancestral home and the Atobe family had been an integral part of Samurai culture since the sixteenth century.

"Takeo was trained by masters in the ancient concepts of Bushido from the time he could walk and he advanced those special skills to levels seldom seen. A big problem materialized when the old Senseis realized they could no longer defeat their teenage pupil. You can only imagine, that within the Samurai community, this caused enormous embarrassment, especially as young Takeo looked more European than Japanese in their eyes. After a high-level, secret conference with his parents, Giorgino and Sakura, Takeo was persuaded to take passage to England to visit his father's brother until the elders could resolve the problem. Then, only days after he left, the bastards bombed Pearl Harbor; luckiest Nip in the world to get out when he did, if you ask me."

"Bloody Hell! But how did he get conscripted into the SAS?"

"Well, that's another weird thing. He was having a beer with this uncle in *The Coach and Horses*, a wonderful little pub close to our HQ in Ricksmanworth—one I suspect you have all visited—when a group of local yobbos decided to declare their own war on Japan by beating up Takeo."

"Holy shit, that sounds ugly! How many were there?" asked Jacqui.

"I've heard as many as twenty, but the consensus is nine." Sergeant Miller paused to enjoy the moment, knowing full well the others were eager for him to continue.

"Takeo persuades the louts to let his uncle leave

the bar safely, by promising he would accompany them outside to take his medicine like a man. Colossal mistake by the yobbos; five minutes later, all nine were rolling in the street with a mixture of broken bones, welts, bruises and severe headaches. Apparently after the fracas, Takeo looked like he had just stepped out of a wedding party."

"How do you know all this?"

"My boss, David Stirling, had just formed Special Air Services, then called 'L' Detachment back in June 1941, and was also in the bar that very afternoon. He stepped out with the crowd, fully prepared to move in with side arm drawn to save the young Jap before it got ugly. He told me that Takeo's shirt did not even come out of his pants though he did have to re-adjust his tie. Claims it was the most efficient demolition of an angry mob he had ever seen and offered him the job of unarmed combat instructor right there in the street. I'll tell you this, lads, Atobe-san might be the most dangerous human being in the world and, by all accounts, even Paddy won't mess with him."

CHAPTER FIVE

The Black Widows

P addy McBride waited three days before announcing his eagerly awaited briefing session. His timing was dependent upon a series of factors; surreptitious conversations scheduled with Brigadier Zumwalt on the secure line and his satisfaction with the chemistry of the squad as they bonded together as a group. By necessity, this diverse band of highly talented individuals tolerated no fools though they gravitated towards infantile practical jokes. Tolerance of this silliness, mutual admiration and respect took time and maturity; Paddy was not going to take his squad into the field if there were any doubts about their loyalty to him and each other.

Siglar, the only woman in the group, disdained any

privilege. Her chiseled features emulated an attractive schoolboy and her cropped black hair, manner of dress and complete aversion to make-up had long since labeled her as a woman who preferred women. If there was going to be a problem in the field, it would be between her and Scotty Miller, a notorious pussyhound who would be oblivious to the lesbian flags she deliberately projected. Gender aside, Major McBride long since concluded no-one could compete with her incredible marksmanship, as she could hit a soup can dangling in the wind at distances curtailed only by terrain and the curvature of the earth. The rest of the squad joked the victim was already dead when Jacqui set up her rifle, not when she pulled the trigger. She simply never missed. Sergeant Miller had to keep it in his pants; Jacqui was on the team.

Those assembled in the Adair Arms dining room had made their way from various arenas of conflict in all corners of the world, owing enough blind respect to the giant Ulsterman to drop whatever they were doing when they received the call to arms. In actual fact, they were given little choice when ordered to report before their respective commanding officers. The scenarios were remarkably similar in their brevity.

"I just received a priority dispatch from Field

Marshal Alexander 'imself. Not the slightest idea what you've done to piss him off but you're to leave here by the most expedient means possible for some special SAS training at Ricksmanworth. You'd better pack your kit and get your scrawny arse to England, old son—tout de suite."

Not one of the prospective squad made it to the HQ in Hertfordshire; in mid-journey, they were individually redirected to an unknown destination. After landing at Aldergrove Airport, unmarked cars picked them up, but it was not until they walked through the front door of the Adair Arms that they realized they were in Ballymena, Northern Ireland.

Three of the twelve-man squad, Podolski, Smolenski and Hoenicke were included primarily for their linguistic skills although all had impressed with combat prowess on prior missions. Specialists Giorgino Blando, Ronnie Martin and Mitch Arnold were simply mean motherfuckers who would follow McBride and Johnston to Hell and back; the thought of not including them in the squad was never a consideration.

Now McBride and his staff sergeant felt ready to reward the blind faith of all these warriors with details of the planned operation.

"Lads—and I respectfully include Jacqui in that epithet—total security is now in effect. What I am about to tell you must never be repeated in your lifetimes. If you are planning on writing a book after this war is over and you include details of the mission I am about to reveal, you will not live to see publication. You are all smart enough to read between the lines of what I have just said. Walk out now and we remain friends 'til eternity with no problems. Stay, and my conditions go into effect." McBride and his ever-loyal cohort, Johnston, waited dutifully for reactions, staring deep into the eyes and souls of each and every soldier, but none waivered.

"Ah well, there y'are now. I thank you all from the bottom of my heart. This mission is black and involves a covert, hot extraction from behind Soviet lines. You need to be aware the target we are going to extract is a personal friend of Bryan Zumwalt, Mike Johnston and, most importantly—myself. This particular man, a Polish freedom fighter known as 'the Spider,' pulled off several amazing stunts against Nazi Germany that were pivotal in the war effort. The War Office figures he alone saved millions of Allied lives—plus one,— that gentleman being Malcolm McClain. I take it you've all heard of McClain?"

"The Blackpool and Ireland full back?"

"Wasn't he the guy who got shot down in Yugoslavia? The Daily Mail ran some story about an international football game he organized on an airstrip after he escaped."

"I'd have paid serious money to watch that game. Heard the score was 10-0 for the good guys!"

"All true, except for the score. It was 8-1. Staff here was referee and let the Yugoslavs have a soft goal that was offside by a mile. The Spider played in goal for us and by that time we'd been around him for quite a while, so very little surprised us.

"Zumwalt had sent us to the Yugoslav Partizani headquarters in Semic to rescue Billy Fagan and his fellow POW's from a camp in Maribor. In a side job, we were asked to equip and train a squad of local guerillas that the Spider was about to lead on a suicide mission into Poland."

Wing Commander William Wallace Fagan yelled his thanks from the back of the room. "Absolutely textbook rescue, old chap, though I might add the Gerrys had long since fled with their tails between their legs after a prior encounter with the Spider."

"Actually, Billy's absolutely correct. Though we didn't realize it at the time, we were underwhelmed with the Spider we saw the first day in Semic, but all that certainly changed. Tell 'em, Mike."

"The Spider's real name is Czeslaw Orlowski; we call him Chez. He is around 5 foot 8 inches of solid muscle and moves like a cat. His mum and dad were both gymnasts—Olympic-level gymnasts—and that might be the secret 'cause I swear this kid can defy gravity. As a teenager, he was thrown into a hard labor camp by the Nazis, escaped and will do anything to avenge his adopted country, Poland."

"Where's he originally from, Mike?" interrupted Giorgino Blando from the back.

"Weimar, Germany, Gino. And oh yes, the little bugger speaks at least four languages and is as good or better than anyone in this room with a gun or a knife. Put it all in one package and he's a lethal weapon that can disappear in the blink of an eye. You have to see it to believe it, right, Paddy?"

"That's why they call him the Spider. He delights in causing mayhem against the enemy and is completely fearless under any circumstances we've seen him in. He leaves a calling card at the scene of his chaos; an oval surrounded by eight legs, and the Germans are scared shitless whenever they see it. As far as the youth of Poland is concerned, the Spider is a superhuman. His legend has kept the whole country's hopes alive throughout this horrendous period of history. Stalin plans to control a strategic geographic empire of subservient slaves after the war and the Spider does not promote that cause. Consequently, the Russians want to crush and publically destroy the myth as soon as they find him."

Several of the squad threw up their hands with questions and Paddy chose Ronnie Martin, knowing it must be important because Ronnie usually kept himself to himself.

"I'm just guessing but this has to be about the suicide mission, right? The fact that this Spider character is still around must mean something went horribly wrong."

"On the contrary, Ronnie, it succeeded beyond anyone's wildest expectations. It's all highly classified but, with your lives on the line, you deserve to know more about why we are going in to get this guy."

The assembled assassins nodded in agreement and mumbled their appreciation.

"Bryan Zumwalt heard about the Spider through the successful Malcolm McClain escape and asked me, if I met him and got the chance, to tease him with a top-secret mission to eastern Poland. To be completely honest, neither the brigadier nor I thought he would be crazy enough to accept. It seemed patently impossible and nobody would have bet a shilling against a hundred pounds on its success. I cannot tell too much about the actual mission, but that damn kid pulled it off in spades and has been officially credited with saving countless lives as a result. British lives, I might add—maybe even your families. Wish I could tell you more. Suffice it to say, the powers that be were profoundly impressed, causing King George to grant Chez and his immediate family British Citizenship in absentia. So you can only assume it was a fucking big deal.

"Our mission will be to bring those folks back to their new adopted country before the Russians track him down."

"Paddy, I hesitate to sound braggadocios but this room is filled with the crème de la crème of Special Forces and there's got to be more to this mission than meets the eye. How come the Spider can't sneak himself and his family into allied controlled territory?" The hardened warriors all seemed in concert with Siglar's shrewd observation.

"Jacqui, I am going to tell you everything I am allowed to, but certain details are going to be buried deep in the Official Secrets Act for generations.

"The Germans are in full retreat to make a last stand in Berlin. Chez and most of his Armia Krajowa rebels have laid down their weapons, disappearing into the anonymity of civilian life with their families. In Chez's case, it's a new bride, her four sisters—and the mother-in-law."

"So the Spider's not very smart?" a wag called out to hoots of ribald laughter.

"Maybe not!" smiled the big man reflectively. "However, the Poles have a whole new problem called Russia and if they didn't have bad luck, they wouldn't have any.

"We believe that Chez and his family live in Silesia. It is technically in Germany for now but behind the Russian front lines. Therein lies the conundrum; the Russians are going to repatriate Silesia into Poland after the war and desperately want to kill the Spider because he is the iconic leader of the Polish nation they wish to subvert. Winston Churchill cannot afford to piss off Premier Stalin, yet acknowledges we owe the Spider for saving millions of Brits from certain death. In short, lads, we have to hot extract our seven targets without anyone on either side acknowledging we were there! Any incident that broadcasts our presence might escalate into a state of war between Britain and the Soviet Union.

"Our covert raiding squad will be known as the Black Widows."

The soldiers in the room started to move uncomfortably and mutter as they tried to reconcile what they had just heard, so Staff Sergeant Mike Johnston took the opportunity to jump in.

"Listen up, lads, as far as I'm concerned, this little fucker saved half the free world, the least we can give him and his family is a new life. I really don't give a flyin' shit if all of you walk away from this right now, Paddy and I will go it alone. We'll get him out or die trying; that's how important this is."

Then, with a quiet grace, Takeo Atobe stood up and for some weird reason, the whole room went deathly silent. "I know more than you think, Mike, and I am in one hundred percent. This man and his family deserve to be extracted."

There was something in the way he spoke that changed the chemistry in the room; a sense of oneness took over, an incredible unity from all twelve people. They were the best of the best; they knew it and nothing could stop them.

"Wow," Paddy cleared his throat. "Okay, our best intelligence from remnants of the AK has the Orlowskis living on a farm in Żagań, a small town in a grey area of Western Silesia. Various countries have owned Żagań over the centuries and I have it from a very high source that the new landlord will be Marshall Josef Vissarionovich Stalin as soon as Germany surrenders. Even as I speak, the Nazis are moving out and the Ruskis are moving in.

"Chez hides in plain sight; his main disguise is the legend that the Spider is a giant of a man over seven feet tall, whereas he is, as Mike explained, quite non-descript. This illusion can end at any second so we have to move fast. The day after tomorrow, Brigadier Zumwalt will have us transported to the American front lines. The United States has just captured the Ludendorff Bridge over the Rhine at Remagen but from there, we'll be on our own, travelling 600 klicks through the enemy's back yard to Żagań. In the simplest of terms, our mission will be to escort Chez Orlowski, his wife, Jadwiga, her four sisters and mother safely back to the Special Raiding Squadron's new base at Dukes Road in Euston. Zumwalt will take it from there."

"You lads ever executed a night LALO jump?" interrupted Billy Fagan.

"I have done about a hundred HALO's," growled Mike Johnston in his guttural Glaswegian accent, visibly upset at the English flyer's interruption. "High Altitude-Low Opening. If you're talking about Low Altitude-Low Opening, the term doesn't exist because it's fuckin' redundant! It's more commonly known as FSID - Fuckin' Stupid - Instant Death."

"Don't get frosty with me, old boy; just trying to save you from dodging and weaving through the entire, retreating Wehrmacht army. I, on the other hand, can put you within five miles of Zagan and, if we get a little lucky, you'll never even see a bloody German or a bloody Russian."

"How low and how dark?" asked an intrigued Paddy McBride.

CHAPTER SIX

Krakow

C hez did not take the obvious route to Leszno, opting to cut across country to Rawicz. He knew he might be seen and heard, perhaps even reported, but with this tactic, almost certainly not apprehended by a strategic roadblock. By using similarly ambiguous routes, the one hundred miles to Lodz took almost four hours to negotiate and when he finally reached the Strykowska Road on the north side of that city, he left his bike parked with the key in the ignition outside a busy café. The traffic pattern in the parking lot was fairly easy to discern, with vehicles en route from Lodz to Warsaw pulling in from the south, so this location was where the faithful Wulgum was left,—as tempting as a juicy plum.

Strolling casually around to the north side of the café, Czeslaw waited patiently for the right person to assist him. Ten minutes later, he approached a middle-aged man engrossed in picking the remains of breakfast from his irregular teeth as he mined his trousers for keys.

"Excuse me, brother, my ride from Warsaw dropped me off on his way to Poznan; I am trying to get into Lodz. Any chance you might be headed that way and can give me a ride?"

The driver looked him up and down before replying. "You'll have to ride with the turnips but jump on board. My store is in Baluty. That be okay?" Czeslaw nodded swift thanks before vaulting onto the back of the produce truck. As they drove away, he saw his freshly purloined Wul-Gum speed off towards Poznan.

Warsaw would have been my preference but anything away from Krakow works for me. My next diversion should throw them into complete confusion, Chez plotted.

But he had underestimated Russian Intelligence.

Once back in Lodz, it did not take too long for him to pilfer a non-descript blue Fiat and head for Krakow. However, the unfortunate soul who stole his Wul-Gum was pulled over just outside Konin by a diligent platoon of Russians and questioned unmercifully for three days. The NKGB wanted the young man to be the Spider, even begged him to be the Spider but in the end, had to accept that they had been duped.

Uncharacteristically, no heads rolled, instead, Moscow used the new intelligence to their advantage by issuing a nationwide directive.

"The Spider's ruse to have his bike stolen at the Lodz cafe leads to an obvious conclusion; he is not headed to Poznan or Warsaw. The People's Commissariat for State Security hereby determines the fugitive is most likely headed towards his last base of operations—Krakow. React accordingly."

Throughout the latter stages of Nazi occupation, the Armia Krakowa had skirmished them with unbridled ferocity. The AK division in Krakow was led by Jan Kowalski, a swashbuckling leader who sported dark curly hair and an impressive moustache. Jan's group had grown to well over one hundred guerrillas and were revered as the Bracia, or brotherhood. When Kowalski died heroically in a firefight, a death he might have scripted for himself, Czeslaw Orlowski took over as leader for the final few weeks before the Germans retreated to Berlin.

The Russian army had been in control of Krakow since Czeslaw disbanded the Bracia in late January and there were noticeable, drastic changes in the city's security and ambience. Scrapping with a retreating Wehrmacht who were singularly focused on saving their own skins had been relatively easy, compared to evading the battle-hardened Russians now dominating the beautiful old city with the swagger of fearless conquerors.

It took less than ninety minutes from his arrival for the Spider to obtain confirming answers to his surreptitious yet well-placed questions. Brunon Mazur, his trusted lieutenant from the Bracia days, was working as a dishwasher in the Pod Sloncem Restaurant in the main market square.

It was backbreaking work and Brunon's final task of the night was, as always, to carry bags of trash into the rear alley for collection the next morning. At the very moment he replaced the metal trashcan lid, a hand clamped over his mouth and spun him against the rough brick wall. His panic focused on a honed steel blade about ten inches long. It's flat surface was pressed against the fleshy point of his nose, the razor-sharp tip only one inch from his eyes.

"Greetings, Brunon," whispered the familiar but stern voice. "Please don't move a muscle. I have a few questions for you to answer."

"Is that you, Pająk?" he managed after the vice-like

grip relaxed somewhat. "I have been praying you survived. Ask all you want; I don't know if I can help you."

"The Russians have tracked me to Żagań. Someone told them I was riding a Wul-Gum and apart from myself, the only two people in the world who knew that were you and Filip."

There was a crack of fear in Brunon's voice as he gulped. "I've been in hiding from the Russians since the moment you left and swear I've talked to no one. Our friend, Filip, was killed that very same day so I am now your only suspect. Fortunately, I've not been given the pleasure of a Ruski interrogation—yet. So I'm at a loss."

The Spider moved the knifepoint down to the shaking man's larynx but his eyes never left Brunon's as they tried to sense the truth.

"Hold on, Pająk, I seem to recall there were at least two other people in the warehouse that day and I think I know where we can find both of them. Believe me, Czeslaw, the NKGB could get Jesus to betray Mother Mary. These bastards make the Gestapo seem like kindergarten teachers."

The Spider relaxed his grip and lowered the knife. "Tell me more about what happened to Filip."

"Filip got into a fight with a couple of soldiers who were trying to shake him down. He decked both of them but was unarmed and they shot him, right in the middle of the street. I know I speak for him when

I say we would never betray you. If they had thought he had any information leading to you, his life might have lasted a couple of hours longer."

Czeslaw looked deeply into Brunon's eyes, into his very soul and could sense the veracity of what he said. The knife returned to his belt and the old friends hugged with considerable emotion.

"I feel the noose tightening around my neck, Brunon, forgive me, please. You and Filip are—were—most trusted friends but I had to find out how I was betrayed. Now, it's beginning to look like I must write off any clues the Russians gathered as a pure consequence of intimidation and the torture of innocents. All is forgiven and forgotten."

Brunon sighed deeply, pulled a bent Russian Belomorkanal cigarette out of his pocket and struck a wooden match against the bricks.

"When did you start with that shit?" Czeslaw challenged.

"Since the day you left, Pająk; the nicotine calms me down. If you were here in Krakow, you'd probably smoke ten packs a day. Can you please get me out of this place?"

"I'll do my best, Brunon, but I am married now and my family is my first priority. Neither you nor I have a future in Poland right now. I suggest you try to get to Yugoslavia and meet up with our old friend Vedran Bozic in Semic." Brunon leant against the wall, closed his eyes tightly and choked back a sob. Czeslaw patted him on the back and the two friends silently and independently considered the hopelessness of their individual predicaments for almost a minute. Then the Spider had an idea.

"Brunon, do you have access to any kind of radio transmitter by any chance? I have to try and reach Brigadier Zumwalt with a few questions."

"I do, but you won't like hearing where it is."

In their heyday, the Bracia used an old building in pasaz Bielaka as their headquarters. It was abandoned abruptly when suspicious characters, determined to be NKGB operatives known as chekists, were noticed scouting the area just before they swooped down to capture a couple of hapless freedom fighters. As far as Brunon knew, the building's secret attic still contained their powerful transmitter along with weapons and sensitive material such as personnel files.

Stemming from his brief tenure as head of the Bracia, the Spider was familiar with the building, but certainly did not know it as well as Brunon. And he remembered that the secret attic was well disguised so there was at least a chance the Russians were oblivious to the concealed stash of AK paraphernalia under the roof.

"It'll be extremely difficult to get into the old headquarters, Czeslaw. It always seems to be heavily guarded; otherwise, I would have done it myself. I worry about it constantly because of those damn files. In the hands of the NKGB, they would spell death warrants for thousands of brave Poles."

It was not that far from Brunon's restaurant to the old Bracia headquarters, so early the next morning the two men took a casual stroll together. Czeslaw scanned the narrow passage several times and analyzed the conditions in silence.

"So, how many of those chekist bastards do you see?" he asked.

Brunon identified four, possibly six.

"I'm going to add those two characters over there," Czeslaw said, indicating a couple of men down the block. "That makes eight and I have to assume there are more inside because the front door handle and stoop have seen recent traffic. That seems like a lot. What do you think?"

"You're right, Pająk, and I don't like it one bit. It's like they're expecting us."

"No, I don't think so. When you put all the pieces together, Moscow is pulling out all the stops to find me and they'd be crazy not to strengthen surveillance in Krakow. It certainly makes things more interesting."

"Pająk, let's just go undercover for a couple of weeks; give the situation time to cool down. You can continue to stay at my place. I might be able to get the use of another transmitter."

"That doesn't work for me, Brunon. Those personnel files are toxic so we have no choice but to break into our old headquarters and destroy them. A dozen chekists cannot stop me as long as I have the element of surprise on my side.

"Tell me, did you add any other doors to the place, perhaps a fire escape?" Brunon paused to think for a couple of seconds. "I'm afraid we didn't. There is, of course, a rear door onto the space beyond the pasaz but we relied upon spotters whenever we had a meeting. We figured by controlling the passage all the way from Stolarska Street to the Market Square—that's over a hundred meters—plus a reliance on picking up on any Kraut activity beyond that, we might have as much as five minutes to get out and disperse before the Krauts got close."

"But I want to get in!" spat the Spider ferociously under his breath. "I'll meet you at the kitchen of Pod Sloncem in one hour."

Brunon glanced along the passage in the direction of the Market Square and scrunched his shoulders, hands in the pocket of his overcoat as he started back. He turned briefly to nod to his friend but was not surprised the Spider had already vanished.

About five minutes later, a couple of the NKGB surveillance team noticed a non-descript figure, clearly soused, an empty bottle of vodka held loosely from one hand. The drunk stumbled towards Stolarska Street, bumping into the wall several times before he rounded a corner to stagger north. Once out of view from the pasaz the figure transformed completely; no longer a clumsy boozer he took another left, this time onto Sienna before locating a service alley that headed back south in the general direction of the old Bracia headquarters. Czeslaw crouched low behind some bags of rubbish, confident the hairs on his neck would bristle at the first sign of unwarranted movement. There appeared to be none and the lack of a spotter in this alley declared that this route would most likely not lead directly back to the passage.

The building separating him from his destination ran parallel to the pasaz, a building that apparently contained a multitude of small offices. He gained entry through a rear door and made his way to the ground floor reception desk to find a very attractive young teenage girl wearing an extraordinary amount of black-market make-up. She was focused on the important task of polishing her nails and he had already memorized the directory before he interrupted her.

"Ahem. Przepraszam, Panno. Excuse me, young lady. I am looking for my architect, Pan Roman Jurkiewicz?" The girl did not even glance up from her nails as she told him what he already knew.

"He's on the top floor." She called to the young man's retreating back, adding that she thought he was out.

There's a bonus, thought the Spider as he climbed the stairs. Nevertheless, when confronted by the stylish, four-panel, red door adorned with a brass plate reading, *Jurkiewicz – Architekt,* he knocked politely once, waited thirty seconds to be sure, then knocked again.

The door lock and deadbolt were too substantial to waste any time on but, as is often the case, the actual door was not. The Spider's knife levered out the thin, upper wooden panel above the locks and forced it inwards, enough to reach through and release the door.

Sorry about the mess, Mr. Architect, but you will know better when you design your next door.

From Roman Jurkiewicz's empty office on the third floor, Czeslaw was able to look south across twenty feet of open space to the old Bracia head-quarters. His vantage was roughly in line with the top of its roof. Carefully studying each of his former building's six rear windows, he picked up movement only on the ground floor. Two bulky NKGB agents were taking a cigarette break outside the rear door as he heard a voice from within call out in Russian.

"Mikhail, Igor, you two will be on your own for the next hour while we go for lunch. I'll bring you back some kielbasa and golabki." The Spider smiled and looked around the architect's desk for some white paper from which to make a fake package. He found a roll of sketch paper and several rubber bands to make a convincing prop.

Czeslaw returned to the reception area and smiled at the young girl. "Dziękuję, but Mr. Jurkiewicz was not there. I'll try again tomorrow." The young painted lady, now in her all-important nail buffing phase, did not even glance up as the most wanted man in Poland walked out of the front door.

"Mikhail? I was asked to bring you lunch," Czeslaw called out in Russian as he rapped confidently on the rear door. One of the thugs opened the door and transfixed on the white package being waved at him at shoulder height. He never noticed the smooth motion which propelled the knife in the Spider's left hand through his lower jaw and into his brain. The other NKGB operative, his back to the door, was absorbed in a newspaper as he sat at a trestle table. Czeslaw eased the limp body down to the floor and was at the man's neck before he had a chance to reach for his TT33 pistol. With one hand clamped at the rear of Igor's skull and the other on his chin, the Spider launched all his body weight off the floor and the large Russian's neck snapped like a twig.

One body at a time, Czeslaw grabbed the ankles

and dragged both into the central hallway to shield them from any windows. He calmly locked both outside doors, jamming a prong of a kitchen fork into each keyhole before vaulting up two flights to the second floor. Memories flooded back as he pulled open the cleaning closet door on the top landing. It seemed to be only two feet deep, filled with brooms and buckets that had to be cleared out of the way to reach the rear-paneled wall. The two latches he remembered were on the lower and upper right-hand sides and when released, the wall hinged outwards to expose a dark and dusty steep stairway up to the attic.

The light bulb still worked at the pull of a string-operated switch but the filament flickered on its last legs as he went straight to the transmitter and powered it up. It would take a good five minutes for the valves to heat so he used his time to gather all the loose paper he could find into a pile into the center of the wooden floor.

Now, where are those damn files?

Searching around the small, dim space, his eyes adjusted to the point where he spotted an assortment of Bracia weapons piled on top of a large cardboard box. He clattered them onto the floor and was rewarded when the box revealed the incriminating personnel files.

The roof was long in need of repair and three or four needles of daylight streamed into the attic to pool on the floor, highlighting millions of dust particles all the way down. He started to cough. Pulling a crowbar from the pile of weapons, Czeslaw jimmied a decent-sized hole into the rear attic roof and breathable air flooded in.

Light to see and oxygen for the fire to breathe: two for one!

Czeslaw knew he would not be able to fight his way out of this situation so he added the weapons, ammunition and explosives to the top of his pile of combustible evidence. Then, with time running out, he studied the list of frequencies taped to the top of the transmitter and tried them one by one. On his fifth try, a crackling Polish voice identified itself as receiving his signal in Radomysl, a town in eastern Poland he remembered well.

"Who are you and why are you on this frequency? The Krakow Bracia has shut down. Over."

"Radomysl? May I speak with Bogdan Dobrowolski. Tell him this is the Spider. Over."

"Odpierdol sie! This is Bogdan. If you are the Spider, tell me where the rockets were being assembled? You have five seconds," growled the legendary AK commander. He had come to know the Spider very well when only last year they had shared a successful adventure together in the village of Blizna. Bogdan was in no mood to take any crap from an imposter. In turn, Czeslaw recalled that the Radomysl division's radio transmitter had proved capable of reaching the BAF base in Brindisi and MI6 in London. He began a quiet chuckle at his good fortune.

"That would be a top-secret assembly plant known as the Heidelager, hidden within dense the forest around the village of Blizna, my friend. And as it turned out, we royally fucked up their V-2 rocket program. Good to get hold of you, Bogdan. Over." Only a very small handful of people in the world could possibly know this answer, so Bogdan replied.

"Holy shit, Pająk. How the hell are you, boy? Over."

"I'm in our old Bracia headquarters in Krakow and in about five minutes all hell will break loose. Please try to get hold of Brigadier Zumwalt or Paddy McBride at SAS, even Malcolm McClain at Blackpool Football Club if you have to. Your transmitter is much stronger than mine is, so we need to relay. Tell them I need help getting out of Silesia with my family. The Russians are so close to capturing us, I can taste the salt mine. I can only wait about two minutes for your reply. Otherwise, send me a status message by courier through Brunon at the Pod Sloncem Restaurant in Krakow. Over."

"I can do that, Czeslaw. Give my regards to Brunon but get the hell out of there immediately. There's another covert transmitter I can reach in Krakow after I get hold of the Brigadier. Out."

Czeslaw's complete concentration on the radio caused him to disregard the banging on the front door at street level, but he heard it clearly now. *I might buy a couple of minutes if they think that Mikhail and Igor have locked the door and gone for a quick bite. But they're going to try their own key pretty soon.*

With increasing urgency, he began setting fire to the box of files in the center of the floor. He had only six matches, the first an immediate dud. Taking a calculated risk, he used the second match to light the remaining bunch of four and held this small torch under a single sheet of paper. It flared into yellow and brown so he patiently built a tent of more paper over the small flame. *If I can light a fire in a damp forest with next to nothing, God knows I should be able to light dry paper with matches!*

All the while, his eyes darted around the dour space for anything else that might prove useful.

Of course, the antennae cable! The transmitter had to have an aerial that was not visible from outside their building, so the Bracia had looped perhaps 10 meters of cable around the inside of the attic ceiling.

As he pulled the cable off the ceiling, a four-foot high pyre was starting to burn nicely, its thick smoke pluming towards the hole he had busted through the roof. Looping the wire around his free arm, he swung back down the stair and through the rear of the closet. Now he could hear multiple Russian voices from the ground floor recoiling with shock as they discovered the two dead bodies of their comrades. No doubt heavily armed, the NKGB squad began advancing cautiously to the first and second floors as Czeslaw fastened the latches, replaced the cleaning equipment and shut the closet door. He spun into an open second floor room on the west side of the building and secured the door behind by jamming the back of a wooden chair under the handle. Then with innate calmness, he slid open the casement window, wrapped one end of the cable around a heavy table leg and rappelled down to the ground. When the cable ran out, he dropped the last two meters into the yard, landing like a cat before strolling nonchalantly away from the smoking building.

The Spider paused before entering pasaz Bielaka but seeing that all attention was focused on the yelling and screaming from the upper floors, he proceeded casually west towards the Market Square. He had not gone ten paces when the heat from the paper fire in the attic exploded some of the ammunition and blew the roof off his former headquarters.

It had been slightly more than an hour but Brunon knew his friend well enough to remain unconcerned. Suddenly, a regular customer scurried breathlessly into the restaurant, eager to be first to gossip about the fire and explosion in the passage. Brunon even cracked a smile, as he could guess the cause. That smile turned into a broad grin when a voice interrupted the customer from behind.

"I heard some Ruskis were smoking cigarettes near a gas line and it exploded. Take note, Brunon, smoking can be very dangerous to your health."

Later, in a secluded corner, Czeslaw sat down in front of a large mug of hot, sweet coffee and walked Brunon through the entire adventure, assuring him that everything in the attic was almost certainly destroyed in the blaze.

Both men were into their second cups when a young boy walked past their table and slid a piece of paper to Brunon. He showed no reaction, waiting for the boy to exit the restaurant before he opened the folded note.

"It's from our old friend, Bogdan Dobrowolski," he said with surprise as he handed it to Czeslaw. The Spider scanned its entirety before revealing the content.

"Turns out Zumwalt is in Paris. He assures me

that my letter reached Malcolm McClain and says my family has been granted British citizenship! However, he could not guarantee that a hot extraction was even possible out from Russian-occupied Silesia, due to political circumstances. However, the message finishes on a cryptic note. Paddy has been assigned the mission.

"Well, Brunon. If Paddy McBride is in charge of getting me and my family out of the Bear's claws, I'd better get to cousin Franek's place immediately and pack. I'm afraid you cannot come with me for obvious reasons and we must part company in Krakow once again. The Spider is persona non grata with the Russians and they will intensify their search until they nail me. But there is one last ruse you can help me pull off before I head home."

The next day, hundreds of leaflets appeared on the streets of Krakow crediting the Spider with the explosion on pasaz Bielaka that killed six NKGB operatives. It finished with the exhortation:

"Brave Poles, follow me and
we will free Warsaw.
The Spider"

CHAPTER SEVEN

Żagań

U pon learning that McBride and the SAS were on the job, Czeslaw now had very good reason to rendezvous with his family in Poznan. However, knowing that the NKGB had confirmed him to be in Krakow and every Russian in Poland now considered him a mass murderer, Czeslaw could not risk using a motorcycle or car to escape their net. Therefore, he decided to sacrifice speed for safety in numbers and took the bus. His disguise was that of a transient plumber and Brunon helped commandeer work overalls and common tools before watching him placidly nod goodbye from the rear window as the bus embarked on its six-hour trek northwest. There was one cursory roadblock at Katowice but the two guards who walked through the bus paid little attention to the young plumber dozing on the back seat. But towards the latter part of the journey he was wide alert as he noticed they were travelling into areas of increasing devastation.

The city of Poznan was a mess. Hitler had designated the city as a 'festung;' a stronghold that the Germans committed to defend at all costs. Consequently, the powerful Soviet army, led by General Vasily Chuikov, took almost four weeks to overrun the determined 40,000-strong, Wehrmacht garrison, resulting in much of the medieval city being reduced to ruins.

A temporary bus station had been relocated to a large open space on the outskirts of the city. Czeslaw was disorientated, not certain where he might be in relationship to the farming community of Komorniki, the small village where Jadwiga's cousin Franek worked his farm. Noticing a small group of transportation employees taking a break, drinking tea and playing a noisy game of Dupa Biskupa, he wandered over and picked a polite moment to ask for directions.

"You're not too far, lad, maybe six or seven miles. If I were you, I'd hang around for the next bus to Żagań. It stops in Luboń and you'll only have a twenty minute walk to Komorniki from there."

"Dziękuję bardzo, when does that bus leave?"

"Should roll out of here in about four hours."

That revelation made Czeslaw's decision an easy one,—he started walking south immediately.

He had met Cousin Franek Lieske at his wedding but never had the chance to visit his farm. Jadwiga always bragged it was quite prosperous, Franek being quite famous in the Poznan region for his high-quality pigs. He also recalled Jadwiga telling him it was situated about halfway to the village of Wiry and had beautiful stone gateposts that Franek had built himself.

Carrying his plumber's satchel in one hand and munching a fresh apple from the other, Czeslaw strode purposefully on his long journey, his mind wandering towards the prospects of seeing his bride. The miles were dissolving in the beautiful spring afternoon as he pictured her smile when he heard a heavy vehicle approaching from behind. An instinct told him not to turn around.

The Russian patrol overtook at speed, pulled to a halt in front of him and leveled their rifles to punctuate a noisy command to halt. Czeslaw put down his plumber's tools and smiled, replying to their broken Polish in fluent Russian.

"Dobry den, (good day,) what can I do for you brave comrades. God knows this country owes you a considerable debt for kicking out the German scum."

"You are Russian?"

"My parents were from Molodeczno, near the border. I grew up with Mother Russia in my blood but got stranded down here on a job when Hitler decided to take over the world. You need any good plumbers back home?"

The Russian soldiers relaxed under the spell of the smiling young plumber and Czeslaw was encouraged to maintain his brazen initiative.

"If you can spare any room in your truck, I'd be most grateful if you'd drop me in Komorniki. Mrs. Smolenski's toilet is backed up and she's the most impatient old bitch I've ever met."

"Can't do that, we're on patrol, but you're only five minutes away. What's your name, son?" yelled a corporal from the back of their truck as they sped off.

"Igor, Igor the plumber," lied the Spider with a laugh and a wave.

Within five minutes of turning onto the Kormorniki/Wiry road, Czeslaw thought he heard and smelled pigs. He continued walking and soon passed an elaborate, hand-painted sign on a farm entrance framed by stone gateposts. It read *Leiske Farms* and he knew he was within yards of his family. Ever cautious of an ambush, he kept up his pace and direction for another half mile before ducking into a copse of trees and doubling back to assess the situation.

As dusk advanced, a night owl started to hoot

its minor annoyance as the Spider crept stealthily towards the farmhouse and waited. After some time, the back door opened and the familiar figure of Ma Brzozowska walked out into the small garden. She sang softly to herself as she gathered some vegetables and came within five feet of the garden's wall when her singing was interrupted by an urgent whisper.

"Ma, it's me, Czeslaw. Don't turn around. I need to know if the farm is safe. Continue singing if there is danger."

In reply, she turned towards the familiar voice with a broad smile.

"Czeslaw, stop these silly games. Why don't you and Jadwiga just come in and join us for supper? We're having bigos tonight."

Czeslaw jumped over the stone wall, hugged his mother-in-law, then paused suddenly.

"But Jadwiga is with you, is she not?"

Once inside the Leiske kitchen, the bad news was shared. Jadwiga had put her mother and sisters onto the train for Poznan but elected to stay in Żagań to wait for Czeslaw.

"Nothing we could do to change her mind, Czeslaw, you know how stubborn she can be. She told us she would stay with friends in the village but we all knew she was going back to the farm."

"I must leave immediately for Żagań. Franek, can I borrow your car?"

"Czeslaw, there's a curfew in effect. Any Pole found on the roads after nine o'clock will most likely be shot on sight. Remember, this family already lost a son to that cruel rule. I will not let you go before first light."

"Okay, I understand, but can I at least get a message to my friend Brunon Mazur in Krakow? It is critical that I let him know where I'm headed."

"I don't have a transmitter but my neighbor does. Do you have a frequency for your friend?" Czeslaw nodded and Franek continued, "Then let's grab a piglet and cut through the back pasture. Fryderk is not the most cooperative man in town but fresh pork is valuable currency and in these times, it should get the airwaves humming."

By dawn, Franek Lieske had loaded his van with another special delivery of pork, this time for one of his clients, Walczak the butcher in Żagań. He waited impatiently for Czeslaw Orlowski to crawl into the passenger seat after his completely sleepless night.

Although a fraction of the physical distance, this ride seemed to take longer than his bus journey from Krakow. Czeslaw was exhausted, hungry and in serious need of a bath by the time he began to recognized the familiar approaches to Żagań two hours later. Knowing the tremendous risk and effort his cousin had taken, he thanked Franek profusely and asked if he could be dropped off at Zelazna Street, estimating that from there he would have less than a mile to walk before being at the Brzozowski farm. The exhaustion lifted like a heavy cloud and he could easily have sprinted that last mile had caution not warned him otherwise. Finally, he turned left of the road and there was the big red barn.

Everything looked normal—yet it didn't.

The powerful Radomysl radio receiver collected another call several hours after Brunon Mazur had passed the Spider's planned whereabouts to the ever-vigilant Bogdan Dobrowolski. This time it geographically identified the source as Ballymena, United Kingdom.

"May I speak privately with Mr. Dobrowolski please? Over."

"This is Dobrowolski. Who the fuck are you? Over."

"A friend of the Spider from Northern Ireland. Is your radio secure? Over."

This prompted a brief hesitation before a cautious question punctured the dead air, "How tall are you? Over."

"Six feet five. Over."

"Well, I am certain Malcolm McClain is not that height so you must be the other one. Major McBride, we have thirty seconds left on this broadcast before a trace kicks in, at which time, I'll have to call you back on another frequency. Over."

"Bogdan, can you arrange transportation within Russian-occupied eastern Germany for up to twenty men within the next twenty four hours. We simply do not know the exact location right now. Details to follow. Over."

"Consider it done, Paddy and I believe I can help you a little bit because I just heard where our boy is headed. Out."

Bogdan recalibrated the radio immediately to a Krakow frequency and left a message for Brunon Mazur to organize the temporary usage of two large trucks through the Bracia in Żagań.

While Czeslaw was causing mayhem in Krakow, the Russian battalion in Żagań had independently tracked down the domicile of the only Wul Gum bike in the area. They were still unsure if they had finally found the Spider's hiding place but it was the best lead they had, so they mobilized surveillance. For the past two days, a squad rotated to a location that over-looked the Brzozowski Farm but reported nothing other than one female occupant and no sign of any motorcycle. Unknown to the current members of this squad, the man they were looking for was observing the observers from within dense bushes not twenty feet from their truck.

Jadwiga, in deciding to disobey her husband by not leaving with her family, was now extremely nervous, knowing with certainty that the farm was being watched.

How could I be so stupid? Those bastards on the hill are using me as bait and I'll never forgive myself if he walks into their trap. I have to leave here tonight and maybe set fire to the farm so Czeslaw will know I'm not here. He'll find me in Poznan—I know he will.

Oh, why the hell didn't I listen to my mother?

Czeslaw heard a car driving towards the squad and hugged the ground. It skidded to a halt alongside the bushes and an overweight sergeant in an ill-fitting uniform stepped out to address the four soldiers. He did not look or sound the slightest bit happy.

"Screw this for a wild goose chase! We can't wait here any longer, because if the Spider ever did live here, he's certainly flown the coup. Latest reports have him in Krakow where incidentally, the bastard murdered a dozen of our brave comrades before heading on to Warsaw.

"For now, we're going to arrest the woman at the farm and interrogate her for the hell of it. She should be able to tell us who—if anyone—owns a fucking Wul-Gum around here. When she's tied down and sees the Russian kielbasa I have for her, she'll sing like a bird. Then I'll slit her throat and we can get back to barracks. Hell, if this really was the Spider's lair, we might even locate some photographs inside. Hey, maybe we'll finally find out what this sonofabitch looks like."

Out of breath, the sergeant ended his rant by leaning against the car and lighting a cigarette. "You've less than five minutes to gather everything into your truck. Then, follow me to the farm, you'll enjoy watching this and there might be some leftovers for you."

The young Russian soldiers, somewhat visibly excited about the potential entertainment, scrambled under the watchful eyes of their superior and were soon loaded up,—ready to roll. The wheezing veteran eased his substantial weight off the car, tossed the cigarette onto the ground and was grabbing the handle of the driver's door when the entire vehicle was lifted off the ground by the sudden *whoomf* of exploding petrol. Fuel soaked the tunic of the unfortunate sergeant and fierce blue flames sought him but milliseconds later. He screamed and flailed in attempt to stop the unbelievable pain, rolling over and over in a blur of frenetic motion before he succumbed to his fate.

The rest of the squad, blown backwards by the force of the blast, took several seconds to recover their senses. By the time they finally summoned the courage to assist, the man was a charred, motionless corpse, emitting a gross smell none of them would ever forget.

Czeslaw had appeared at the rear of the farm a few minutes earlier. Jadwiga opened the door in grateful surprise when she recognized their special knock but her relief could not mask the abject fear in her eyes. The Spider hugged his bride as he pushed her into the shelter of their kitchen.

"A Russian patrol will be here in less than five minutes. Don't ask any questions, don't even pack. We must leave here immediately and beg a ride out of this immediate area,—to Komorniki if possible." Holding hands tightly, they made it safely to the cover of the trees behind the farm when they heard the horrendous boom of the explosion.

"Oh my God! What was that?" cried Jadwiga.

"I cut the fuel line in one of their vehicles and a spark must have caught it. Should distract them for a while but let's keep moving."

The Russian patrol did not head directly for the farm, choosing instead to retreat at great speed to their headquarters; all four soldiers crammed into the cab, the sergeant's unrecognizable corpse was wrapped in a blanket, and the only object in the bed of the truck.

"So you are telling me that Sergeant Piotr Vasilevich was killed just as he was about to interrogate the Brzozowska woman? Coincidence? I think not." Major Boris Ivanovich, a tall, career soldier in his late fifties, had a wicked dueling scar running from the corner of his right eye to the base of his cheek. Having served Mother Russia loyally for the past thirty years, he had been wounded enough times to be elevated from the front lines to a desk job and was currently in charge of the small Żagań garrison.

"I think we can be fairly certain that the Spider is protecting his web. My bet is that they are now on the run to a new hiding place. Mobilize all twenty men and lock down the immediate area. I shall personally take care of this vermin before nightfall.

"I want roadblocks set up on a five mile radius from that farm. They have to be on foot so we shall search every farm and possible refuge within that circle. Shoot any Polish peasants that don't give you complete cooperation.

"Oh, and in case the rats have a secret nest; the attic or a basement, have a couple of men search that Brzozowski Farm from top to bottom. Rip it apart then burn it to the ground. Remove all the contents, box 'em and hand everything over to the NKGB.

"Let's go!"

As the two fugitives crouched within the cover of the copse behind their farm, Czeslaw was well aware the NKGB would soon be focusing all available resources on this geographic area and there was no way to outrun the seemingly limitless resources of the powerful Soviet Union. He was more depressed than he had ever been in his young life. His own existence meant nothing but now he had full responsibility for a very scared wife whom he loved dearly.

There is only one thing I can do, he concluded. *I must trade my surrender for her safety. Now, how the hell do I make that deal with the Devil?*

CHAPTER EIGHT

The Mission Begins

Major Paddy McBride and his Black Widows left Northern Ireland's Aldergrove Airport on a military transport plane that officially carried mail and supplies to the rear of the British Eighth Army, an army now enjoined by the US Fifth Army under General Mark Clark. The plane's inventory listed no personnel beyond crew, as a blind eye was turned on the Black Widow squad when their leader produced Downing Street stationery stating—in no uncertain terms—that their passage was not to be hindered or questioned in any way. Closer scrutiny would have revealed the signature to be that of *T. T. Hoar-Stevens,* the given name of Terry-Thomas, a well-known, gap-toothed comedian of the time and a man with absolutely no connection at all to His Majesty's government.

After a final refueling stop in Sicily, the Armstrong Whitworth Albemarle lumbered over *'the heel of the boot'* to touch down at the Royal Air Force maintenance facility outside Lecce-Galatina, Italy. The seven-year-old aircraft taxied to a large remote hanger at the far end of the taxiway on its unique tricycle undercarriage. The pilot then shut down the engines and a tug truck pulled the plane inside while an impressively efficient ground crew began shutting the wide hanger doors, completing the task as soon as unladen the tug truck re-emerged. Within the privacy of this building, the Black Widows unloaded their gear into the waiting AEC Matador and were on the road to the remote SAS base in Apulia with reasonable confidence that no Allied or Axis bureaucrats knew of their whereabouts.

By scheduling a very public visit to London during this time, Brigadier Bryan Zumwalt, secured the imperative that the British army had absolutely no knowledge of any unauthorized, covert operations McBride and his rogue friends might be cooking up; officially, the records showed all personnel in the squad attending a two-week course in martial arts in Ballymena.

During that tedious and noisy 1,500 mile flight from Aldergrove, Staff Sergeant Johnston combatted the droning engines to review and refine details about the mission with each member of the squad. As a result, all that was left for the warriors to do once they arrived in Brindisi was to check weapons, eat some delicious bolpette with pasta and wait for the aircraft they were going to 'steal.'

Billy Fagan did a double-take when he first saw their new plane. He knew perfectly well it was a Douglas C-47 Skytrain military transport but the fresh paint indicated it to be a Douglas DC-3 passenger aircraft belonging to LOT Polish Airlines.

Maybe no one will notice the cargo door, mused the veteran pilot to himself.

"Billy, will this crate do the job? And can you get us behind Russian lines by tomorrow morning?" Paddy had moved beside Billy and the two of them were peering through disappearing daylight as the ground crew worked furiously to pack the plane with equipment.

"I can certainly get you there, old boy, but it is 800 miles to Western Silesia and that plane has a range of 1,600 miles."

"So you will not be able to get back?" asked the big man.

"Not if we hit any kind of weather or spend an extended period under 25,000 feet."

"But you have a plan, right?"

"That's the problem du jour, old boy. We still don't know exactly where we're going but the flight will take at least six hours. We are on a mission to nowhere unless we're able to pick up final coordinates for the actual drop zone as we sweep over Radomysl. This character, Bogdan Dobrowolski, is understandably insistent about not jeopardizing his friend, the Spider, by broadcasting details over the airwaves; preferring to toss them up to us in a quick, low power burst as we fly over his base. Pretty smart really and minimizes your chances of parachuting into the waiting arms of a Russian patrol."

"And if we don't manage to get the coordinates from Bogdan?"

"I'll turn the crate around and bring you home."

"That is not an option, Billy, we're going in regardless. We need to figure out a back-up landing zone."

The Black Widows were loafing in the base NAAFI, drinking tea, playing cards, and reading comics. The general atmosphere and casual laughter belied a group about to fly an extremely dangerous mission. Paddy walked in with Billy and a third man.

"Clear the bar, Staff." Johnston obeyed without

question by glowering as he approached a group of non-comms at the far end of the club. The five rose immediately and left through the nearest door.

"You too, son," he said, staring down a server who, still wearing his apron, scurried after his mates. The sergeant did a quick reconnoiter of the back rooms.

"All clear, Paddy, what's up?" Paddy nodded for Billy to do the honors.

"First, allow me to introduce a new Black Widow. The base is lending us Ted Robinson, an excellent navigator and second seat as my crew. He's American, has tons of hours in Dakotas and knows this part of Eastern Europe much better than I."

The lounging assassins looked Ted up and down but said very little. Approval of membership into this group was not easily gained, so Paddy stepped forward and placed a large hand on the nervous Robinson's shoulder.

"We are ready to take off but as you're all aware, we have no bloody idea where the hell we are going! The grand plan has a local AK group scrambling to commandeer a couple of trucks to rendezvous with the Black Widows once we hit the ground. In an ideal world, we will end up within ten minutes and a couple of hundred yards of each other—all without the Russians knowing anything about it. However at this time, to protect the integrity of our mission and the location of the Spider, the Polish radio operator with the coordinates is refusing to divulge the drop zone to either the local AK or us until the last possible moment."

"Define 'last possible moment,' Paddy," interrupted the introverted Ronnie Martin. But the reply came from Billy Fagan.

"Bogdan Dobrowolski is our liaison. He will shoot us the drop zone coordinates in a ten-second untraceable transmission as we fly over his base in Radomysl. He'll duplicate the burst to the drop zone's local AK militia."

With uncharacteristic tenacity, SAS Specialist Martin continued to press.

"Way too many moving parts, Billy and high odds we'll be no wiser about our destination than we are in this NAAFI."

"Spot on, Ronnie. I came to the same conclusion and want to brainstorm a back-up plan. When it all boils down, we are certainly better off landing anywhere in Poland rather than fighting our way to the Spider through Nazi Germany. Our best intelligence puts Chez in Krakow and his family in Żagań. I suggest we vote as a group to pick one of those locations if Dobrowolski fails to get through on the radio."

"Democracy is a beautiful thing, Paddy, but let's not get fuckin' crazy here. You and I both know if Chez does not want to be found. We'd be wasting our time in Krakow," the crusty Glaswegian grimaced.

"We should drop in the vicinity of Żagań and locate his farm—hopefully before the NKGB does. We'll get his family to a safe location and leave Chez a message to come find us."

Paddy waited for dissention but there was none.

"I am in complete agreement, Mike. What do you think, Billy?"

"It is the lesser risk but still dangerous as hell. Ted has identified some flat land to the east of Żagań that we could use by coming in from the southeast at treetop level. I'll pull up to 800 feet to allow you and the lads to swing off a static line into the field. You won't have any ground transportation if we don't get the bloody coordinates but it's the best I have for now.

"Anyway, once you drop, I'm planning on coughing the engines to try and fool anybody listening into thinking that I'm a commercial flight with a minor problem before climbing back up to cruising altitude and heading north to neutral Sweden."

"Eight hundred feet will give us one swing of the chute before we hit the dirt. Should be okay, even in the black of night." Paddy's response was so matter-of-fact, Billy was not sure if it a clinical assessment or a wry sense of humor.

"Show me where the hell Żagań is on this map, Ted."

The squad convened by the cargo door of the plane to double-check their individual gear as the clock ticked down. The thought that they might never return was not lost an anyone but they had all been in similar situations before and as the boarding process began, Scotty Miller used his expected jocularity to relieve tension. The procession had just started meandering up the ramp when an adjutant approached McBride with a large white envelope. The major said nothing and stuffed it into his bag, returning Takeo's stare with a knowing wink.

It was just after nine o'clock on a starless evening when the fully-loaded, C-47 transport took off to head north over the Adriatic in the general direction of Budapest, Hungary. There was heavy cloud cover below 15,000 feet so little likelihood of encountering Bomber Command if they kept the fully lit appearance of a commercial DC-3 airliner cruising at 25,000 feet, though to do so, the occupants within the unpressurized military aircraft were swathed in wool blankets and never strayed far from the portable oxygen tanks.

Almost four hours into the flight, LOT flight number P670 crossed into Polish airspace, now technically controlled by Russia but the risk was essential. Flying Officer Robinson doubled as navigator and radio operator so at his command, Billy dropped below the clouds to 8,000 feet for the briefest of moments to attempt contact with Bogdan Dobrowolski in Radomysyl.

"Bracia, this is Black Widow. Over."

The grizzled AK veteran commander had been fidgeting with his receiver since midnight for this moment and switched to transmit immediately with his short, crisp burst of information.

"Fifty One Thirty six Nan. Fifteen Twenty One Easy. Good luck. Over."

"Roger that. Dziękuję bardzo. Thanks for your help. Out."

After the twenty second burst, the radio airwaves quickly reverted to total silence as the plane rose back above the clouds towards the coordinates of the anticipated landing site, now less than two hours away. Robinson walked back into the fuselage to find Paddy and grinned proudly.

"Great minds think alike. The landing zone is less than a mile from the one I picked for the back-up plan."

"Then I have to think that great Russian minds might come to the same conclusion.

"I have a bad feeling about this."

As he sensed the Russian patrols closing in, Czeslaw knew his chances of escape were diminishing by the minute—at least with Jadwiga beside him. It was a couple of hours after midnight, and the night was dark and overcast. As they passed behind a small neighboring farm, he noticed a light within. He turned to his bride, marveling at how calm she remained as he revealed his desperate strategy.

"Jadzia, you need to beg shelter in this house, it looks like someone is still up. Do you know them?"

"Sure, it's the Jaglowski Farm. They're an older couple whom I see in church every Sunday and I'm certain they'll recognize me even though we've never really talked."

"Get them to hide you while I lead the Russians away. Tomorrow, you must find a way to get to Poznan. I'll be fine on my own and will meet up with you soon as I can get to cousin Franek's house." He paused upon hearing a very low flying plane cough and splutter in the distance and could not help a distracted thought. *Those poor souls are not going to make it either. The whole world has its own troubles.*

"Everything will be okay, ukochanie. Trust me, my love."

Jadwiga knew in her heart she would never see

Czeslaw again but recognized their only chance this night was to separate. After a long kiss, they lovingly tapped their foreheads together. She smiled and patted him on the cheek before turning to crawl slowly from the tree cover to the back door of the farm and wrap on the glass. He sensed their catastrophic mistake as soon as the door opened. Seconds later, a tall Russian major stepped out to press his TT33 pistol against her temple.

"Mrs. Spider, I presume? And where, might I ask, is your eight-legged fool of a husband?" A pair of uniformed men materialized to drag the kicking and clawing Jadwiga into the farmhouse, leaving the major to turn and shout towards the dark. "What good fortune for both of us, Spider. You are lucky to choose the same farm as me as you will find me much more lenient than any of my men occupying the surrounding houses. I am going to give you five seconds to show yourself before I shoot your wife. Others would give you much less. One, Two Thr…"

"Niet! Octahobka!" The Spider yelled out from the shadows in frantic Russian. "No - Stop! Do I have your word that my wife will have safe passage if I surrender?"

"Of course, my word as an officer and a gentleman."

Czeslaw walked slowly towards the back door; his arms stretched vertically above his head. The major and his two soldiers trained weapons at him from point blank range. "You look much too puny to be the famous Spider. Give me some proof. How many NKGB did you murder in Krakow?" Major Ivanovic asked dubiously.

"I murdered no one but I'm guessing five or six were killed by a mysterious explosion in a house on pasaz Bielak after I had already left," replied the dejected captive.

"Possibly true, but I have many, many more questions. Step inside."

"What about my wife?" Czeslaw spat angrily as his arms were pinned to his side by strong rope.

"I suspect you will be more inclined to honesty if you are able to look into her eyes as you both die, asshole. Let's be honest, neither of you are going to see this morning's sunrise. It is really more a question of how much pain you are willing to see her suffer as I begin her death by a thousand cuts.

"Your choice. She dies regardless—but you can pick when."

CHAPTER NINE

The Cavalry Rides In

B illy Fagan's melodious baritone crackled through-out the fuselage of the plane.

"We are ten minutes from our landing zone; heavy cloud cover, next to no wind. I am dropping down to treetop and opening the cargo door. Gear up and prepare to clip onto the static line. I'll be pulling up through eight hundred feet at which point Ted will indicate a 'green light.'

"Go with God, my friends; bring the Spider home safely."

Flying Officer Robinson left the cockpit and gingerly walked the length of the plane by using short steps and any hand supports he could grab until he was in a position to release the rear cargo door. The special equipment bags strained against their straps and the squad braced as the change in aerodynamics shuddered the big gooney bird before Billy made the necessary corrections from the front seat. Through the whistling void at the rear of the aircraft, the Black Widows watched the ground rushing by below for what seemed like an eternity before the noise from the twin Bristol Hercules engines increased in pitch to indicate a climb.

"Four hundred ...... Five hundred ...... Six hundred ...... Seven hundred ...... Eight hundred and holding .... Green light, green light, green light!"

Ted Robinson slashed through the equipment straps with a machete and the muscle of Hoenicke, Blando and Miller supplemented the angle of the climbing plane to slide the equipment bags out of the hatch. Then, without any trace of trepidation, the line of Black Widows ran fearlessly towards the cold darkness until gravity took over.

Ronnie Martin, the last to leap, snagged his static line but without hesitation grabbed Robinson's machete to slice the attachment away. He tossed the big blade back into the plane and turned to Ted with a smile.

"Hope my fucking rip cord works!"

Once on the ground, Paddy blew softly on a small wooden hunting device that simulated the croak of a frog. The Black Widows were clad in dark green camouflage with no insignia, their faces blackened beneath woolen balaclavas. Indistinguishable from shadows or each other in the dead of night, this 'ribbet' sound gave them direction for assembly. After the squad had gathered behind a low hedge, Mike Johnston performed a brief roll call and made his report.

"Sorry, Paddy, we're down to ten. Jacqui Siglar might have a broken ankle but Ronnie Martin's chute never opened and he pancaked. Brave little fucker flew past me on the way down and never let out a sound beyond the thud when he hit the ground."

The staff's terse report was met with silence.

Four of the squad retrieved the two large supply bags, dragging them into the gathering as he was speaking. "Where to from here, Paddy?"

"Scotty, take Edmund and bring Ronnie's body over here while we wait for Takeo. I sent him on a recce of the area to see if our local friends managed to get the message to meet us with transportation." He was interrupted by a whisper from the other side of the hedgerow.

"I'm right here, Paddy and have already checked out the two trucks parked over there. The drivers are sitting together in one of the cabs but I don't think they even saw us arrive. I need Jurek to come with me to check these guys out."

Brunon had done well under the circumstances. Though too far for him to personally get to Żagań on such short notice, he had dealt with Szymon Grabowski on many occasions and the old postmaster had leaped at the chance of helping the Spider by driving one of the trucks to the rendezvous himself. The fact that both trucks were emblazoned with the gaudy logos a local produce distributor was not lost upon Scotty Miller.

"It's three o'clock in the bloody morning. Anybody worried that a ton of veggies are unlikely be on their way to market at this time?"

"Scotty," Siglar laughed through her pain. "Anything on the road this late—or this early—is going to cause a Russian shakedown regardless. So just get over it."

Sergeant Jurek Podolski had been born in London to a Russian mother and Polish father but he would have made the Black Widow squad regardless of the added bonus of his linguistic skills. After he had received his sealed orders, he took time to meet secretly with his parents based upon a weird precognition that it might be the last time they would ever see each other. No details of the mission could be revealed but the extreme risk was evident in his eyes.

His mother did not take it well but the father grasped his shoulders to look Jurek squarely in the eye.

"Son, are you certain in your heart that this mission is important enough to give up your life?"

Jurek hesitated, then leant forward and said softly, "Dad, the Spider needs my help."

Old man Podolski recoiled. As far as he was concerned, the legend of the Spider was as important to Poland as the Royal Family was to any Brit; Babe Ruth to any American.

"Then go with God, Jurek and please, come home safely."

And so it was Jurek that translated for Paddy, as the leader of the Black Widows brought Szymon and the other driver up-to speed.

"First things first, we have a team member who died in the drop. We'll show you where we're burying him tonight but sometime in the near future, we want him re-buried in your local churchyard as a hero. Can you promise me you'll do everything you can?"

"Absolutely, Major, the local priest is my cousin."

"Thank you, Szymon. Now, what word of Chez?"

"I know him better as Czeslaw but the news is not good. The Russians are closing in on him and I give him little chance of escaping their trap. His in-laws have made it to Poznan but his wife stayed here. As soon as the Ruskis identified his farm, they've been using her as bait. I did hear a rumor that Czeslaw got back into town earlier today, I mean yesterday, but he's about to walk right into a trap. Our intelligence reports that for some reason, the Ruskis have rousted every farm in the immediate area, so he might already be dead…"

"Or on the run? Never give up on the Spider, Szymon. Get us to the vicinity you are talking about and we'll check out every one of those farms ourselves. I think it a fairly safe bet that the Orlowskis have flown the homestead, otherwise the Ruskis would not be searching the surrounding farms. No doubt they have a secure perimeter set up. I swore to Zumwalt that we would remain strictly covert but we might have to crack a few heads to get out of this one."

The Black Widows gathered their equipment and squeezed into the two grocery trucks, leaving the landing zone to drive cautiously in the direction of the Brzozowski farm. They used no lights and after about three miles, the first vehicle almost crashed into the blackened burned out shell of a car. The drivers pulled off the road and into the shelter of nearby trees where the Black Widows set up a perimeter.

"The Brzozowski Farm is just on the other side of that hill. This car looks like it exploded quite recently, I'm surprised I heard nothing about it!" Paddy had a grim smile as he commented on the wreck.

"This has the Spider's fingerprints all over it. How large is the local Russian garrison, Szymon?"

"Oh, it's not large, maybe twenty troops but led by a genuine sonofabitch called Major Boris Ivanovich. He's almost your height but has you beaten in the ugly department. I've only met him perhaps three times but believe me, the cruel bastard would have been perfect in the SS. So much so, he's probably pissed he was born a Russian and not German. I shudder if he gets his hands on Czeslaw and Jadwiga."

"Can't wait to meet him. Let's stage here in these trees. I'm going to take a quick peek at the farm to see if I can figure out our next step."

With the trucks parked behind the late Russian sergeant's funeral pyre, the Black Widows unloaded their gear and moved further away from the road. If a Russian patrol came by, Szymon and Piotr could claim they were looking through the car wreck for loot. Ten minutes later, Paddy rejoined his men, Kershaw field binoculars still around his thick neck.

"No signs of life at the farm and no signs of a fight. Szymon tells me the entire local garrison numbers about twenty troops. If and whenever they meet up with Chez, he will not run from those odds so I'm encouraged that he and Jadwiga are on the run. I'm also informed that the Ruski commander is a seasoned veteran, in which case I expect him to do what I would do; form a noose—then tighten it.

"We'll spread out from here in small teams, looking for any clues that might reveal the Spider's location.

Jacqui will stay here to coordinate radio traffic between the teams. If you see anything suspicious, report in so we can consolidate. Don't try anything on your own; if we get pulled into a fire fight, Russia will declare war on Britain by the end of the week.

"Move out."

For the next thirty minutes, the Black Widows floated silently through the shadows, staying within tree line as they studied each farm they encountered. There were quite a few military trucks driving along the roads but none with any apparent urgency. These trucks were noted to be methodically stopping at each house they encountered to wake up all occupants as they searched for their prey.

The Black Widows got lucky very early in the game when Scotty Miller's team noticed a small farm with all its lights on. As they watched, the vehicles seen earlier began arriving from all directions.

"This is team three, Jacqui; I think we've got something and I'm calling a re-group. Over." Scotty Miller and his team watched this farm for a further two full minutes before retreating like ghosts to the trucks and their staging area.

"You pretty certain this is the place, Scotty?" asked Mike Johnston in a way that left Miller in little doubt the grizzled Staff was in no mood for bullshit.

"There are about twenty Russian soldiers there, Mike, which has to be pretty much the entire garrison from what I've been told. We watched them drive in from all points and park. They're relaxed, sitting around, laughing and joking. My opinion is that the search has been called. Not only that, somebody in that farm is getting the crap beaten out of them. I heard male and female screams."

"I like your thought process, Scotty," Paddy broke in. "I doubt they would have called in their search pattern if they had not caught their prey. Let's go take a wee peek."

Within fifteen minutes, the entire Żagań garrison of the Russian army was under the deadly collective gaze of the Black Widows. Their numbers had not swelled much beyond those Sergeant Miller had seen earlier and they were evidently still enjoying some kind of victory; lolling around and smoking their cigarettes, cheering when sounds of distress emanated from within the building. Hidden under the cover of surrounding trees, Mike Johnston organized his men in complete silence through practiced hand signals.

The Black Widows spun off into their small teams, each able to creep within eight to ten feet of the raucous soldiers by using the protection offered from the dark side of parked headlights. Two of the young soldiers left the bright circle of light to relieve themselves, never to return. The numerical odds were still heavily in favor of the Russians but elements of surprise and Special Forces training caused them to be completely shocked and hopelessly out-gunned when Johnston's men stepped into their world with Sten guns aimed at their heads. The stunned Soviet soldiers instantly obeyed Mike's universal signal for complete silence as they sank to their knees, hands behind their heads.

Inside the farmhouse, the major was nearing the end his patience. He strutted slowly around the wooden kitchen chairs that held his trussed victims. His sadistic temperament made no attempt to conceal his theatrical sharpening of a vicious knife old man Jaglowski used for skinning rabbits. The Russian Major pulled up his own chair and sat backwards astride the seat, putting his battle-scarred face within inches of Czeslaw's.

"From your reputation, you are a very tough man but believe me, you will spill out your very soul until I am satisfied you have told me everything. Then, you will die. How am I able to predict this? Because I am going to give you a ringside seat to watch how a Russian man pleases a woman. You will both beg for death but it will come only after I am satisfied with your confession."

In fluent Russian, Czeslaw immediately launched an incredible bluff.

"Major, I am but the Spider's half-brother. You must have heard he is well over two meters tall; that's even taller than you! How can that possibly be me? But, I do know where he is. I spoke to him not four hours ago on the radio transmitter he keeps hidden in our farmhouse. That's how I heard about the explosion in Krakow.

"Please, let my wife go and I will take you straight to his secret hiding place. I know you will kill me but my wife is pregnant and it will be worth it for my chi…"

"Total bullshit!" derided Major Ivanovitch, his wicked scar now a brilliant red line indicating his peaking blood pressure. He signaled one of the two henchmen he was using for muscle to smash a rifle butt into Czeslaw's kidneys to repay what he considered an insult. Jadwiga immediately screamed her outraged protest.

"You low-life, cowardly bastard. Release me and I will kick your ass in front of these idiots. Or do Russians need three men to fight one Polish woman?"

"They have used up the only chance I was prepared to give them. Slice the bitch."

Jadwiga was stoic as one of the soldiers approached her with the razor-sharp hunting knife but an unexpected change in her focus to the rear of the kitchen caused all three Russians to glance around in curiosity. What they saw caused a palpable shock wave in the room. An enormous man, ominous in threatening camouflage, was peering at them through the small eyeholes of an olive green balaclava as he casually leant with arms folded against an antique china cabinet. For a moment, the sheer size of this apparition made the major think he was face to face with the legendary Spider. Then his fantasy shattered when he noticed a second interloper, much stockier but in the same outfit, standing about four feet to the giant's side. Boris Ivanovitch had trouble comprehending how they could have mysteriously appeared and he paused to wipe his eyes; but both of his compatriot bullies grunted into action and began to raise their guns.

Takeo's left and right arms blurred across his body, a matt black, six-pointed throwing star appearing at each soldier's throats almost instantly. The two henchmen collapsed in agony to the floor, grasping their necks as they gurgled on their own blood.

Ivanovitch, still unwilling to comprehend what was occurring, slowly pushed himself off from his chair as if dismounting a horse. He puzzled how these two could have slipped into the kitchen past his entire garrison stationed outside in the farmyard. His brow furrowed and he cocked his head as he strained to hear any sounds that might have encouraged him to summons help. There were none.

His eyes began to fixate on the nonchalant swinging of a 9 millimeter Browning in the large man's hand.

This makes absolutely no fucking sense. I would think it was a dream if my men weren't bleeding all over the floor. Where are these two men from? Are they Nazis? he wondered.

Neither intruder had spoken to this point so the mystery compounded until Ivanovich heard something he thought might be English, though clouded by a very strange accent.

"Chez, my friend, good to see you again. After Takeo gets you and your bride out of those uncomfortable bindings, I would like you to inform this arsehole in Russian that his future well-being depends upon …"

Unable to comprehend any of Paddy's side conversation with Chez, Major Boris Ivanovitch Comenchenkyo decided to take his chances as a gunslinger and his right hand darted for his holstered pistol. The TT3 did not even clear leather when McBride's dum-dum bullet caused a neat 9 mm hole to appear in the center of major's forehead, scrambling everything inside before exiting a much larger hole that painted the entire farmhouse wall above the Spider in reds and grays. Paddy stood up, removed his balaclava and bowed to Jadwiga.

"Apologies, ma'am. It was not my intention for you to see that."

At the sound of the shot, Staff Sergeant Mike Johnston bust through the door like a bull elephant, Sten gun ready. The relatively passive scene confronting him contained three very dead Soviet soldiers, Takeo Atobe bent over retrieving his stars and Paddy McBride assisting Chez and a young lady restore circulation to their unbound limbs.

"Well hello, Chez." He grinned. "This beautiful lady must be Jadwiga?" Chez nodded back with appreciative recognition but kept his attention on his bride who was throwing up violently onto the floor.

"Time to move out, Boss. I'm pretty certain those Ruskis outside have not heard any English spoken. Edmund and Jurek have been gossiping loudly to each other in Polish in an attempt to create subterfuge."

The remainder of the Russian soldiers were bound, gagged and blindfolded before being locked securely into the small adjacent barn. When they were finally found and released two days later, they debriefed their rescuers that they distinctly heard their attackers speaking Polish to each other about belonging to the Armia Krajowa in Warsaw.

The very ripe bodies of the major and his underlings had squares of paper pinned to their chests. On each was inscribed an oval surrounded by eight legs.

CHAPTER TEN

Flying Blind

E dmund and Jurek began the one-mile jog to where Szymon Grabowski was waiting with Piotr, Jacqui and the two trucks. The Polish drivers had been instructed to wait no later than dawn and were getting very nervous as the birds started to chorus their anticipation of the event. The two men started to pace around the vehicles, their eyes scouring the sky as if looking for a way to accelerate the inevitability of sunrise. Jacqui Siglar noted several furtive glances towards her and although she spoke not one word of Polish, she detected their conclusion that, were it not for her, they could be on their way back to the relative safety of their beds in Żagań.

A woman's intuition is almost infallible; it is an

instinct evolving over millions of years that has helped protect women from the irrational curse of male testosterone. So Jacqui decided to pull herself away from the radio and onto her good leg with the help of a nearby tree branch. She could hear their nervous mumbling as they walked continuously in a loose loop around the vehicles. She made ready her BAP by thumbing back the hammer of the Browning Hi-Power and checking the safety catch before tucking the barrel into the back of her belt.

I'm a female cripple and these guys have to be reckoning they can overpower me, she thought. *I wish I could calm them down for another ten minutes so Edmund and Jurek can get here to explain what went down. But they don't understand a bloody word of English.*

Of course, they also don't understand that this lady can shoot the eyes out of a potato at twenty paces, so I truly hope they keep their cool.

The two men re-appeared from behind the rear grocery truck but stopped when they saw her standing beside the radio. They had their fists and jaws clenched and moved several feet apart as if deciding their next move. Jacqui beamed a broad smile that disarmed them; she raised her left hand with the thumb raised and shouted.

"Good, good, everything is good."

Szymon and Piotr frowned, relaxed their fists and then smiled to each other.

"She must have received a message from her squad. I think 'good' means '*dobry;*' sounds like '*gut*' in German. Plus, I don't think she would be smiling and shouting so loud if there were any Russians around.

"Oh thank God we didn't do something stupid."

Within seconds, two jogging Black Widows entered the scene to see both Poles shaking their raised thumbs in the air and laughing. Jurek filled them in with news of the Orlowski rescue while Edmund moved towards Siglar, noticing she had turned her back to the trucks to shield her movements. With practiced expertise, she released the hammer on the BAP and holstered the weapon, giving her only witness a nod and a wink.

"Trouble, Jacqui?"

"Not for me, Edmund, but our friends might have just dodged a bullet—make that two bullets!"

While Jurek and Szymon drove back to collect Chez, Jadwiga and the rest of the squad from the Jaglowski Farm, Edmond conscripted Piotr to begin de-camping the gear into the rear truck as Jacqui made a necessarily brief transmission to SAS headquarters in Brindisi:

The Black team is winning at half-time. Repeat. The Black team is winning at half-time. Acknowledge? Over.

She switched to receive and waited. It seemed like an eternity but closer to one minute when a crackle preceded a distant voice.

Acknowledged. Have a good game and bring home the win. Out.

With that, she shut everything down to allow the vacuum tubes to cool as she watched all traces of their staging camp disappear into the gaudy vehicle. The last item, her radio, was being loaded just as the first truck returned.

The Black Widow squad that piled out onto the road were now divested of their camouflage and dressed as typical local workers. The transformation was amazing. Notwithstanding, no disguise could hide the sheer size of Major McBride—and more than one recognized it might prove a problem as they now attempted their repatriation.

"I got through to HQ, Paddy, told them we were ready to come home. Where're the rest of the family members. I thought Chez had a bunch of in-laws in tow?"

"Minor plan amendment, Jacqui, he has them hidden in a farm about 140 klicks northeast of here. Our mission includes extracting seven people, so we have to make a detour to Poznan."

"Poznan is a bloody hornets' nest and even further behind Russian lines," Mitch Arnold chipped in. "I don't have warm and fuzzies about this, Paddy."

"Ah well, there y'are then." The subject was dropped and the Black Widows piled into the trucks.

"Where to now, Czeslaw? Better make it quick." the postmaster asked, delighted to see both him and Jadwiga again.

"If you can drop us somewhere north of Żagań, we'll jump onto the early morning freight train to Poznan leaving you in peace with our eternal thanks."

Jadwiga, who had worked for years at the Żagań railway station, knew the schedules better than anyone, so she turned to Chez. "We are too late for today's train; it went through Żagań at midnight but there's a morning freight to Leszno we could jump on. Leszno is only 40 miles south of Poznan and a much bigger hub than Żagań."

Chez translated to Paddy as they bounced along the country roads. "Jadwiga says that freight trains are frequently used to transport supplies for the Russians and if that's the case, there might be an armed guard or two to contend with."

"And how exactly do we jump onto an armed, moving train with all our equipment, Chez? Remember, we're not supposed to be behind Russian lines."

Czeslaw Orlowski laughed confidently. "That's a job for the Spider! Don't worry, Major."

An old steam engine pulled eight boxcars through Żagań just after five o'clock that morning, relentlessly chugging its load of produce to the market at Leszno. Apparently, the content was not important enough for armed guards as none could be seen where they might be expected. Nevertheless, the Black Widows meticulously scoured every inch of the train through their binoculars as it trundled towards their treed hiding place just beyond the small road to Meksyk. Soldiers assigned to guard slow-moving trains usually sit on the roof of each carriage and just in case any were taking a break below before they resumed their duties, Specialist Siglar had 'Betsy' her Enfield Sniper rifle, set up on a makeshift tripod to send them into early retirement.

The train was picking up speed after slowing through the market town of Szprotawa and doing perhaps thirty miles an hour when the engineer noticed a large, brightly painted, produce truck immobilized in the middle of the Meksyk road crossing. The bonnet was raised and two men were diligently working on the engine until they heard the approaching train. They both looked up in horror before running frantically to the side of the track, leaving their disabled truck to its fate. But the train had plenty of time to stop, steam belching everywhere. The Polish engineer was not a happy man as he jumped from cab with his fireman and strode to confront the miscreants.

"You idiots were almost killed. We will help you push that piece of garbage off the crossing and you can fix it over there. If it will not move, there'll be no choice but to run the train through it."

"Any more muscle on the train?" asked the Spider innocently. "I think six men could push our truck quite easily. Four just doesn't seem enough."

"No, you dumb Polak. What you see is what you get. We are due in Leszno in two hours or the damn Russians will kick our dupas all the way back to Żagań. One try, then I am going to have to crush it out of the way." Chez had all the information he needed to know and wiped his forehead with his cap; a signal to the Black Widows that there were no unwanted surprises on the train and they should all get into the last box car on the blind side of the curve.

"Okay. Piotr, if you steer, these kind gentlemen and I will push from behind." The old truck began to move and with great effort and relief, cleared the tracks to park safely out of the path of the train. The whole debacle took several minutes and would have been a lot faster had Piotr not had his foot on the brake. He and Chez shook hands with the two railway men and waved to them as they mounted the engine to shunt on to Leszno.

"Dumb Polak! Where's the love, Piotr?" Chez

whispered through the frozen smile of his clenched teeth. "Thank you, my friend and also to Szymon. We owe you a lot. Travel safely back to Żagań and keep your heads down for a while. I've a feeling things are going to get pretty hairy over the next few days."

With that, he shook hands and vaulted effortlessly into the last boxcar as it passed by.

Jadwiga and the Black Widows were sitting comfortably on crates of cabbage and Chez gave her a quick hug before turning to Paddy. "Any bright ideas, Paddy?"

"Well, first things first, we have to get Jadwiga's family out of the farm near Poznan, then figure out a way to get us all safely back to jolly old England. So far, I don't think our noble allies, the Soviets, have any idea we're here but the Russian body count is rising and they'll figure something's not right soon enough. Zumwalt will be very relieved if we can get everybody home without that change in situation occurring." He called over to Specialist Siglar. "Jacqui, as soon as our radio picks up reception, I need to confer with headquarters and get some intelligence on where the hell the German and Russian front lines are in this part of Poland; seems like they change from day to day. At least we're allowed to shoot Germans.

"And find out if Prague is still our best option."

Thirty minutes into the journey, Siglar reported it was not.

At the briefing in Ballymena, several escape contingencies had been mapped out and just as well. First choice had been to get everyone to Czechoslovakia as fast as possible and have Billy Fagan fly the group out of Prague to London. This option started to fall apart when a few wayward USAAF bombers accidently mistook Prague for Dresden and carpet-bombed the city last St. Valentine's Day, killing almost one thousand civilians in the process. Now, MI6 now considered Prague an increasingly pernicious environment and most likely to remain so for years to come.

Another option involved heading north to the Baltic Sea to steal a boat, shipping everyone from Swinemunde to Trelleborg in neutral Sweden. Eleven men and six women, travelling north through 150 miles of war ravaged Poland as the Russians fought the retreating Germans for every inch of ground, had more than a few details that needed to be worked out, but it might work at a pinch. Beyond that, the options became very thin and perilous at best. The sullen attitude in the boxcar after Jacqui's communication about the Prague option, betrayed everyone's fears that the group was flying blind without a plan.

They wracked their brains but could not seem to evolve any escape solutions that had even a slight chance of success until, out of the blue, Chez cut the Gordian knot with a painfully simple idea. "Jadwiga reminds me there's a landing field outside Leszno. Why not have our friend Billy pick us up there? Didn't you say he had to fly up to Sweden after dropping you in Żagań? Be a bloody site easier for him to fly to Poland than for us to walk to Sweden!"

Paddy and Mike looked at each other and started laughing, shaking their heads in wonderment. "Chez, for somebody who has not spent one day of his life behind a school desk, you never, ever cease to amaze me.

"Jacqui, see if can you raise anybody at HQ to find out where the hell Billy Fagan is. He should still be in Sweden and I would start by searching anywhere that serves gin." Then, turning back to Chez, Paddy said, "Please tell me everything you know about this landing strip."

"Jadwiga knows Leszno better than I do but it was made quite famous before the war as an ideal place to fly bi-planes, tri-planes and gliders; World War One antiques, Red Baron stuff. A flying club—The Leszno Bandits, I believe they were called—maintained a grass flying field there. It was called Aeroklub Leszno Strzyzewice and should be pretty easy for us to check out. I was going to suggest we jump off this train in Strzyzewice anyway to avoid looking suspicious as we wait for our next ride. We can always circle to the north and pick up some form of transportation beyond Leszno to get us to the farm in Kormorniki if the Aeroklub idea proves infeasible."

"How far is this airfield from where we jump off in Strzyzewice?" After talking briefly to Jadwiga, Chez responded, "Less than a mile."

Scotty Miller was sitting on the planked floor idly trying to score points with the injured sniper.

"Jacqui, how's the foot? You know, sometimes the best thing for a broken ankle is a back massage. Just let m...." Jacqui scowled fiercely and was just about to let him have a piece of her mind when Miller fortuitously heard the radio trying to reach them and turned away as Specialist Siglar spent next two minutes patched through to Brindisi.

"Paddy, they've finally located Billy. They have him on the radio from the Con Tower of Bullofta military airfield in southern Sweden. He still hasn't relinquished that Polish C-47 he stole and Headquarters is reminding him they would like it back. Got any instructions for him?" Paddy was pouring over a map but looked up.

"Have HQ ask the Wing Commander if he would be so kind as to pick us up from a grass field southwest of Leszno, Poland, coordinates 51 degrees 50 minutes Nan, 16 degrees 31 minutes Easy. Early tomorrow morning should be fine. Let's say nine o'clock?"

Chez was peering over Paddy's shoulders to catch a glimpse of the map as he felt the freight begin to slow down in preparation for its upcoming stop in Leszno.

"I'll be right back. Get ready to jump off the left side of the train once we slow down to walking speed." With that, he opened the sliding door of the boxcar and pulled himself onto the roof of a train that was still doing a respectful twenty miles an hour. He jogged towards the engine, leaping the six-foot gaps between boxcars effortlessly.

The engineer and fireman almost had simultaneous heart attacks when the man they recognized as having left with a disabled truck almost two hours ago was now standing behind them in the cab.

"Ah, dzień dobry once again, gentlemen. I trust you are both proud Polish patriots like myself?" Both men looked at his questioning raised left eyebrow and then at each other before nodding a cautious yes. "Doskonały, then I need you to begin decelerating this train down to a walk,—hold that speed for one minute—then resume your journey. Do not look back until I leave, then you can be on your way. Czy rozumiesz? Do you understand?" The two railway men were puzzled but discretion told them it would be better to do as they were told so both turned away to stare stalwartly at the track ahead.

The train was just south of Strzyzewice when it slowed enough to inch along for the sixty seconds requested. It was only then that the stranger concluded his conversation with, "Dziękuję bardzo, moi przyjaciele. Know that you will have done your part for Poland by keeping both our opportune meetings a complete secret. You may now resume your speed.

"Oh, and if I ever hear you disparage our countrymen by calling them 'dumb polaks,' I swear you will regret it. In the meantime, please accept this small souvenir with my thanks." The engineer felt something being thrust into his pocket, which he cautiously removed only after he sensed the stranger had gone.

"Odpierdol sie! What the fuck is that?" asked the fireman, catching his partner staring at the paper with very wide eyes. With an uncontrollable shake, the engineer slowly turned it around so the fireman to see the infamous oval with eight legs.

"Holy Mother of God!"

CHAPTER ELEVEN

Hot Extraction

C hez leapt off the speeding train, tucking into a ball as he landed. As soon as he regained his feet, he sprinted at speed to catch up with the group. Having been led by Jadwiga, who knew this part of Poland well, they were soon all standing at the southern edge of a large open field in less than twenty minutes.

"Paddy, this is the Aeroklub Leszno Strzyzewice, home of the Leszno Bandits. The grass looks pretty short for an airfield that hasn't been used for the past six years. If you will excuse me, I'm going to go from here get my in-laws from Kormorniki, it will be best if you all remain in hiding here to wait for Billy. Please look after Jadwiga."

"Need some help?" several of the squad chorused.

"Thanks but it will be much better if I go alone. It's only a seventy mile round trip, so I should return here with my in-laws by nightfall.

"Now, before I set off, I'm going to check all the farms around this field...."

Takeo Atobe interrupted with a cold smile. "That's my job, Spider. Get on your way to Poznan," he said sharply to prompt an awkward five seconds of silence.

"I'm not checking for security, Takeo. I am going to try to negotiate some shelter and fine Polish food for you all. Hey, maybe I'll get lucky enough to borrow a car!" The rest of the hardened SAS warriors shrugged and laughed nervously at the minor confrontation but Mike Johnston caught McBride's eye with an unmistakable expression that telegraphed trepidation.

The Spider was good to his word and the Black Widows, an unlikely sobriquet they now quite enjoyed, ate a wonderful dinner of potato-cheese pierogi accompanied by long, thin kielbasa that, when broken into three-inch lengths, were enough for everyone in the squad. The meal was hosted in the rear barn of the Babik family farm and although the men were fairly certain their hosts were sacrificing their own dinner, they were equally sure to refuse would have been an insult. In addition, Zenon Babik had not hesitated to lend the Spider his Polski Fiat 618 when he heard who needed it.

After Chez drove off into the dusk, the squad lounged within the barn on bales of hay. Jacqui Siglar's foot was wrapped tightly and for the first time since the jump she was able to get about independently on a makeshift cane. An air of relaxation coupled with optimism infused everyone.

Conversations indicated emerging feelings amongst the Black Widows that they might even get out of this one alive.

"Ya know, a couple of weeks ago, I'd never heard of the Spider," mused Mitch Arnold. "However, it's now apparent that every man, woman and child in Poland worships him. I don't think I'll do anything more worthwhile in my life than to get him home safely."

"I feel the same way," agreed Edmund Smolenski. "Jurek and I had heard about his legendary exploits through friends and relatives but I'll be honest, I thought it was all bullshit propaganda."

"Apparently not," nodded Jurek.

"I'll bet a fiver that Billy brings Swedish dumplings for breakfast in the morning!" laughed Gino Blando, changing the subject.

"Swedish crumpet would be more like it," retorted the eternally one-track mind of Sergeant Miller.

As the night crept on, some soldiers caught sleep,

others played cards, Jadwiga was a guest on the floor of the small farmhouse. Shortly after midnight they all started upon hearing a car engine approaching. Mike Johnston woke last to find the rest of his men already covering the large barn doors with their automatic weapons.

"What do you think, boss?" he whispered.

"Takeo's out there keeping watch and it sounds like a small car. I doubt he would have let them get this close if they were not friendly," the big man mused. Sure enough, the large wooden doors eventually creaked open to reveal the trim silhouette of the Spider and behind him, five ladies carrying suitcases. Jadwiga ran into the barn from the house and the Brzozowskas squealed with excitement.

Poznan had only been in the hands of the Russians since the beginning of March and the new occupiers had been systematically looting and plundering the old city. Another week and there might have been no escape. Czeslaw had offered Jadwiga's cousin, Franek, the opportunity to escape with them to England but he declined, preferring, like many Poles, to rebuild Poland from within.

Just after breakfast, Wing Commander William Wallace Fagan and his navigator Ted Robinson left Swedish airspace at 15,000 feet on a southeasterly course towards the destination coordinates transmitted to them from the SAS headquarters in Brindisi. The three hundred and fifty mile flight would take just under three hours and they expected to attract little or no attention from marauding fighters. Fagan correctly predicted that only one side would have air support for the battles raging below to control the Baltic coast, the once-dominant Luftwaffe having withdrawn in its entirety to defend Berlin. Consequently, there was little concern when a couple of inquisitive MIG-3's climbed up for a peek but the Russian pilots did not seem too interested in a non-threatening, non-German, commercial carrier.

At twenty minutes before nine, Zenon Babik walked Chez and the squad to the center of the large landing strip. He explained that the grass was kept perennially short by grazing sheep and cattle, every one of which had now to be removed from and kept from straying into a long central rectangular swath he was defining by sticks with red tape knotted to the tops.

Off in the distance, they heard a low rumble, a dull, rolling noise that increased rapidly to cause some consternation when no one could make out its source.

"Try looking directly downwind towards those trees," suggested Scotty Miller. "I don't think the fat bastard has ever flown higher than fifty feet above the ground his entire life!"

Sure enough, from roughly that location, a Douglas C-47 Skytrain with LOT Polish Airlines insignia suddenly materialized over the surrounding trees and loomed towards them. Billy touched the plane down onto the grass strip with his usual artistic grace and then taxied towards the small crowd. Dropping the rear cargo door before the plane had fully stopped, Ted Robinson de-planed and ran towards them urgently.

"Get yourselves on board as fast as you can, there's a Russian patrol about ten miles away and headed right towards us. We can only figure some fighters we saw must have reported us. Don't know how they knew this was where we were going to land but they have a jump on us and we've no more than twenty minutes to get back in the air."

Paddy raised his eyebrows and tossed a quizzical glance at Staff Sergeant Johnston.

"Ah well, there y'are now. Mike, I'm thinkin' there might be another reason.

"Let's roll, folks. I want every trace of our existence put onto that plane so these good people do not suffer for their generosity."

Chez excused himself to persuade Zenon to get his family into Strzyzewice by car immediately and plead ignorance if asked about any strange visitors to his farm.

"I parked your Fiat behind the barn. It is full of petrol but let me show you where I hid the key." The two men ran to the farmhouse and gathered the rest of the Babik family, anxiety and with fear mounting, they all disappeared towards the barn.

Paddy was raking through his personal gear and suddenly spun back around to Mike Johnston. "Where the fuck is he, Mike? Someone's been in my bag and the file is missing. I warned you to keep a close eye on him throughout the mission and it's not bloody over yet."

"Damnation, Paddy. I haven't seen him for over thirty minutes; been too busy herding fuckin' sheep off the landing strip. Do you think he's flown the coup?"

"With that file gone, perhaps, but I'll wager he's the reason a boatload of Ruskis are headed our way. I blame myself for not sleeping with that envelope strapped to my chest. Never believed in coincidence and this is his last chance to spike us. My gut tells me he's still around to make sure we don't take off before his friends get here. Life'll be a lot easier for him if all the witnesses die in a firefight.

"Everybody prepare for a rapid take-off. Mitch, Jurek, under no circumstance do you allow Atobe to get within twenty yards of that plane until we return. Mike, grab your Sten and follow me. Chez was headed to the barn."

Both men sprinted around to the far side of the

barn, Paddy getting there a full twenty yards in front of the older Johnston.

Jacqui Siglar limped forward to the cockpit and talked with Fagan and Robinson.

"Give me a word picture of the Russian patrol you saw headed towards us. I might be able to buy us a little time."

"There are four troop carriers; each with maybe ten soldiers in the back; machine gunner beside the driver. I figure they'll have to pass through that village over there; Strzyzewice according to these charts, before swinging into the airfield...."

"Let me see those charts, Ted, and describe anything you might have seen in that village."

"Well, the main road is typically narrow and winds over a small river right by the church. You can see the steeple from here. Look over there."

Jacqui said thanks and retreated towards the cargo door, pausing to have a brief word with Sergeant Miller.

"Make yourself useful, Scotty. I need Betsy set up on the starboard wing and some assistance from you and Gino to get me out there without busting my arse."

Special Forces obey orders without question and even though Specialist Siglar's demands seemed strange, Miller went immediately into the cargo hold to comply with her crisp command. With the exception of Specialists Arnold and Podolski, the rest of the men hurried around the farmyard to find anything that might afford an easy means of transporting the invalided sniper onto the wing. Several sacks of grain did the trick and by the time she was safely secured in position, Betsy, her 1944 Enfield No.4 Mk1T Sniper Rifle had its matching No. 32, Taylor–Hobson Scope in place and was resting on two ten pound bags of rice in lieu of a tripod.

"Anything else, Jacqui?" asked Scotty with uncommon sincerity and respect in his voice.

"No, just get everyone off the plane, mine is the only heartbeat I can control and I don't need any vibration beyond these bloody engines, which I guess I'll just have to adjust for."

With practiced skills, the ace sniper calibrated her scope onto the church steeple in the village and accounted for any wind movement she saw indicated by birds and trees. Then, she professionally scanned the village for a target. The extra elevation from the wing helped, but her view of the bridge was limited to a very narrow window between two buildings; the range was close to one thousand yards.

Siglar noticed a logging wagon moving slowly towards the center of the village. An easy shot for Jacqui would be to kill the old horse on the apex of the bridge but animals meant more to her than people. She had grown up on a horse farm in Essex and deliberately let the nag pass through her shot window without pulling the trigger.

I am better than that in every sense of the word and besides, it's the logs I'm after. I need a mess they cannot clear up for a couple of hours. With that in mind, the scope focused on the ropes at the rear of the wagon; she held her breath and squeezed.

The magazine held ten rounds of .303 ammunition but Jacqui Siglar needed only six before the weight of the massive logs released through what was left of the shattered ropes, causing the entire load to crash onto the road, completely blocking the bridge. The squad had no idea what she had chosen as a target as the retorts cracked out of Betsy's barrel but when they heard the chaotic noise from the village, they figured she had somehow been successful.

"A little help?" Scotty reminded Gino and they reversed their earlier efforts, getting both Jacqui and Betsy safely back off the wing.

Once he reached the far side of the barn, Paddy held up his hand and Mike skidded to a halt, his eyes transfixed on the four prone bodies of the Babik family lying beside their Fiat. No sign of anyone else so he cautiously cracked open the rear barn door to see and hear Takeo Atobe and the Spider engaged in mortal combat. He was tempted to watch; two exceptional athletes, one with a lifetime of formal, martial arts training, the other a kid who had grown up learning how to fight for his very existence. Then McBride extended his arms into a shooter's grip and calmly walked in, his single-action, semi-automatic pistol pointed directly at the back of Takeo Atobe's head. Atobe had gained the advantage and was sitting astride the taught body of the Spider, moving his knuckles into various pain pressure points; the intense grimacing of his prey making him oblivious to any movement behind him.

"Where are the fucking car keys, you piece of shit?" he kept yelling until McBride interrupted.

"You have exactly five seconds left on this earth, Takeo; one if you do not release Chez immediately." The Samurai froze, his head slowly turned, black eyes refocusing from the bruised face of the Spider onto the steady 9 mm Browning held a sparse fifteen feet to his rear. In one continuous, fluid movement, he released his hold on Chez and assumed a crouched stance, his arms in Shotokan's manji gamae position, ready for combat—or to die with honor.

"If you even flinch towards those throwing stars you keep in your sleeves, it won't be a nine mille that kills you. I can cut you in half from here with my Sten, you fuckin' bastard and I can assure you it will be my pleasure." The hardened Glaswegian Staff had come in behind Paddy but moved 45 degrees to McBride's right, straight out of the military manual.

There was still no visible reaction from Atobe, but his eyes darted between the two men as he assimilated his slim chances against their professional cone of coverage.

"Captain Atobe, the brigadier and I have long suspected that your easy infiltration into the SAS was a plan by the Japanese to set up a fifth column. You have been groomed since birth in the ancient culture of Bushido yet wanted us to believe your loyalties were to Britain through a once-met uncle in Ricksmanworth! I never bought it for a second and neither did Bryan Zumwalt.

"It was the brigadier who suggested you join the Black Widows and then sent me bait to dangle in front of you; a mysterious file containing our intelligence regarding the soon-to-be-defunct Soviet-Japanese Neutrality Pact. Information so potentially critical to your empire, we felt your handlers would risk the exposure of a top agent such as yourself.

"I figured I could use your skills regardless but if you took the bait, a loose end would be cleaned up and Zumwalt could collect on a few bets at the Officers' Club."

Absolutely no emotion showed on the face of the Japanese warrior but both McBride and Johnston noticed a slight involuntary tremor take over the young man's left hand.

"This mission also gave you an irresistible opportunity to bag a personal trophy; more specifically, my death. The Japs have had a bounty on my head since I caused your Port Moresby Operation to fail in 1942.

"You never cared about rescuing the Spider. He is nothing more to you than an enticement to elicit Russian support if the Black Widows succeeded in their mission and looked like they were going to escape. I knew as soon as I noticed my file was missing and we heard a Soviet patrol is headed this way, this became your final play."

The Samurai's eyes finally blinked within the disbelief that his cover had been so transparent but his disciplined Bushido training soon took over. He tossed out a derisive taunt with bravado.

"So I have the immense satisfaction of finally knowing what it takes to kill me—two yellow cowards with guns. I wish to die completely unarmed to stain both your souls forever. You were wise never to spar with me, McBride. I could always smell your fear." Sneering contemptuously, Takeo Atobe stripped off his upper battle tunic with slow, unhurried grace to reveal his ripped muscular torso.

"Yet another big disappointment coming your way, wee man. I never sparred with you because I was persuaded your ego would not know when to quit and I was afraid I would seriously hurt you." The Ulsterman uttered this with a tone of such undisguised condescension, it transmitted more uncertainty and fear to the martial arts expert than Johnston's covering Sten. The major then flicked on his Browning's safety catch and tossed it towards Johnston.

"Mike, if you would be so kind as to take charge of my pistol, I'm figurin' we have no more than ten minutes until his friends show."

There was no Shotokan positioning for McBride, he went straight into the classic boxer's defensive crouch that won him the British heavyweight title, but with the subtle difference that he kept both his forearms perpendicular to the ground and the backs of both fists towards his adversary. The Samurai was momentarily confused by this unconventional form of defensive posture but at the first opportunity, he yelled out a primordial battle scream and lunged forward with a vicious spinning back kick. The Ulsterman fainted to his left and then pushed back hard onto his right foot, swaying low as Takeo's rigid right leg whistled over his head. Paddy did not even try to block the kick, pivoting instead through ninety degrees as his left forearm led the extension of his body to full height. This move not only redirected the smaller man's energy, it accelerated it in a flailing upward direction. Then, as if delivering a fastball in Yankee Stadium, Paddy McBride's weight transferred back onto his left foot to unleash a hard straight right punch to Takeo's exposed kidneys as he flew overhead. The major hopped lightly to the side and the Samurai crashed back to the baked earthen floor of the barn. To his credit, the martial arts expert used amazing agility in breaking his fall from almost ten feet in the air but excruciating pain in his lower back caused him to lose sight of his quarry for a critical half-second. Too late; as he spun around, Paddy was already within his defenses; the back of both wrists simultaneously slamming like a closing rattrap onto the younger man's ears.

"Jesus Christ, that hurt me, and I'm only watching," laughed Mike Johnston.

Takeo Atobe's crushed ego found energy in the staff sergeant's mockery. Staggering backwards in his immense agony, he dropped all semblance of the Bushido code by reaching into a pant leg pocket to retrieve a hidden throwing knife. With one fluid motion, the knife whirled towards the startled veteran, piercing Johnston's arm before he could react and causing the Sten gun to clatter onto the floor. Then a deadly throwing star materialized in the Samurai's hand, with plenty of time and space to hit any square inch of the unarmed McBride's body he chose. Even with his head feeling as if was about to explode, he was going to savor this victory and a wide, crazy grin pre-empted his joy.

The contorted face transmogrified into shock when a powerful blow, resembling a steel piston, hammered into his injured back from behind. He reached back and spun around but there was no sign of anyone. Another blow from behind, this time catching the backs of both his knees. The legs of the Samurai were swept away and he began to fall backwards. But before he hit the ground, powerful, sinewy thighs cartwheeled into a locked position under his jaw and his neck snapped almost immediately.

Atobe was dead before his lifeless corpse crashed onto the ground but his last earthly thought puzzled to blackness as it tried to resolve the unseen force that had defeated him.

Death by the Spider was swift and unmerciful.

The three friends left Takeo's body where it lay and sprinted out of the barn towards the loading door of the plane.

"You okay, Mike? For the record, I had him exactly where I wanted him when you guys busted in. Did he kill the Babiks, Paddy?"

"I think he took 'em out with sleeper holds so they should be okay. Anyway, rather than running, they'll have a better chance with the Ruskis if we get the blame for their demise.

"Then let's get the fuck out a here."

The wing commander began taxiing as soon he saw them leave the barn. The rear cargo door was wide open to allow the three warriors to sprint level and scramble into the fuselage. Robinson winched the cargo door closed while Fagan turned the plane through 180 degrees and headed back to the point on the runway where he had originally touched down. Another slow 180 turn into the wind and he eased the throttles wide open to rotate the plane almost to the second a dozen, out-of-breath Russian turned into the field on foot.

From the starboard window beside his seat, Chez could make out several of the soldiers had binoculars pressed to their eye sockets.

"What happened to their trucks?"

"Annie Oakley and Betsy distracted them," laughed Scotty Miller, his voice betraying an uncharacteristic, amorous tone.

"I need to know more about that but it can wait until Billy gets us to cruising height," McBride said, as they climbed through 1,000 feet en route north to the Baltic Sea, eventually crossing the coast just east of Kolobrzeg.

CHAPTER TWELVE

A Visit to the Art Gallery

Marian Holmes, Winston Churchill's personal secretary, put her ear to the heavy mahogany door of the War Leader's study in Number 10, trying to pick up any sounds of snoring before she knocked. A grunt from within translated as permission to enter. During the war years, Churchill spent most of his time in this pleasant room, installing a day bed where he could cat nap on occasion.

"A courier dropped this off for you, sir. From the envelope, it looks like it might be from an art gallery but somehow, it managed to breeze through security." This odd fact peaked the old man's interest as he used his ivory opener to slice the red sealing wax from the expensive bond envelope.

Mr. Prime Minister,

*I would be most grateful if you could pop
by the shop at your earliest convenience.
I have a few baubles you might be
interested in adding to your collection.*

Most sincerely,

C.

Winston let out a soft chortle, "Ah yes, the Art Gallery at 54 Broadway," referring to the headquarters of Britain's Secret Intelligence Service. The original director of intelligence, Sir George Cumming, always signed his directives with the single letter 'C' written in green ink, an idiosyncracy that became a tradition for subsequent SIS directors who also used the letter 'C' when signing their missives. Since the beginning of the war, the Agency had been under the guidance of Lieutenant Colonel Stewart Menzies. The extent and contribution of his department's code breaking skills would not be fully appreciated by the world until several decades later but in this time of war, it gave Mr. Churchill a massive advantage over his antagonists.

"Holmes, please have Lieutenant Morton bring my Daimler to the front door."

Churchill's personal Daimler DB18 drophead coupe was an absolute beauty; chocolate brown with a convertible hood over gleaming silver and black coachwork by the Carlton Carriage Company. A mere eight of these automobiles were manufactured before the war and Winston's was one of only three that survived the London Blitz.

"Put the hood down, Robbie, the great British public needs to see their Prime Minister is alive and well, even though it looks like we might get a little wet. I'll be back out in a few; got a couple of letters to sign."

Churchill's personal driver of many years, Lieutenant Robin Morton, squinted up at the grey London skies and shrugged, his lips pursing into an inverted 'U.' After the hood had been folded carefully back to his satisfaction, Morton stood dutifully at the rear left hand door and waited. Five minutes later, the prime minister strode out of the black front door of his famous residence and climbed into the Daimler.

"No problem, sir, I think it'll hold off for a while. Be wonderful to give the old girl a run. Where to today? Chequers, Chartwell?"

"Ha-ha, our final destination is 54 Broadway, less than half a mile away but I would like you to drive up to Trafalgar Square and take the Mall down to the Palace so I can wave at Queen Victoria. Then we can circle around Her Majesty and get to Broadway by way of Buckingham Gate and Petty France. Once you drop me off, put the hood back up. I will be spending some time in the Art Gallery but another passenger will be taking my place for your ceremonial return to Downing Street. Take him by Westminster Abbey and the House; should be loads of people that will enjoy seeing 'me' and the car.

"Mum's the word, Robbie, and with any luck, prying eyes will see this little excursion as an innocent shopping trip and Max Aitkin's minions at *The Daily Express* will think it not worth the ink to report."

As soon as the car swept left out of Downing Street onto Whitehall, Londoners flocked to the edge of the pavement, drawn by the sight of the open-topped limousine carrying their hero.

"Go get 'em, Winnie!" Churchill, puffing his ever-present cigar, doffed his homburg and enjoyed every minute of the short ride.

When Lieutenant Morton eventually brought the elegant car to a halt, it was outside a non-descript Art Gallery at 54 Broadway and he moved swiftly to attend the rear door. His famous passenger stepped out, acknowledged a few surprised pedestrians and was greeted by staff before disappearing inside. By the time Morton had re-installed the hood, a line of bobbies had cleared the street for fifty feet around the car. This buffer proved more than enough distance to convince the curious, persistent crowd that the man with the cigar and homburg who hurried from the gallery under Lieutenant Morton's umbrella and into the back of the Daimler, was once again their legendary war leader, but of course, he was not. The beautiful automobile began a slow processional journey down Victoria Street towards Westminster Abbey, to the joy of Londoners gathered on both pavements to cheer the hand waving at them from the rear window.

Colonel Stewart Menzies had steered the Prime Minister through a discretely guarded rear door of the Art Gallery and then down two flights of brightly lit, concrete stairs. The bottom landing presented a tall, brick-vaulted space that once served as a maintenance facility for the St. James' Park Station on the London Underground; now it was the epicenter of Britain's Secret Intelligence Service and most specifically Section Six of Military Intelligence.

As Churchill and Menzies entered the central map room, two senior naval officers cut short their conversation and sprang to attention.

"Mr. Prime Minister, I believe you know Rear Admiral John Godfrey and Commander James Fleming?"

"Of course, gentlemen, please be seated. Now, what has caused MI6 to create this elaborate yet thoroughly entertaining subterfuge? Perhaps you are finally going to deliver me the elusive mole who has been reporting our every move to Hitler?"

"As you bring that delicate subject up, Prime Minister, we are getting very close. Turns out our main suspect for the past several months, Lord Halifax, is now almost certainly deemed innocent. However, the mole is someone very close to Halifax and a couple of traps we have set should deliver the culprit to us within the month.

"Apart from that, sir, the main reason we invited you to headquarters is potentially far more important. Commander Fleming, will you bring the Prime Minister up to speed, please."

Fleming opened a fat manila folder, removed four stapled sets of mimeographs and passed them around the table, keeping the last set for himself.

"Gentlemen, these are Ultra decryptions and I am obligated to ask for their return after our meeting so I can ensure their destruction in the acid bath.

"As you peruse the five pages, I would respectfully ask you to pay special attention to the anomalies I have underlined."

Menzies, Godfrey and Fleming allowed Mr. Churchill as much time as he needed to catch up with the Intelligence information they had studied intimately over the past two days and, knowing the prime minister would read every single word, a full five minutes ensued before he grunted his completion.

"Well, gentlemen, it looks like Bletchley Park has done it again. But are you certain the Huns are not planting misinformation in the hope of an over-reaction from me?"

Churchill was one of the very few politicians privy to the goings on at this top-secret facility in Bucking-hamshire where, led by the pure genius of Dr. Alan Turing, a small group of mathematicians was evolving a decryption intelligence called *'Ultra.'* Unknown to any in the Axis or Nazi high commands, Bletchley Park was currently able to decode almost all the German Enigma and Lorenz machines and consequently, any ciphers that flowed between Hitler's upper echelon and his battlefield commanders. Needless to say, this intelligence proved priceless.

"If I may, sir, the tone of this traffic indicates a gross underestimation of the importance we have been assigning to Reichleiter Martin Bormann. These very private communications leave little doubt that he is surprisingly belligerent when orchestrating Hitler in what to do and what to say; a complete reversal of Bormann's cowering public persona. We now have a strong hunch that Bormann might be the real leader of the Third Reich and Hitler not much more than a gifted orator used by him as a front man…"

"Not so fast, Commander, I need a bloody sight more than your hunch. This is quite incredible, but I am intrigued, so please, continue."

"Certainly, sir. For example, we know that Hitler moved out of Wolfschanze , or as we call it, the Wolf's Lair, about five months ago. Hitler has been operating from the relative safety of these massive concrete bunkers in Eastern Prussia for most of the war. Then, just ahead of the Russian advance, we intercepted a top-secret message from Bormann that orders Hitler to a command bunker under the new Reich Chancellery in Berlin. Based upon current conflicting evidence, we have reason to believe this decision made very little sense unless it was done for propaganda purposes—or as an important step in a grandiose escape plan.

"I base the latter assertion primarily on our results from Project Goldeneye, a clandestine operation MI6 is conducting on the Iberian Peninsula. Goldeneye has uncovered a highly sophisticated Nazi escape route, embarking the port of Vigo in Spain by U-boat to an unknown destination somewhere in the Southern Hemisphere. I have personally been gathering and corroborating this intelligence for over two years and it all points empirically to the Nazi top brass, perhaps orchestrated by Martin Bormann, taking this option to escape the wrath of the Allies and any responsibility for their crimes against humanity.

"Sir, I repeat, for Adolf Hitler to die a hero in a last stand against the Russians is absolutely incomprehensible to me when he could live out his days in the lap of luxury and under a cloak of complete anonymity."

Churchill pulled himself out of his chair, leaned on the table and glared at Fleming.

"Commander, you have not linked all the dots to my satisfaction. If Bormann is the main man, why would he give a royal shite about Hitler dying in Berlin. It gives him perfect cover to escape to Spain or wherever!

"What does make perfect sense to me, Fleming, you have all heard me state publically on many occasions. If Germany had invaded Britain in 1940, I would not have run; I would not hidden. The Huns would have found me in front of Buckingham Palace holding an empty revolver, spent casings at my feet as I awaited their bullets. I expect Herr Hitler is well aware the war is lost and is preparing a similar last stand in his nation's capital." The stirring words were delivered as only Winston Spencer Churchill could, tears trickling down his cheeks, the gruff voice rising to address a multitude rather than the other three men in the room.

A respectful silence followed before Admiral Godfrey offered a polite cough.

"Ahem, with the greatest respect, Prime Minister, we believe Reichleiter Bormann needs Adolf Hitler for a reprise role. We have increasingly credible suspicions that might prove Adolph Hitler's plan for a similar grand defense of the Fatherland will be theatrical at best."

After several seconds digesting the implications of this revelation, Winston Spencer Churchill chomped down on his Cuban cigar and growled,

"Tell me more; tell me everything."

The prime minister's rounded back listened to Commander Fleming's comprehensive analysis whilst his eyes focused on an enormous linen map of Europe tacked to the wall of the conference room. After Fleming concluded, he waited for a response, not entirely sure if Churchill had heard even one word. Without turning, the P.M. exhaled a thick cloud of grey cigar smoke and uttered his soft reply directly to the map.

"Now it all makes sense.

"As every member of MI6 in this room is aware, when we were at the Yalta Conference and staying at the home of the British delegation, the so-called Vorontsov Palace, it was bugged by the Russians. Apparently, this is what one does at these events, so to return the favor—though I might add with only my tacit approval—a couple of my female translators started taking their smoke breaks with the Russian kitchen staff. As luck would have it, one of the cooks had a brother serving as valet to Lavrentiy Beriya and all sorts of good gossip leaked back to my ears, none of which I assigned the slightest veracity, except perhaps until this afternoon."

"The same Beriya that heads up the Secret Police,

Stalin's notorious NKVD?" Admiral Godfrey whispered incredulously.

"The very same, John, and a dead fish has more personality. But, if we are to believe his valet's sister, he brags like a village bully from within the security of his dressing room."

"With the greatest respect, Mr. Prime Minister, pray do tell."

Winston sat down and gestured the three top intelligence officers to join him before reminding them that for several months, urban legend rumored that Beriya had his own mole within the upper hierarchy of Third Reich, a source referred to as 'Sasha.'

"I gleaned that one night, at a hotel in Moscow, Laventiy Pavlovich Beriya and another high-ranking NKVD officer woke the valet with loud drunken singing fueled by many litres of vodka. The valet was shocked to overhear the tail end of their conversation, the general gist of which he relayed to his sister."

"The cook?"

"C'est cela même, mon ami. The conversation seemed to go something like: *So Sasha is actually inside the Fuhrerbunker with Hitler?* To which Beriya laughed long and loud before replying,

Hell no, Sasha is in the bunker with a man who looks like Hitler. Hitler is most likely in Barcelona by now."

Commander James Fleming rubbed his temples before exhaling a loud sigh.

"I don't know, sir, our girl shares a ciggy with a Russian cook who has a brother who overhears two drunk NKVD officers talking…wha, wha, wha. It's extremely farfetched we must all admit. Yet, there are a remarkable number of common threads between the Yalta gossip, these mimeographs and what we have learned from Project Goldeneye.

"I do not believe in coincidences and with your permission, C, I need to find a way to check this out."

"I rather wish you would, James," responded the head of MI6.

CHAPTER THIRTEEN

Bienvenue à Paris

I n the airspace over the Baltic Ocean, Fagan had just readjusted his course due west, when in a classic deja-vu, two MIG-3s re-appeared out of nowhere. From their distinctive graphics, they were undoubtedly MIGs from the same squadron they had encountered on the way in. Their long snouts slowed to each side of the bogus DC-3 and one of the pilots signaled the cockpit with the palm of his hand down, indicating he wished the Polish aircraft to turn around immediately. Billy smiled with thumbs up and pointed forward, shrugging that he did not understand. In the right seat, F.O. Robinson was on the radio in a desperate attempt to raise help.

The MIGs made it obvious they wanted the

disguised Skytrain to land in Poland by emphasizing their request with a short staccato of cannon for effect. Billy circled his finger and thumb to wave an *okay* out of his window and reduced altitude, but he still did not turn. He knew he was now closer to Sweden than Poland—and about to shave the coastline of Nazi-held Denmark! The unlikely convoy of three planes sank lower and lower, the MIGs seemingly confused about their right to shoot down a civilian aircraft when suddenly, the C-47 Skytrain was buffeted hard by a completely unexpected thump. Paddy stumbled forward into the cockpit and caught Billy grinning as he fought to hold the plane steady.

"What in Holy Hell was THAT? Are we hit, Billy?"

"Paddy, my boy, THAT was three of His Majesty's Royal Air Force Supermarine Spitfire IXs passing by at over five hundred miles an hour. When you combine our airspeeds, the delta must have broken the sound barrier. My old squadron, Number 19, just refueled in Bullofta and came by to say hello. Ted gave them a 'heads up' less than two minutes ago. Quite a co-incidence, what?"

"Yes, Billy, quite a coincidence. Do I take it the MIGs will not want to mess with your friends?"

"You might say that, old boy. They would be rather silly if they did."

They were enjoying an uneventful and smooth crossing of the North Sea, but as Robinson was readying to tell the back of the bus that the English coastline would soon be in sight, an urgent radio message crackled into the cockpit.

"Brigadier Zumwalt for Major McBride. Urgent. Over." Ted went back into the raucous passenger compartment and whispered into the Northern Irishman's ear.

The major came forward to sit in Robinson's seat and spent some time recounting the Takeo Atobe episode before listening to the brigadier in silence. When he got off the radio, he immediately requested Billy to turn south and head for Orly Airport in Paris.

"Ted, can we make it?" asked the concerned pilot.

"It will be close, Billy, very close."

Originally known as Villeneuve-Orly Airport, the facility in the southern suburbs of Paris activated in 1932 as a secondary airport to Le Bourget. Since the recent liberation of Paris, 50th Fighter Group flew their P-47 Thunderbolt fighter-bomber aircraft from the airport to support the push towards Berlin.

USAAF Colonel Mark David Estrin, the current base commander, knew RAF Wing Commander Fagan rather well as he had spent many evenings losing countless games of gin rummy to him when the 50th trained briefly in Lymington, Hampshire.

"LOT flight number P670 requesting permission to land. We are low on fuel and need to come in from the north with the wind on our first approach. Over."

The American flight controller, Lieutenant Robert S. Pribell, had joined the 50th in Orlando, Florida and responded to Billy in completely professional and emotionless tones. "P670, we have no flight plan for you nor do we have any official records that you even exist. I will need identification and clearance before permission can be granted. Over."

"Much obliged, Orly, but I'm not joking about being low on juice. As for identification, tell Mark Estrin that just because he's embarrassed to have lost Oklahoma Gin *'every single time we played in Lymington,'* this is no way to treat a friend. Over."

The joke was lost on Pribell. "We have you on radar P670 and you are about to be joined by two Thunderbolts. Imperative you await my instructions or they will shoot you down… regardless of your card playing skills. Out."

However, within seconds, the radio buzzed back, "Billy, you lyin' cheatin' bastard. What the hell are you up to flying a fake Polish DC-3? Over."

"Mark, old boy. I will tell you over G&T's tonight if you let me land this gooney bird before the fumes run out. Over."

"Billy, come around. Wind is swirling at up to 10 knots from the north northeast. I cannot allow aircraft to come straight in with that wind, not even you; too much risk over the suburbs. You are prioritized to land from the south on Runway Zero Two. Good luck, Buddy. Out."

For a pilot as insanely gifted as Billy Fagan, anything less than a strong gale and a muddy grass runway took all the fun away. The Dakota touched down so smoothly that when he announced, "Welcome to Paris. We have enjoyed flying you today and hope you will continue to choose us for your next destination," several of the passengers did not believe they were safely on land until they looked out of the windows. Then a spontaneous, "Hip, Hip, Hooray," rang out.

Once standing on the tarmac taxiway, the Orlowskis and Brzozowskas were numbed and quiet as they began to soak in the knowledge that there might be a happy conclusion to their plights.

Billy and Ted remained at Orly as guests of the 50th, everyone else was instructed to make their way into Paris where a representative of Brigadier Zumwalt was scheduled to contact them at the Austerlitz railway station.

The most efficient transportation for the short journey was by train, as many of the Parisian roads were still under repair, so all seventeen piled into a carriage that soon became theirs alone, existing travelers quickly deciding there was something strange, sinister and distinctly *un-French* about this group.

Mike Johnston procured a bottle of Scotch from the USAAF NAAFI and in a heavy, unintelligible Scottish dialect, began to treat all within earshot to his loud version of *'the Tam o'Shanter'* as he passed his bottle around. Only Mike could comprehend the Robbie Burns' classic but the poetic meter was so infectious, even the Polish women were joining in stridently.

It was the perfect excuse to blow off steam.

The train eventually pulled into La Gare d'Austerlitz, a beautiful station built in 1840 to serve the Paris-Orleans line and the motley group disembarked and waited on the platform for the promised contact. The Black Widows, wearing dirty, civilian farm clothes, lounged beside and on top of three black, Special Forces equipment bags, bags that were somewhat out of context with the 'Polish farmer' look the group portrayed. Consequently, a nattily dressed gendarme took notice and walked over imperiously to demand identification. Four other police officers joined him almost immediately and began yelling loudly at the squad. Edmund Smolenski, one of the SAS linguists, spoke reasonably fluent French but decided to play dumb.

"Paddy, they say they are French Immigration Police but the bastards are really looking for a cash kick-back. If they don't get their palms greased, they are threatening to arrest us," he whispered to McBride.

"Everybody on your feet but stay cool. Chez, move your womenfolk to the rear. Lads, if these clowns so much as touch their guns, take them out hand-to-hand, no firearms, no knives." That proviso elicited one or two grumbles.

More French gendarmerie hurried to back up their friends and a comical standoff ensued right there on the platform. The two groups, now only five feet apart, glared at each other, one completely silent and unblinking, the other yelling obscenities in French and gesticulating wildly.

The situation escalated rapidly and, although they were unaware of their pending predicament, the police grew bolder and more frenetic in the face of a total lack of response from the Black Widows. Fortunately, a man in a beige mackintosh appeared from nowhere and positioned himself between the immigration police and the scruffy, unwashed travelers. The French sergeant kept up his bluster as he turned to the new arrival.

"Et qui êtes-vous, Monsieur?" As a reply, the man slowly pulled open his mac., making absolutely certain the paranoid sergeant got an eyeful of the insignia adorning his uniform. He slowly removed an envelope from his left-inside pocket and handed it to the gendarme.

"Lisez cette lettre, s'il vous plaît."

The letter was hand-written in French and the sergeant snapped to attention when he saw the signature at the bottom. He nervously returned it to the envelope and stammered to his men, "Step aside immediately." Then to the immigrants, "Bienvenue à Paris."

The tension melted as the courier whispered, "Je vous en prie—you are welcome, arsehole." Then, turning to the easily recognizable Ulsterman, he smiled warmly.

"Major McBride, a great pleasure to meet you. I am Staff Sergeant Timothy Levin, your escort assigned by the brigadier. On his behalf, thanks for not sending those idiots to hospital. We need the beds right now.

"We're going to take the Métro from here to our headquarters where you can wash up and relax. It's only about ten minutes away, in the Saint-Germain-des-Prés area of the 6th Arrondissement."

Within the promised time, the underground train squealed into the Sèvres-Babylone Métro station and Sergeant Levin led them up into daylight at the intersection of Boulevard Raspail and Rue de Sèvres. Mike Johnston stared at a magnificent Art Deco building in front of them.

"Forget fuckin' headquarters, why don't we stay there, Tim? It says Hotel on the front though I have no bloody idea what the second word is, L-V-T-E-T-I-A," he spelt out, turning to Levin with a laugh. "How the hell do you say that, there aren't enough vowels?"

"Never understimate Brigadier Zumwalt, Sarge. We've been slumming it there for the past week while you bastards have been gallivanting around Poland. First thing the Old Man did when we got to Paris was make sure the SAS had first dibs on The Hotel Lutetia; it's a fancy 'U' not a 'V.' We have the entire upper floor; top brass in the French and American Forces use the rest of the building. Oh, in case you were wondering, that letter I carry to ensure your safe passage was signed by General Charles De Gaulle at the request of Mr. Churchill."

"Little wonder Edith Piaf was shittin' his pants back there."

As the bawdy laughter died down the SAS men were suddenly aware of sobbing and all hushed as they noticed Chez trying to comfort Jadwiga and her relatives. The Polish family, completely overwhelmed by the occasion, the grandeur and realization that they had made it unharmed to the City of Lights, now knew with certainty that their lives would change forever.

CHAPTER FOURTEEN

L'Hôtel Lutetia

The next evening, after he felt an appropriate amount of relaxation had been granted, Brigadier Bryan Merfyn Zumwalt formally requested the pleasure of the Orlowski and Brzozowski families to join the Black Widows in the Bar Lounge for drinks, followed by dinner.

The old saying, *the worst meal in Paris could be the best meal in the world,* rang true and afterwards, Chez stood and tapped his glass.

"My dear comrades. I have been truly blessed by being able to call on two powerful, powerful friends in our time of extreme desperation; Paddy McBride and Malcolm McClain. A man could not ask for more and my family and I will be eternally grateful for everything you have done. Na zdrowie!

"I've seen those two in action before and I would not doubt they might have pulled off the extraction on their own but Malcolm had a couple of games to play...." The hoots and whistles at this tongue-in-cheek remark were unmerciful but the Spider held his hands aloft to beg continuance. "Lucky for me, Paddy has some powerful friends of his own. Gentlemen, the Black Widows. Na zdrowie!"

"Na zdrowie!" chorused the room loudly.

"Words will never be able to thank you all for the sacrifices you have made for us. None more so than SAS Specialist Ronnie Martin who gave his life in Żagań. Szymon Grabowski assures me that Ronnie's name will never be forgotten in Poland. The Spider solemnly echoes that pledge.

"Ladies, gentlemen, to Ronnie. Na zdrowie!"

Everyone stood somberly to toast their fallen comrade, followed by a moment of reflective silence.

"And now, with your permission, my wife and her sisters would like to sing a couple of Polish songs for you." The Special Forces politely prepared to tolerate some caterwalling but after Jadwiga and her sisters began singing, it became apparent that all assembled were in for a world-class treat. These girls sang together in the cathedral choir of Vilnius when they were children and now created their own problem in that the warriors would not allow them to stop.

The memorable evening progressed until well after midnight. As the festivities began to wind down and everyone drifted towards their assigned rooms, Jacqui Siglar, perhaps a little tipsy from champagne, picked her moment to brush up behind Scotty Miller and whisper teasingly, "Maybe now would be a good time for that back massage you promised," before continuing her way out of the bar towards the stairs. The super-cool SAS sergeant momentarily choked on his brandy but left the bar in pursuit a respectful five minutes later.

Zumwalt signaled clandestinely and pulled the Spider and McBride aside to join him at the fireplace. In a gesture to the start of the adventure in Boodles, he filled three fresh snifters with vintage Aberfeldy Scotch Whisky and lowered his voice.

"Gentlemen, I have to share troubling news. I gave you my word that this was it; the final mission. A career of your choice, well-funded by an extremely grateful government, awaits you both in Britain. God knows you have done more than your share in this bloody war.

"By the way, congratulations, Paddy. It is Colonel McBride from now on. The ceremony, along with another couple of well-deserved baubles for your chest, will take place at Buckingham Palace when you get home. It is a field promotion, effective immediately, whether or not you decide to go along with what I am about to tell you."

The two men smiled at each other with questioning raised eyebrows then back at the brigadier. Each sensed he was extremely troubled and this was something more than a congratulatory wrap up.

Paddy stepped forward, put his massive arm around the shoulder of his long-time comrade, and whispered softly, "Bryan, spit it out. Chez and I are big enough to handle whatever is causing you concern."

Zumwalt sucked in a deep breath before speaking.

"As you both know, this war should end any day now. We all believe Hitler and his cohorts have retreated to a command bunker under the Chancellery; a literal mausoleum surrounded by a tightening noose of two million Soviet troops. The Americans and British are pushing to swoop in and grab his scrawny arse but President Roosevelt cut a deal with Stalin to allow the Russians that honor. Something about payback for the treachery of Barbarossa.

"Problem is, any surrender must be unconditional and Hitler knows it. He also knows that the Russians, left to their own devices, will exact ferocious retribution on any Nazis they find - most especially him. So what do you men think?"

After a reflective pause, the strongly accented voice of the Spider concluded, "If I was Hitler, I would not let them take me alive. I'd shoot them 'til I had one bullet left in my gun and then blow my own brains out so as not to give them the satisfaction."

"Aye," added Paddy. "Remember the Alamo! Jim Bowie ended up fighting the Mexicans with his knife after his bullets ran out."

"And that is what any honorable, ethical soldier would do," Zumwalt continued. "However, honor and sanity are not traits high on Hitler's resume and what I have to tell you is strictly *'Top Secret'*—it comes from the very top—W.S.C. himself."

The brigadier paused to let the seriousness sink in until the two men nodded for him to continue.

"MI6 has solid intelligence suggesting a long-standing plot is under way to stage Adolf Hitler's suicide. This sham will be theatrical to the point that Russian euphoria in finding any corpse that remotely resembles the Führer of the Third Reich will satisfy their lust for revenge. As we stand here tonight, Adolf might have already subbed in his stooge and be miles away from Berlin.

"We are all tired of this war and, after six long years of sacrifice, eager to get back to normal, marry our sweethearts and start families. Even the Russians must be sharing those dreams with us.

"Meanwhile, the bastard-in-chief, along with several million pesos, will be spirited down to Barcelona to catch a U-boat to Argentina."

"Well, Holy shit, Bryan. I cannot speak for Chez, but I am not going to sleep very well knowing that scumbag is playing Gaucho and dancing the fucking fandango in Buenos Aires! I'm not holding you to any promise you have made me—if that's what's worryin' you."

The tough brigadier was already speechless with emotion when the Spider interjected with a simple, calm request, uttered in a strong, fearless tone.

"I need two promises, Brigadier; can you get Jadwiga and my family safely to England and can you make sure Malcolm McClain knows his efforts were not in vain?"

"You have my absolute assurance on both counts."

PART TWO

CHAPTER FIFTEEN

The Parting

A s Chez eventually returned to his room in the early hours of the morning, a strong feeling of guilt was beginning to overpower his bravado. He grimaced as the key clicked within the brass rim lock and then eased opened the door as quietly as possible, hoping to slide undetected into the darkness within. He was still undecided whether to wake Jadwiga or tell her Zumwalt's request in the morning but her voice whispered at him almost immediately and the bedside light clicked on.

"Czeslaw, when you stayed to meet with the brigadier, something happened didn't it? I know it must be important but please don't break my heart."

"Jadzie, ukochanie, you read me like a book." He

paused and took a deep breath. "You must forgive me if I do not accompany you and our family to England tomorrow. Zumwalt has asked Paddy and me to check out a rumor—that's all. Hey, he has lined up a beautiful big house in southwest London for us to live in—all expenses paid—including a Polish housekeeper! I'll join you in a couple of…" But Jadwiga was not listening to or fooled by the change in direction. Holding her head in her hands, she started to sob.

"Czeslaw, stop it."

The Spider looked sheepishly down at the floor, took a deep breath and decided she needed to hear the truth,—or at least a cautiously sanitized version. "It's best you don't know any details and I doubt you would believe them anyway but I will be in no danger and should join you and the family in England within the week." His bride said nothing in reply, but turning rapidly away from him and grabbing the preponderance of the covers spoke volumes.

Despite an elegant breakfast, the troubled night's events caused an uncharacteristically introverted Czeslaw to accompany Jadwiga, the other Brozowska women and a limping Specialist Jacqui Siglar back to Orly Airport. This time, instead of an awkward train journey, they were regally transported in a convoy of three large dark blue Citroens, festooned with French tricolors over their front wheel wells. Due to road repair throughout Saint Germain de Pres, the forty-minute journey detoured by necessity onto the right bank of the Seine, a journey that showcased Paris's past six years of horror. But, within the gray landscape of burned rubble, the resilient Parisians smiled and cheered loudly as the limousines sped by.

Crossing the famous river onto the Ile de la Cité gifted them a breathless view of the Cathédrale Notre Dame. The driver of the lead car, Alaine Grangé, had fought in the Resistance for the entire occupation of his beloved city and lost his father and three brothers. When he heard his passengers crying out in wonderment at the sheer magnificence of the cathedral, he started to well up. The proud Frenchman made an impromptu executive decision and the convoy followed his limousine in peeling off the most expeditious route. Grangé treated everyone to a stately tour of the first and second arrondisements, pausing at the Place Vendome and L'Opera de Paris before eventually turning south at the Place de La Bastille to head for Orly Airport.

"I am surprised so much of the classic architecture has survived the Nazi penchant for looting and pillaging!" Jacqui commented aloud to herself as she stared out a rear window. Sergeant Roger Edwards, charged by the brigadier with escorting the party all the way to Ricksmanworth, heard the whisper and turned from his front seat.

"If I may, mademoiselle, Paris has been spared mostly intact mainly because, after Hitler specifically commanded the city be destroyed, the German Commandant Dietrich von Choltitz, stalled the order until he could surrender to Leclerc. He probably knew the game was up and did it to ingratiate himself to the victors. Worked a little bit 'cos they haven't kill him. Not yet, anyway."

Squadron Leader Fagan and Colonel Estrin were nervously checking their watches when the three Citroens finally rolled into view considerably behind schedule. The two men constituted a reception committee at the bottom of the loading door of the familiar C-47. The plane, maintained and fueled by the USAAF, had been ready for take-off for the past ninety minutes. The cavalcade pulled right up to the two old friends and everyone piled out, stretched their legs and sorted which of the newly provided suitcases belonged to whom. Fagan and Estrin escorted them up the ramp to find Flying Officer Ted Robinson, a case of French Champagne and delicious pastries welcoming the entourage aboard.

The ladies squealed excitedly in Polish as their adventure took this luxurious turn for the better. Then the laughter stopped as Jadwiga's unhappiness from the prior late night's incident welled through the silence. Chester was holding her tightly, his hand patting her back until it was time for him to return to the runway. Billy followed him down and had a few words.

"Don't worry, old sport, Mark has a couple of Thunderbolts escorting me across the Channel and Sergeant Edwards will send a message to the Lutetia once everyone is safely tucked in at home. Take care of yourself—and look after the big man."

The Spider did not bother to explain the true cause of the tears and appeared stoic as he remained to watch the Dakota bank slowly to port. The troubled Pole continued to stare silently into the skies long after the black dot disappeared into the western sky. He needed the time for his internal emotions to calm and Alaine Grangé, waiting patiently by the lone Citroen, understood perhaps as only a Frenchman can. Chez finally wiped his cheeks with his shirt-sleeve and walked to the car, commenting quietly to Grangé in French,

"D'accord, nous devons retourner à l'hôtel."

The journey took place in silence, Alaine glancing periodically into his mirror to check on his passenger's emotional stability. But he need not have worried, when Grangé pulled to a halt in front of the Hotel Lutetia, the limo driver noticed a fundamentally different demeanor in the man who stepped onto 'le trottoir.' The eyes were a colorless grey that sent shivers up his spine. After the Spider entered the lobby and was out of earshot, the drivers agreed. "That is one very scary *salop*. I would never want to get on the wrong side of him!"

At four o'clock that afternoon, Chez met Paddy and together the two men knocked on the door of Brigadier Zumwalt's suite. He opened the door himself and welcomed them into the sumptuous interior. There were two high-ranking Royal Navy officers already seated on the couch but both stood up smartly when Zumwalt introduced them. Admiral John Henry Godfrey and Commander James Fleming betrayed almost schoolboyish delight to be in the presence of the highly decorated SAS colonel and the legendary Spider.

"Tea, gentlemen?" All present accepted; in British society, the etiquette of allowing your host to serve you is an important ceremony that breaks down barriers created by rank or class. When all had their cups doctored with milk and sugar to their satisfaction, the brigadier returned the accoutrements to the antique sideboard, prepared his own cup and sat down with one final superfluous comment.

"Ah, delicious, I much prefer Assam tea to Darjeeling."

Then, it was straight down to business. He put his cup down on its saucer and focused on McBride and Orlowski.

"What these men and I are about to share with you will most likely shock you. You will have many, many questions but I ask you to try to hold them until we have finished.

"You both might be aware that Hitler wrote his manifesto, *Mein Kampf*, whilst in prison twenty years ago. When eventually liberated, he had the equivalent of only ten pounds sterling to his name, yet today he is by far the wealthiest man in Europe, just ahead of Herman Göring and a bunch of other Nazi thieves and bandits. They gained their colossal wealth by plundering the treasuries and museums of every country they have occupied over the past six years. To the victor go the spoils, so to speak."

Sweeping his right hand in the direction of the two other guests, he continued. "My Royal Navy colleagues represent Military Intelligence, Section Six and have been instructed by the Prime Minister himself to analyze what might happen to this immense wealth when the imminent and expected demise of the Nazi regime comes to pass."

"If I may, Bryan?" Commander Fleming waited for and received an affirmative nod. "For the most part, the Nazis have made no attempt to hide this plenitude; flaunting it in fact. That fat pig, Göring, has an estate called Carinhall just north of Berlin that makes the Victoria & Albert Museum look like a flea market. Billions of pounds of plunder, incredible opulence beyond anything you could possibly conceive.

"However, we at MI6, along with our American friends in the OSS, have been monitoring a very interesting anomaly; to be specific, a relatively recent and massive increase in the treasuries of Argentina and Brazil. We have not positively confirmed where this wealth came from but if you connect the dots, the influx of gold reserves into these two South American countries began shortly after the German defeat at Stalingrad."

Chez concentrated hard to follow the tale as Fleming's language was liberally sprinkled with idioms from his Eton College education. After all, the young freedom fighter had learned his English under the entirely different circumstances of a POW camp worker. He was grateful when Paddy McBride, having his own problems with the commander's upper-crust accent, decided to interrupt.

"Commander Fleming, may I call you Jimmy?" he asked. In such discrete circumstances, he had certainly earned the right to drop rank and besides, who was going to deny him. "I hope you're not suggesting that we're going to finish this war as treasure hunters?"

Fleming grinned, took a long pull on the cigarette holder between his teeth and rejoined the banter. "I would be honored with James, Paddy; haven't been called Jimmy since I was three. However, I am a little miffed you might think it is all about the loot but I have probably not got to the punch line fast enough, so if I may continue?"

"Ah well, there y'are now, Jimmy,—James it is. Carry on, my friend," laughed the Ulsterman.

"Since early 1943, our intelligence services suspected the upper echelon of the Nazi Party has been planning their escape into anonymity; a mass disappearing act which we have reason to believe is masterminded by Reichsleiter Martin Bormann and not Hitler. If successful, it will allow the bastards to get away with the murder of millions of innocent people, escape justice and live out their lives in the lap of luxury funded by their ill-gotten spoils…"

"…In South America," completed the Spider in an ominous voice. "Anonymity? How can they possibly pull that off? I saw Adolph Hitler once and his image is burned into my memory. If I ever see that sonofabitch again, he will die within seconds. And I don't care if he is dancing on the center circle of Wembley Stadium with thousands in the stands; I will take him out without hesitation."

"Well then, I seriously doubt either of you will like hearing what I am about to tell you next." Fleming paused briefly for a nicotine boost then continued.

"A female Nazi Intelligence Officer, Magda

Zeitfeld, works in Berchtesgaden. She has been sending us information since late 1944 because she is convinced the SS murdered her father and brother under very mysterious circumstances. Her late father owned the largest plastic surgery clinic in Berlin. He was a pioneer in the field, and well financed by the Nazis due to their obsession with physical perfection. Dr. Zeitfeld specialized in implanted facial prosthetics, using highly advanced silicates to build up weak jaws and noses to fit the German penchant for a look of chiseled strength.

"Fifteen months ago, three exceptionally high level Nazi officials were brought to her father's clinic under a shroud of extreme security. According to Magda, her father and brother were ordered to alter the appearance of each of the men. Two weeks after these men left her family's clinic and sufficient time passed to be sure there was no need for follow up treatment, the hospital was raided by a group of masked terrorists and the entire staff, including Magda's father and brother, were brutally murdered. The clinic was burned to the ground, files and all. Magda figured out that these 'terrorists' were in fact from a division within the SS."

"So…even though I saw Hitler, it might not be Hitler and if I do see Hitler I might not recogni…Wait a minute; now I am completely confused," complained the young Pole. Fleming continued unfazed despite the interruption.

"Magda had discrete conversations with both her father and brother after the operations and according to her later reports to us, two of the men were definitely Martin Bormann and Adolf Hitler. She thinks the third might have been an SS Lieutenant General called Hermann Fegelein. This might make perfect sense when you consider Fegelein just married Gretl Braun at the Berchtesgaden and she happens to be the sister of Adolf's main squeeze, Eva.

"All the top Nazi brass were in attendance and open comments were made, not just about the fading bruises, but the overall aesthetic success of the plastic surgery. Magda stated that the alterations were subtle but evident. Apparently, the new Hitler has a fatter nose and perhaps different ears."

Paddy joined in with a laugh. "As long as he keeps that stupid black toothbrush under his nose, we shouldn't have a problem." To which Admiral Godfrey interjected an immediate, sharp response without any hint of humor.

"Do either of you gentlemen think you could recognize Hitler without his moustache? Not to mention identifying Martin Bormann, who it is becoming more and more apparent, might be the true leader of the Third Reich. Conveniently, this man has next to no photographs on record; he might as well be a bloody ghost! Sorry James, please carry on."

"Thank you, John. We now believe quite positively

that these three war criminals, along with cohorts Heinrich Himmler, Adolf Eichmann and Dr. Paul Joseph Goebbels, all plan to escape from Berlin in the guise of priests on Vatican diplomatic passports. I am also betting they take the Braun sisters with them, so add two nuns to the entourage."

Fleming dragged on his cigarette again, the exaggerated silence indicating he had finished for now so Bryan Zumwalt turned to the head of Naval Intelligence. "Anything to add, Admiral?"

"Well, James has all the details. He uncovered a lot of this as he put together *'Project Golden Eye'* for us. Golden Eye maintains a network of undercover agents throughout the Iberian Peninsula and everything points to this Catholic Entourage embarking to obscurity from either Vigo in Portugal or more likely, Barcelona in Spain.

"But let me give you some additional evidence. For several years, Adolf Hitler, Rudolph Hess and Heinrich Himmler have each been known to have at least one physical double—or doppelganger—for security purposes, and after all, Winnie uses one on a regular basis but mostly in his perennial jousting with *The Daily Express*. It is possible that all of the top Reich leaders keep look-alikes as part of a master contingency plan to escape unnoticed should the need arise, no doubt presenting the world with the bodies of doppelgangers, most likely disfigured to an extent that their own mothers would think they were the Nazis they replaced."

James Fleming, now revitalized again by nicotine, enthusiastically re-entered the conversation as he pulled a sheaf of photographs from his briefcase.

"It has been confirmed independently that Hitler has undergone some sort of cosmetic surgery. We have a couple of agents working within the cleaning staff at the Reichstag who see Hitler on a regular basis. Over time, they noticed strange alterations in Adolf Hitler's physical appearance, especially his nose."

Fleming passed a series of photographs across the table. "Just look, the originally thin, straight nose of the late 1930's Hitler has now given way to the large, exaggerated nostrils of today's Führer. Shave the hair and signature moustache off and he could walk amongst us undetected! The only way to tell if you are in the presence of the real Adolf or one of his doppelgangers is when the bastard opens his mouth. No one can realistically duplicate the maniacal voice of the original!

"A further visual clue might be that the genuine Hitler has had either progressive syphilis or more likely, Parkinson's Disease, for over a decade. His left arm currently shakes uncontrollably and he self-consciously holds it with his right or keeps it out of sight behind his back."

"All well and good, James. You can fake an arm

shake but how the hell do you know whether the changed physical appearance of these clowns is due to plastic surgery or their replacement with sacrificial lambs?" Colonel McBride asked, puzzled.

Bryan Zumwalt stood up and took over the conversation. "You have nailed the conundrum, Paddy. Need a drink anyone?"

The brigadier decided to avoid an information overload at this first meeting by indicating it was time for cocktails. All five men gathered at the Louis Quinze sideboard, recently cleared of tea service and now stocked with a couple of single malts and several fine cognacs.

"I trust I don't need to mention this entire conversation is classified to the highest level but I want Paddy, Chez and the Black Ops Group to have real facts to chew on before they decide to risk their lives getting to the bottom of this mystery. Common knowledge has most of these Nazi scumbags confined to a concrete bunker beneath the new Reich Chancellery. There is absolutely no possibility of them begging mercy from the Russians. However, Mr. Churchill is desperately afraid that at the conclusion of this horror story, we will find an empty nest or unidentifiable bodies from a mass suicide. In either of these scenarios, I don't think any of us will rest to our graves knowing that these bastards might be living it up in South America, brainwashing the next generation of Hitler Youth to start the Fourth Reich and World War Three."

"Golden Eye indicates a distinct possibility that they might have already left. The escape route has been in place since before Christmas," interjected a concerned Commander Fleming.

"So, Bryan, you would be able to rest in peace if the Spider and I went into the bunker, capped them all and brought you their scalps?"

Paddy was laughing as he tendered this plan but the brigadier came back with an immediate and perfectly serious response.

"Yes! Provided you get positive identification."

CHAPTER SIXTEEN

Preparation

S even SAS soldiers and the Spider had all received the personal request from Colonel McBride to meet him at 1900 hours in room 714 and now, within a silence pregnant with anticipation, Paddy studied the eight serious faces staring back at him.

"Well lads, you are probably well aware that the brigadier has something on his mind and as a result, Chez and I are not going home just yet. It could be a very dangerous mission but same rules as always; leave the room now and we'll meet you later for a drink before you head back home. I'll only give you the scoop if you want to stick around; we'll be grateful for the company—and the muscle." Not a soul moved. Mike Johnston made eye contact with every man and each returned his gaze with a solemn nod. "I guess we're all in, Paddy. What's the plan?"

"Don't have one yet, but I'll tell you what Chez and I learned from Bryan this afternoon." McBride related salient points regarding the astonishing MI6 briefing, finishing with, "And that's about it. Have I left anything out, Chez?"

"No, it still sounds as bloody ridiculous as it did three hours ago, but I've been tossing a few ideas around in my head. Mind if I throw some options on the table? They might generate something we can fine-tune as we go along." Paddy appreciated this initiative, as experience had shown the Spider's ideas to be liberally laced with street smarts and hard to top.

"I see three or four scenarios that need to be sorted out before we can do anything.

"First of all, I need to get inside the Führerbunker to find out which Hitler is in residence; the real one or the fake.

"Second, if he's already been replaced by his doppelganger, we can regroup and hunt the bastard down to the ends of the earth.

"Third, if the real Hitler is still there, I'll try and learn when he plans to leave. At that point, we'll hunt the bastard down to the ends of the earth.

"Fourth, if he has no plans to leave, I will; we'll sit back and watch the doors until the Ruskis go in and finish the job for us." Chez was not trying to be funny but his matter-of-fact, rapid delivery in the face of impossible odds had all the men, even Paddy, rolling with uncontrollable laughter. It all left a confused Spider trying to comprehend the source of the joke.

"And, Chez…ha-ha-ha, how are you…ha-ha, going to get into the bunker…ha-ha-ha-ha. Got a key? Heee-Haaa," wheezed Mitch Arnold, the taciturn corporal who normally just sat quietly in the background.

"I have no bloody clue," responded the Spider without a hint of humor. "That's where I thought you guys could help."

Mike Johnston had tears rolling down his cheeks. "Sounds like the entire plan revolves around hunting the bastard down to the ends of the earth. I'm all in favor of th…." He suddenly paused, frowned and stood up, arms raised to calm the room into silence.

"Well wouldn't you know it? That little fucker has done it again."

The room fell silent. Gino Blando asked, "Done what, Sarge?"

"Chez is right on the money like always. Think about what he just proposed and not how he's going to do it." The rest of the squad started to mumble amongst themselves and conceded Mike could be right.

"I agree," said Paddy. "If we cannot find out where Adolph is and what he is up to, there is no mission. Kudos, Chez—as usual!

"I suggest we treat Chez's four scenarios as the

freestyle elements of our plan, none of which can be considered until we get the compulsories out of the way; the most immediate of those being to transport him from this hotel room and into the Führerbunker to find out exactly who the hell is in there."

After an intense two hours, there were reams of paper discarded all over the floor. The most meritorious ideas, condensed into one page of information, was now held in Colonel McBride's hand.

"Okay, lads, I think we might have it. To recap:

"This morning, we learned the US 84th Infantry captured Hanover. This city is a designated British, post-war occupation zone, so we'll set up 30 miles from there in Braunschweig. This is about as far east as we can go without crossing front lines. We regroup tomorrow morning to check our equipment before flying there by transport. Mike, Scotty, Gino and Mitch will establish our rear support base at the Braunschweig airport. There should be enough transmission power in the control tower to maintain communications with our designated forward base in Berlin.

"Subject to further confirmation, forward base will be in the basement of the Hotel Adlon. It's located on Pariser Platz, close to the Brandenburg Gate. A field hospital is currently operating out of this hotel and we have a reliable contact there called Hans Dorff. Not surprisingly, several of the hospital staff are now sympathetic to the Allied cause. Jurek, Edmund, Günter and myself will hide out there with Chez 'til we figure a way to get him into the bunker. I'm the only one of the four who doesn't speak fluent German but we should be able to swing it with a little luck. Depending upon what Chez manages to find out, we'll extract him and retreat back to Braunschweig. Then it's home to Rickmansworth and the beers and steaks are on me.

"Everyone okay with that?"

"How are you guys planning to travel the 100 miles from Braunschweig to Berlin and back?" asked Johnston pointedly.

"Well the first 40 miles are protected by the good old U. S. of A. The Yanks are officially holding at Magdeburg at a front line defined by the River Elbe. They're not supposed to advance any further in deference to letting the Soviets officially accept the surrender of Berlin. Notwithstanding that stupid political arrangement, we just learned today that the Russians and the Americans are in a balls-to-the-wall covert race to capture the Kaiser Wilhelm Institute in southwest Berlin. Rumor has it the place is chock-a-block with uranium oxide and first there gets to kick-start their country's nuclear weapons program. Starting about an hour ago, both sides are bombing the shit out of the very part of Berlin we have to go through.

"As an aside, it's becoming increasingly apparent that a whole new war is looming; a war that will be decided without a shot being fired when one side beats the other to successfully explode an atomic bomb,— whatever the fuck that is. Anyway, those in the know attach great importance to it and apparently, if the Russians win the race, we're all up shit creek without a paddle."

"Regardless, I still need details of your plans to get into Berlin," pressed the focused, gruff staff sergeant.

"Seeing as how our destination is a field hospital, I was thinking about somehow commandeering a German military ambulance, uniforms and papers. We'll cover the damn thing with the stars and stripes until we reach the American front lines and then hope the guise gives us protection from there to Berlin. I'll be the patient, too badly wounded to speak and Chez, who knows Berlin pretty well, will drive."

Although Johnston was deliberately pressuring Paddy to think fast on his feet, the plan seemed just crazy enough to have a chance. The colonel continued on his line of thought.

"The Wehrmacht has a lot more on their mind right now than to search an ambulance headed back to a Berlin field hospital. With any luck, we should be able to park it right outside the Hotel Adlon and carry me, as a wounded patient, into a controlled area inside."

"Any ideas how we're going to carry you? There's only four of us?" laughed Edmund before a distracted Scotty Miller jumped in at a tangent.

"Paddy, I'm looking at our maps and see a bigger problem. I've identified the actual location of the Kaiser Wilhelm Institute in southwest Berlin and you could not have picked a worse place to drive through. It is the epicenter of three armies going at it hammer and tongs!" Sergeant Miller was genuinely concerned and wore no sign of his trademark grin. Chez was not fazed at all.

"Scotty's right but what's to stop us driving around? If we can get north to Hennigsdorf, Mullerstrasse eventually brings us right into the Pariser Platz. If I recall, the Hotel Adlon is right there on Wilhelmstrasse just beside the Brandenburg Gate."

"Ah yes, Chez, as I was just saying, lads, we will be circumventing Berlin and entering from the northwest." The colonel went over and gave the Spider a friendly tap on the head.

"You see the world with a refreshing clarity that is unmatched, my friend."

Unknown to the Special Forces in room 724, five hundred and forty four miles northeast of the Hotel

Lutetia in Paris, the chancellor of the Third Reich, Adolf Hitler, was meeting with Reichsleiter Martin Bormann in the Führerbunker. The two richest men in Europe sat on metal chairs in a dank concrete box some twenty-five feet below the Reichskanzlei in Berlin.

"Champagne, Martin?"

"Don't mind if I do, Adolph. Everything is in place and if all runs according to schedule, the Russians will be sitting at this very table in about three weeks. Our generals are actually putting up a more competent resistance than I anticipated, though in fairness, Georgy Zhukov is nowhere near as brilliant as Stalin gives him credit for."

"Excellent. By the way, Martin, Gerda and your ten children, I trust they will be taken care of?"

"That's really none of your damn business, Adolph. Just pay attention to what I ask you to do. You will make one more public appearance, maybe award some medals to the Hitler Youth. I'll get Herr Goebbels to send photographs out to the newspapers—that should be more than enough—then we can trigger the final act."

"Excellent, excellent, Martin, I am excited about das Gehmütliches Leben."

CHAPTER SEVENTEEN

Braunschweig

At 0700 sharp, Colonel Estrin sent two large trucks with distinctive USAAF stars on the canvases to pick up the nine-man squad from the Hotel Lutetia. The Black Widows were assembling in room 749 when a polite knock tapped the door. Zumwalt was admitted and shook every man's hand.

"Gentlemen, I've never been so proud!"

"Know this; you are the best of the best. Although hindsight vision is perfect, Hitler never had a chance of winning this war when the United Kingdom and Poland could produce a band of warriors such as yourselves.

"God speed."

Another knock and an orderly poked his head

around the door. "The trucks are outside, chaps, good luck."

Each man shook Zumwalt's hand again, made their way down to the service yard and climbed after their gear into the USAAF vehicles.

As soon as the trucks rolled out onto the street, McBride's Black Widows were so absorbed in working out the fine points of their mission, they hardly noticed the one hour drive to the 50th's base at Orly Airport. When they jumped out onto the tarmac, the men observed they had parked equidistant between two large aircraft; the very familiar LOT C-47 Skytrain that had extracted them from Poland and a dark grey, beat-up Curtiss C-46 Commando that looked much the worse for wear. They were at the mercy of the USAAF's tight schedule, weather and enemy activity, but forewarned the 450-miles to the rear command post at Braunschweig might take most of the day, so the men silently prayed the flight would be on the Skytrain and not the Curtiss.

"Let me guess, Paddy, we're not flying commercial to Braunschweig?"

McBride's reply was to point over Johnston's shoulder. "Why don't you ask the pilot, Mike?"

Although his back was towards them as he examined some of 'The Whale's' bullet-torn fuselage, there was no mistaking the rotund Billy Fagan.

"Load up, lads," chortled the squadron leader as

he turned to face them, "it'll fly. Ted and I dropped off our esteemed guests in London but the SAS has unreasonably demanded their Skytrain be returned to Brindisi. We stopped off here with some special supplies for you—courtesy of the brigadier—before Ted flies her down to Italy. Thought I might tag along with you chaps to Braunschweig in case you need a pilot to get you home, what?"

"That's a damn fine idea, Billy, and solves one of our unanswered questions—as long as you don't mind? You positive this piece of shit will even get off the ground?"

"Paddy, my boy, don't let its nickname, *The Flying Coffin*, worry you. I will be flying number two seat beside U.S. Marine Corps Captain, Steve Davis. Take off is in twenty; coffee and croissants are on board. Should touch down around 1400 hours. Tally-ho!"

From the Curtiss' windows at 15,000 feet, the men of the Special Air Services, Special Raiding Squadron were able to look down upon the ants that comprised the advancing allied armies. All armor and materiel moved inexorably towards a coup de grace as the noose of superior numbers constricted the neck of the Nazi Third Reich.

They approached the 9th century town of Braunschweig right on schedule under the clear, blue skies of a pleasant afternoon in Lower Saxony. The Wehrmacht 31st Infantry Division had used this town as headquarters for the past five years before they were decimated trying to extricate themselves from Russia after the ill-fated Operation Barbarossa. Those few who survived to return to Braunschweig proved little challenge for the US 84th Infantry— a division proudly nicknamed 'Lincoln County' in recognition of a former captain who went on to be president.

The Braunschweig Airfield was north of the city and had only one runway orientated east/west. On this occasion, the safest approach regardless of wind conditions, was deemed straight in from the west to avoid any possibility of over-flying the fluid front lines. The narrow runway looked even shorter than the 5,500 feet listed in the log and cross winds caused Captain Davis to 'crab' the plane in at a severe angle. The wheels squealed contact with the concrete barely twenty feet beyond its beginning and Billy Fagan slapped his thigh with uncontrollable glee.

"Nice job, Steven, my boy. I know a carrier pilot when I see one; am I right?" Steve Davis looked over and smiled sheepishly. "USS Saratoga out of San Diego. This runway is six times longer than the one I learned to land on, though the width is about the same."

"You chaps always take great pride in touching down as close to the edge of a runway as is humanly possible, whether it be floating or concrete. I like that a lot. Shows spunk!"

The squad de-planed and were helped to stow their gear within the 1930s terminal building by a half dozen fit and eager GIs. Major David Rogner introduced himself to explain. "I understand you guys will be staying with us for a few days. We billet in the town but have a platoon stationed here at the airport for security reasons. There's pretty good radio communication from the con tower and Corporal Jinks will assign you some specific frequencies that you are welcome to scramble with our B-2. Apart from that, is there anything else I can do for you?"

"Any chance the Gerrys left a large ambulance behind anywhere?"

"Well, they pretty much left everything, though I can't swear to an ambulance. Have a couple of your men come back into town with me and we'll swing by the Wehrmacht's former barracks. I know I can get you a nice troop carrier, low mileage and only driven by a little old lady to church on Sundays but won't even ask what you need an ambulance for. However, I've been ordered from the top to assist you in any way I can. So let's go take a look."

Two hours later, Gino Blando and Mitch Arnold returned to the airport driving a 1.6 ton Phaenomen Granit ambulance with giant red crosses in white circles plastered on every side including the roof.

"I don't suppose?......" asked an incredulous Mike Johnston.

"......Of course we did, Staff; inside are six Wehrmacht medical uniforms, a ton of bandages, stethoscopes and multifarious medical paraphernalia. Got the biggest uniform we could find for Paddy but he might still need a little alteration. I figured if he's supposed to be wounded, we can just rip the seams wherever we need to."

Early next morning, a variety of weapons were stashed under the two cots in the rear before Paddy and Billy lay down to assume their roles as badly wounded soldiers. Their heads were swathed in bandages and liberally daubed with red Stephens' Ink Gino had thought to liberate from the front desk of the Lutetia for the specific purpose. Chez and Jurek would ride in the front, Edmund and Günter tending the 'wounded' in the rear. A large stars and stripes fluttered proudly from the siren on the roof and their German tunics were hidden for now with the weapons. As added insurance for safe passage to the front, Major Rogner gave Chez, the designated driver, a very official letter on Lincoln County Division stationery. Even in the short time they had to know him, the Black Widows had come to appreciate Rogner's dry acerbic wit as he added straight-faced. "This letter should work fine on our side; the Russian and German sides,—not so much."

Staff Sergeant Johnston climbed into the ambulance to cast his critical eye over the patients, double-checking for any breakdown in authenticity.

"If I didn't know better, Paddy, I'd think someone had beaten the crap out of you."

"Mike, we'll be contacting you every day. If we miss two consecutive days, something has gone terribly wrong and I am hereby giving you a direct order to get these lads back home. I'm thinking we'll need four to five days to get to the bottom of Zumwalt's mystery but really won't know 'til we get into Berlin."

"With regard to your direct order, Boss—Fuck off. We'll come and get you; count on it.

"Take care of yoursel' Paddy." He got out, closed the door and the ambulance revved up, turned left and drove the fifty miles to the US front at Magdeburg without incident.

Throughout 1944, the Royal Air Force had systematically destroyed most of Magdeburg. Even when not the prime target, it became a convenient place to discard unused bombs on the return leg from Berlin as the city's main industries formerly revolved around the supply of petroleum, oil and lubrication products (POL) to the Nazi war machine.

Now the city served as a holding point for massive American armed forces, ordered by Eisenhower not to advance past the River Elbe in the vague hope Soviets and German divisions would eliminate each other in the final battle for Berlin. Since the Yalta Conference, Britain and America had no doubts about the most dangerous threat to peace in the post war world; as such, the West saw any diminution in the 450 Russian divisions as a positive.

CHAPTER EIGHTEEN

A Red Flag to a Bear

Through the middle of Magdeburg, the River Elbe splits around Werder Island before continuing north through rich German farmland and eventually flushing out the Hamburg docklands into the North Sea. Since the Emperor Charlemagne, Werder Island was attractive as an easily defensible place for settlement as here, the wide river could be bridged in two sections. The retreating German army had failed to destroy all the bridges to and from Werder Island so, after Chez showed his letter of passage, the ambulance was directed past St. Hans church, east across the Zollbrucke and ultimately into a no-man's land of potential death stretching all the way to Berlin.

The idea behind the ambulance was good in concept, but in the real-time fluid dynamics of the Second World War, their vehicle became an easily targeted red flag to a bull, or it this case, a bear. As soon as they lost the protection of the massed US army front lines, the atmosphere morphed to one reeking of panic. The ambulance bogged down within a sea of white flags waved by fleeing Germans as they advanced towards the Yanks—not to fight, but to plead for mercy from Russian reprisal. Vengeance was running at a fever pitch, fueled by enduring memories of Stalingrad. The Russians, given no quarter on the eastern front, now discarded all regard of the Geneva Convention as they shredded through centuries of evolved human civilization. Any male speaking German was murdered immediately, any female raped repeatedly.

Under these circumstances, a German ambulance was far from the safe haven they calculated and Chez and his compatriots began to feel more and more like sitting ducks.

"Adopting German disguise once we left the Allied front lines seemed like such a good idea; now, I'm not so sure." Jurek voiced his mounting concern to Chez as they plowed onward. "I'm thinking we'd be better off not wearing this Wehrmacht shit?'

"Agreed; tell the lads in the back," responded the Spider and struggled to remove his jacket as he drove.

All hell was breaking loose as they approached Potsdam; terrified, teenage German soldiers and civilians came at the ambulance in waves as they frantically attempted to escape marauding Soviets.

"You are headed straight into a Russian battalion," yelled a middle-aged fraulein, flailing her arm at the streets behind her.

"Time to head north, Jurek. This is the worst possible time to be German and we need to circumvent Russian lines to enter the relative safety of Berlin. Boy, I never thought I would say that!

"I'm going to swing around the Templiner See to find out if any back roads are open to Spandau. We can make a decision when we get there whether to go further north to Hennigsdorf or risk going east into Berlin on Heerstrasse. If I recall from the last time I visited my cousins, Heerstrasse becomes Kaiserdamm, the processional road through the Tiergarten that ends up right under the Brandenburg Gate."

"Nothing wrong with arriving at the Hotel Adlon in style, Chez. Let's go for it."

They had been on the detour less than twenty minutes when a Russian armored patrol bolted out of a side street and screeched to a halt in front of them to block the road. Six high-cheekboned soldiers poured out of the wagon and aimed Kalashnikovs at the front windshield of the ambulance.

Chez slammed on the brakes, held a white towel out of the driver's window and screamed urgently in Russian, "Hold on just a minute, comrades, we are Russian. We are on your side." The leader of the patrol motioned for his men to keep their weapons aimed but not to shoot—for now.

Günter's quiet voice whispered from the rear into Jurek's ear, "How many we got, Jurek?"

"One each," was his ventriloquist reply. The patrol leader was studying him from no more than three feet away so Jurek maintained a stoic forward stare. Chez, on the other hand, smiled broadly even though he was aware that the Asian battalions of the Soviet Forces were infamous for exacting extreme brutality.

"Got a couple of badly wounded German officers in the back. I thought I might get useful information out of them before they die. Where is your HQ?"

The leader, whose insignia indicated he was a praporshchik, (a warrant officer,) was intrigued but not sold. He gestured for three of his men to check out the rear compartment and demanded that Chez and Jurek climb down from the cab.

Smolenski and Hoenicke hurriedly divested themselves of their Wehrmacht jackets and when the rear doors clanked open, they greeted the three Mongolian scowls with Russian pleasantries. The two soldiers held their Kalashnikovs menacingly in front of them as they climbed in to examine the patients; the third held his distance outside.

It all unfolded like a slow motion ballet. Within the cramped compartment, Edmund Smolenski 'accidently' backed into one soldier and held up both his hands in apology. The man lost his balance and fell on top of McBride's combat knife, held rigidly at an angle under his blanket. Edmund's distraction caused the second soldier in the ambulance to turn away from Günter Hoenicke who rewarded him with a sleeper hold that evolved into the quick snap of a broken neck. The third, who had remained outside, managed an urgent alarm. He had only to raise his Kalashnikov a few inches to enter the fray, but a Browning 9mm slug entered his brain before the barrel even moved.

The action at the front of the vehicle was much less theatrical. Smiling and in mid-sentence when he heard the alarm being sounded, the Spider kicked the officer in the crotch, spun him around and collapsed the back of his knees while pulling backwards on the scruff of the Russian's neck. Chez pointed his Browning at the two remaining men from over the kneeling praporshchik's shoulder. Realizing their hopelessness, the men dropped their rifles and froze with hands raised.

"Get their guns, Jurek, and have them lay face down along with their fearless leader. Double tap the first one that move while I check the back." Glancing to verify that Podolski had the situation covered, he slammed his pistol butt under the officer's left ear and was halfway to the rear door before the body crumpled onto the road.

Günter and Edmund had already dragged the three corpses into the rubble of a roadside building so they joined Chez in asking the bandaged-swaddled Paddy what to do next.

"Knock the live ones out, tie their thumbs behind their backs and throw them in the rear with us 'til we cross German lines. They might have some value as bargaining chips—but I doubt it.

"Let's get the hell out of here."

CHAPTER NINETEEN

The Hotel Adlon, Berlin

T he route through Spandau proved a wise choice and by the late afternoon of April 16, the four members of the SAS plus Billy Fagan and the Spider had broken through the contracting German lines surrounding Berlin to head in the general direction of the Brandenburg Gate. Chez stopped briefly to dump the hostages and revert into his Wehrmacht uniform before cranking the wailing ambulance siren to ensure clear passage under the pretext of transporting wounded Germans from the front lines for emergency medical treatment. He even wound down his window several times to loudly demand directions to their destination knowing it currently served as a field hospital. With enlisted assistance from numerous well-meaning citizens, the Wehrmacht ambulance negotiated numerous roadblocks and rubble, eventually pulling to a halt behind the Hotel Adlon.

The 1907 hotel was located where the famous Palais Redern once ostentatiously ruled Berlin society from Pariser Platz at Unter den Linden Boulevard. Their ambulance blended in with five others that identified the once-magnificent building's conscripted use.

Chez and Jurek knocked loudly several times on the rear service door before it was eventually opened to a crack by a wide-eyed orderly.

"What the hell do you want?"

Chez tried the agreed pass-phrase, "Is my cousin, Hans Dorff working here today?" The face at the door was soon replaced by a tall smiling orderly who opened the door wide and grabbed Chez in a bear hug as he cried passionately, "Pietr, is it really you? Please come inside and I'll get you some tea."

"Good to see you, Hans, but we have a couple of badly wounded soldiers in the ambulance so, if you would be so kind, please hold the door open for us."

Chez and Jurek ran back to their ambulance to return promptly with a stretcher weighed down by a large body, the head wrapped in blood soaked bandages. Not a couple of paces behind, Günter and Edmund followed with a similarly packaged Billy Fagan. Once inside the bowels of the Adlon, Hans spirited them all down to the basement.

"Sorry for calling you Pietr. I knew to expect you but had no idea what you look like or what your names are.

"Welcome to hell!"

Hans Dorff was commander of a cell within the German Resistance Force. The G.R.F.'s numbers had swelled since early 1944, encouraged by common knowledge the Nazi scourge that had been poisoning their beloved country for over a decade was about to end. The Dorff Cell now numbered over twenty brave German patriots, most surreptitiously employed in some capacity or other at the Hotel Adlon's field hospital.

"This basement is secure, Gentlemen. We have a couple of doctors within our group and they have designated this area as having an unacceptably dangerous level of bacteria. A twenty-four hour guard at the top of the staircase will ensure that unwanted guests never come down here. Grab some coffee, freshen up and we'll talk."

Paddy and Billy replaced their German uniforms with green hospital scrubs and the bandages were tossed, but the Stephen's red ink left indelible stains everywhere it had touched. However overall, they had made it unscathed to their forward base and the chicory-based coffee tasted great. As they waited for Hans Dorff to join them, Edmund Smolenski muttered the harsh realities of their situation. "Hard to believe that was the easy part of the mission." Then the door opened to admit Dorff accompanied by three other members of his resistance cell.

"Okay, we were told you needed architectural plans of the Führerbunker and lists of the regular personnel and daily routines. The best we could do is spread out on the table but they are little more than sketches from the memories of construction workers. Quite honestly, not many people even know about the bunker's existence for obvious reasons."

Chez poured over the different drawings, noting many inconsistencies but quickly getting a good general feel for the layout. Hans then added his own concerns.

"I know you have all taken tremendous risks to get here but I do hope you are not planning any kind of assault on the bunker? Trust me, it is completely impregnable and, in my professional opinion, a death trap for those within. The Russians will eventually overrun the place by sheer numbers and will show no mercy to any and all occupants. You are most welcome to stay here and eyewitness the final days but your chances of escaping Russian-occupied Berlin will not be high. If I were you, I would seriously consider turning around to go home immediately."

The Spider smiled coldly at the brave German but declined to comment on anything Hans had suggested. Instead, he returned to his study of the plans, pausing finally to ask, "How do they get their fresh air? There must be a shaft? We might be able to poison the rats."

Dorff sighed in the realization that these fierce warriors were not wavering from the focus of their mission. "You are two days too late for that, I'm afraid. There used to be an airshaft hidden in some bushes close to the garden entrance. We only discovered it last week and planned to do just what you proposed. We had the cyanide gas all ready but the Nazis must have coincidently recognized the potential problem and relocated the shaft into one of the guard towers."

"You sure somebody within your group didn't warn them?"

"First thing I checked but it was just an unlucky break. We verified that the redirection of the airshaft had been planned several weeks ahead of when we discovered the old one."

Chez then focused on the bunker's listed personnel and asked a strange question. "Any of the lower, non-descript staff about my build? Think of somebody who might perform the more mundane tasks? Don't worry about specifics; the general build is all I care about."

Hans read between the lines and took several

seconds to ponder this request before pointing at a list to embellish his replies.

"Three men come to mind: Johannes Hentschel, the maintenance engineer; a little taller than you but about your age. He's very loyal and worships the Führer.

"Wilhelm Becker has been with Hitler for years and is the only person Adolf allows to make the apfelstrudel he eats every day at 4 p.m.—rain or shine.

"Then there's Koch, the janitor. He could be about your height if he wasn't hunched over. Besides, he's a lot older than you and not a real match. Koch was badly wounded in the Great War, has a heavy limp and wears thick glasses. He acts a little retarded but cleans the toilets and takes care of the rubbish. I think his first name might be Albrecht."

The Spider's interest peaked immediately. "Where does Albrecht Koch live?"

"No idea; all the staff live in the bunker full time. They're not allowed to leave for security purposes as Hitler is understandably paranoid about assassination attempts."

"But what if they get sick? Maybe a really bad case of diarrhea?" Chez persisted. "Wouldn't they be allowed to get treated somewhere in preference to stinking the place up? Koch must have had a place around here before they all retreated into the bunker. Maybe if he needed a clean set of clothes...."

"Perhaps, but the bastards are more likely to just shoot him." The agent mused as he picked up on the Spider's train of thought.

"I doubt that. A decaying body will only add to the bunker's malodorous problems." Dorff raised his eyebrows in agreement with the Spider's logic.

"I must agree. Causing the diarrhea will be the easy part; a couple of our sympathizers work in the Reich Chancellery kitchens and all we have to do is get a heavy dose of laxative into Koch's breakfast. I can get the industrial strength from the drug cabinet upstairs.

"Before you ask, poisoning Hitler is not an option. He and his close advisors have their own cook, Frau Konstanze Manziarly; been with Hitler for a couple of years and a devout Nazi. She taste tests every single thing before a morsel passes the bastard's lips. But I'm fairly certain we can cause Herr Koch a severe case of the shits."

"Unless anybody has a better plan, I would like a personal interview with Albrecht Koch as soon as possible and the only way I can see to get him out of the bunker is the hope he will be granted dispensation to change soiled clothing. Our mission is to verify if the real Hitler is in the Bunker—nothing more. If Mr. Koch can convince us of that, we can report back to the Brigadier and leave the dirty work up to the Ruskis."

CHAPTER TWENTY

The Führerbunker, Berlin

B y the middle of April 1945, the Vistula-Oder offensive had steamrolled two million Soviet troops into the outskirts of Berlin. Adolf Hitler had been commanding the German armed forces from his Führerbunker in Berlin since January but, despite his apparent blind optimism, the German army simply did not have the resources to halt the pincer movement of Marshalls Zhukov and Konev. The Wehrmacht, running out of able-bodied men, resorted to conscripting younger and younger soldiers. Any thirteen and fourteen year-olds caught evading their duty to the Fatherland were publicly hanged by the neck from lampposts as a gruesome deterrent to their peers.

German officers in the field presented continual assessments of the debacle to General Heinz Guderian, a former Panzer commander who had risen to chief of staff. However, Hitler chose to ignore his depressing reports and replaced him with General Hans Krebs, someone the failing Führer could better trust to tell him what he wanted to hear. Under these surreal circumstances, Adolf Hitler maintained an expectation that the German army would defeat Zhukov's eight armies once they entered the confines of central Berlin.

Sycophantic aides gathered for the daily briefing in the bunker's main briefing area, an open space between Hitler's office and the Göebbels rooms. On this particular day, there was a rumor rampant that their adored leader had perfected a secret plan, one with grandiose German armored formations guaranteed to defeat the Soviets. Anticipation within the gathered group was electric, though understandably tinged with urgent desperation.

"The Führer is a pure genius. He has lured the entire Russian army into the confines of Berlin where he will exterminate them like termites—pure genius I tell you."

"Yes, my friend, it would have been nigh impossible

to beat 500 Soviet divisions in the open fields of Poland; the streets of the capital give our smaller, better equipped forces a distinct tactical advantage. Remember how difficult it was for us in Stalingrad when the Russians made full use of their home-field advantage?"

"No question. The history books will portray our visionary Führer as the greatest military commander of all ti … What the hell is that rank smell?"

An uncomfortable distraction slowly captured everyone's attention. A strong, vile odor from some-where behind them rose to become the main topic of conversation, coupled with accusatory glares and personal indignation. Finally, just before the Führer made his entrance, General Krebs could not stand it any longer.

"Got im Himmel! Misch, take Günsche with you and get rid of that awful smell. There must be a toilet backed up and I would sooner smell Dettol than crap. Close the damn door after you."

The two high-ranking soldiers were just about to object vociferously that this was not in their job descriptions, when the door from Hitler's office burst open and Obersturmbannführer Heinz Linge strode in. Linge was Hitler's personal valet and a Pavlovian trigger for the room to snap to their feet, right arms extended forward at 45 degrees. The Führer followed a theatrical five seconds later to the bellowed, "HEIL

HITLER," and climbed three steps of the staircase which led upwards to the garden before spinning around to glower down upon his ever-loyal staff. He raised his right arm in a limp effeminate manner which contrasted by design to the angled ramrods of the staff below. Then his nose crinkled and he glared at Linge.

"Heinz, what is that disgusting stench?"

"It is being taken care of Mein Führer," General Krebs barked in reply.

Hitler coughed to clear his throat and went straight into a patented rant.

Oberscharführer Rochus Misch and Sturmbannführer Otto Günsche hunted the putrid smell through the corridor and lounge areas, noticing an increase in intensity as they approached the toilets. It was there they noticed a non-descript bald man lurching furtively backwards towards the massive blast wall that separated the Führerbunker from the guards' quarters. A steel door in this wall led up to the Foreign Ministry and the New Chancellery Building.

"Alt! Who are you?" The partially crippled man steered a bucket with his mop as he attempted to erase the footprints of his retreat. He lifted his head slowly at the command and peered back through large, horn-rimmed spectacles at the drawn Walther pistols. His fear and general demeanor left no doubt that the offensive odor came from numerous soggy brown stains that discolored his grey work clothes and squelched into his shoes.

"I'm Koch the janitor. I apologize, Mein Herr, I have severe food poisoning but I am forbidden to leave the bunker. I have to get out of here, even if the guards shoot me. I have lived here for three months and all the fresh clothes I own are in my apartment about two miles from here. I am so sorry…I promise to come back when my stomach pains stop."

"Das ist mir furzegal, du hurensohn. I should shoot you but that won't make the smell go away. Get the hell out of here right now and take that bucket with you. Otto, escort him upstairs and throw the arschloch out of the first exit door you find. Then get back here with some detergent and a couple of janitors as fast as you can. Leave me that mop, you cretin. I will start cleaning up. Hurry for Got's sake."

Albrecht Koch limped his way from the moldy basement passages, eventually finding the light of day at the Old Chancellery Building, a beautiful edifice built in the mid-1700s for Count von Schulenburg. A spotter from the underground resistance picked him out the moment he emerged onto Wilhelmstrasse. Hans Dorff had positioned his available men to observe the most likely ways that Koch might be thrown out of the bunker should their sketchy plan reach fruition. Fully expecting the janitor could die or simply be shot for having eaten the tainted pork, now the plan was apparently going exactly as they had hoped. The spotter signaled another of his fellow dissidents and the pair followed the rancid janitor at a discrete distance. As luck would have it, Albrecht's route to his old apartment off Behrenstrasse would have taken him within a block of the Hotel Adlon so the underground was able to wait until the last possible moment before they whisked him under protest through the service door of the field hospital and straight down to the basement.

Koch was certain he was going to die when one of his captors suddenly disappeared and the other pulled out a pistol, which he leveled it at his head.

"There is a shower over there with soap and towels. Get in as you are and try to get as much shit off your clothes as you can before you strip down. Leave your old stuff in the shower; clean clothes and shoes are on that bench."

I don't understand this at all but at least I will go to a God who will not be repulsed by my smell when he meets me. Why do these men want me to be clean? The janitor puzzled. He enjoyed the shower as long as he could, the hot water stinging him as he scrubbed away his humiliation with a large bar of yellow lye soap.

When he finally stepped out and reached for the

towel, the man with the pistol was still waiting on the bench. He handed the naked, shivering man a shot glass filled with a thick white liquid.

"This will settle your stomach, Albrecht. Chug it, then hurry up and get dressed."

Maybe I'm not going to die; otherwise, why give me medicine? Just a minute, how could they possibly know my name? This is crazy! But Koch obliged and chugged the medicine as he quickly got dressed in fresh clothes he thought he recognized.

He was led into the next room where his heart began to race at the sight of a dozen fierce looking men, several wearing Wehrmacht uniforms. They stopped talking and turned to stare at him as he entered.

"Please sit down, Albrecht. I am Czeslaw Orlowski and I just want to ask you a few simple questions." The young man had a pleasant smile, looked exceedingly fit and spoke with an accent that betrayed his roots as a Berliner. They faced each other across a planked, trestle table.

"I'm obliged to begin by stating the obvious. Should you choose not to cooperate, we will have no choice but to kill you because you already know too much about our organization. If there is any good news in this, it would be that the Third Reich has only days left before it collapses, so you would have died in the bunker anyway."

Koch was startled by this harsh reality but the

young German fixed him with clear pale gray eyes, continuing in a soft voice that held menace, yet was almost comforting.

"However, if you are able to help us over the next couple of hours by verifying some critical information, you will be transported out of Berlin to Damsdorf, your family village in Klostersee and left under the protection of the parish priest to live out your days in relative safety. Please take your time, but I need your response before I continue."

The two men stared at each other in silence for several seconds and, with his choices being extremely limited, Albrecht Koch decided he had to trust this young man.

He certainly knows a helluva lot about me, Koch thought. *These clean clothes are from my apartment so he must have been there. How else could he know I was born in Damsdorf?*

"You poisoned me, didn't you? You took a gamble that they would send me home to get cleaned up. What if they had just killed me in the bunker?"

"Yes and yes, but don't flatter yourself that they need you back. They wanted rid of the smell and probably are running side bets on how far you got before a Kalashnikov popped you." Though Chez's expression remained stoic, the janitor's sudden retort was hardly that of a simpleton. *So, Albrecht is not as stupid as he would like everyone to believe. Interesting indeed,* Chez thought.

"What information do you need and how will you know if I am telling you the truth?" Koch pleaded.

"You live with the truth; you die with a lie."

Koch paused and bit his lower lip before reaching out an open hand for the Spider to shake, which he did, confident that the janitor was going to provide him with at least some of the vital information he lacked.

"Okay Albrecht, who exactly is inside that concrete box? I need names and physical descriptions." The janitor replied methodically, staring up at the ceiling of the basement as mental pictures flashed through his brain. When he stopped, his eyes returned to Chez. There was a moment of silence before Jurek Podolski, the man charged with scribing the list questioned their prey incredulously.

"That's it? That's every single person you know of in the bunker?"

"Ja, I'm pretty sure I have ... no, wait a minute, Traudl Junge. How could I forget Traudl; pretty as a picture...."

"What about fuckin' Hitler? You haven't mentioned fuckin' Hitler. Are you telling us he's not in the bunker?"

Koch looked stunned at this apparent omission and started to stammer.

"Of...of...of...c.course Hitler is there. He...he has lived there since the start of this year. Didn't I say Hih...Hih...Hitler?"

"No, actually you didn't, Albrecht." The Spider's eyes were now chips of ice and the room chilled to a deathly quiet. "Do not fuck with me, Koch. You have ten seconds to convince me you are telling the truth with one of only three possible answers:

"One. Hitler, the Führer und Reichskanzler of Germany is in fact in the bunker.

"Two. A man masquerading as Hitler is in the bunker.

"Three. HITLER IS NOT IN THE FUCKIN' BUNKER." Albrecht Koch started to shiver although rivulets of sweat were popping out of his forehead.

"I am waiting, arschgeige. Only the truth will extend your life beyond the five seconds you have left."

"Wait, wait, wuh…wuh…wait. I swear to you the Führer is in the bunker. It is the Führerbunker for Got's sake, I cannot believe I had to list him. I see the bastard every day." Then a puzzled look clouded his face. "And wuh…what did you mean by 'a man pretending to be Hitler?' The man in the bunker is definitely Hitler, no doubt about it. I know the Führer. I hear him yell at everyone. They are all scared of him, except perhaps Reichleiter Bormann. He never yells at Herr Bormann. I cannot believe I forgot the F…"

"Enough, Albrecht, calm down. I believe you but nevertheless, a seed of doubt has been sown. We must move on to other questions. This time, think your answers through and don't forget anything."

Edmund Smolenski stepped forward with the

rough sketches of the Führerbunker for Koch to update. Subsequently, every moment of the janitor's typical day was mapped out and catalogued.

After almost four hours of repetition—versions of the same questions being re-posed by several different men—Chez stood up, stretched and announced, "Albrecht, that's it and we thank you. For about a week, you will be our guest in another Berlin location before being escorted to Damsdorf, assuming of course that you have told us the truth.

"Oh, one more thing. Please hand over your glasses to Karl, frames with your prescription will be issued to you before you leave.

Koch left the room in the custody of a couple of Hans' men. The next two hours had Colonel McBride and the SAS squad trying to identify any holes in Koch's story. There were many but it was all they had.

"I think we all agree that Albrecht Koch was not lying to us in that he believes the real Adolf Hitler is still in the bunker. However, Zumwalt's first question will be 'How good does a doppelganger have to be to fool a brain-damaged old janitor?' I'm afraid I don't think this plan worked. We need more proof. What do you think, Chez?"

There was no reply from the Spider and as they scanned the room, they were shocked to see the bald janitor with the horn-rimmed glasses standing off in a corner.

"What the hell, Koch, you were supposed to be out of here a couple of hours ago."

"You must excuse me, Paddy, I have some toilets to clean," smiled the Spider.

CHAPTER TWENTY ONE

The Plant

S oviet artillery began the concerted bombardment of Berlin on April 20, Hitler's 56th birthday. The New Chancellery building—The Reichskanzlei—was supposedly bomb proof, complete with its own air recycling plant, yet provision of an adequate communication system had been overlooked. Prior to Adolph Hitler arriving, no one in the Third Reich imagined that the final stages of the war would be conducted from three levels below this location. Now, the chips were down, and the only way German staff officers could ascertain the extent of the Red army's movement into Berlin was to phone civilians at random to ask if the Red army was in their vicinity.

Chez used this confusion to his advantage. Armed

with Koch's credentials, he made it all the way through the guards' quarters and down to the steel door in the blast wall of the Führerbunker without anyone questioning him.

This is too easy. Maybe the sonofabitch has already made his escape!

Suddenly a voice behind him barked, "Alt! Who are you?" Chez froze and then turned slowly to show Albrecht's badge.

"I am Koch, the janitor for the Führerbunker. I had to get some medicine for my stomach but I am back and ready for duty. Could you please call Oberscharführer Misch or Sturmbannführer Günsche to let me back in?" The guard picked up a phone, reached Otto Günsche and a brief conversation ensued. Eventually, the bolts on the steel door slid back and it swung silently inwards. Günsche, a humane man despite his present, dead-end situation, closed the door behind Koch and hissed angrily in his native Bavarian slang.

"Mench bist du blöd; You stupid idiot, I gave you every opportunity to escape—or at least die in your own shit—yet you return? Well, your loyalty to the Führer is impressive; you might as well get back to work."

The Spider had memorized every aspect of the bunker so he left Günsche and scuttled towards the toilets, where a small electrical switch room revealed a worn blanket and Koch's sparse possessions. His mannerisms and hunched walk were a close imitation of the janitor, as was the slightly slurred speech impediment of the older man. Chez knew that his shaven head and horn-rimmed spectacles, now retrofitted with clear glass, would be the over-riding images of identity that allowed him to blend in. Albrecht Koch had warned him that he had to stop cleaning and leave any room when a Nazi official entered but he discovered a fantastic bonus within minutes of entering the Führerbunker.

My luxurious bedroom is also the main electrical distribution hub for the entire bunker. I know there's a ventilation room on the other side of Hitler's bedroom and I would be very surprised if I cannot get across this entire area by crawling above the ceiling and following these pipes.

He pulled himself up to the horizontal void where conduit and wires disappeared into darkness above Hitler's suite of rooms. Although this presented real potential, he dared not risk exploring any further until he was sure Hitler and Eva Braun were in the central conference room. A voice called from beyond his closet.

"Koch, where the hell are you?"

Chez dropped silently back down to the floor and limped out into the toilets. "Right here, sir."

"Our glorious Führer will be celebrating his birthday tonight. I want the briefing area to be spotless before

AND after his party. Start cleaning now but leave the moment the staff begins to gather. You can return to clean up ONLY after the last person has retired."

"Ich verstehe, Mein Herr. I understand."

The Spider waited patiently for the party to begin and seriously considered taking out Hitler, his girlfriend and all the top staff of the Nazi hierarchy by commandeering a machine gun from a guard and raiding the conference room in a suicide mission.

But I still do not know if it's the real Hitler or a fake. The lucky bastard escaped assassination at Wolfschanze and I have to be completely certain before committing to anything that radical. A vision of Jadwiga flashed before him to bury further foolish thoughts.

He returned to the electrical room, took off his shoes and hauled himself up and into the dark horizontal space. He could not risk his weight causing the collapse of any portion of the ceiling so chose to hang horizontally within the thirty-inch space by using major conduit and plumbing pipes as support for his hands and feet. Emulating a giant rodent, he was able to scuttle rapidly over the private bathroom, Hitler's sitting room and finally his bedroom before reaching the new ventilation shaft. His eyes had adjusted to the dark and his innate gymnastic ability was in full Spider mode.

The recent construction of the airshaft flavored the air with saw-cut pine. Needles of light through knotholes and leakage from the rooms below afforded him a faint but welcome awareness of his surroundings. His mind was encouraged by this potential escape route as he headed back from his first exploration. Then, he picked up the faintest of sounds as he was passing over the ceiling of Hitler's sitting room. He froze immediately and held his breath. It sounded like a key turning, followed by footsteps entering the room beneath. Clamping both legs and one arm around some thick metal conduit, Chez positioned his head so his right ear was close to the gap around the room's central light fixture.

"Martin, my friend, please close the door. What is so important that you need to interrupt my birthday?" This voice was unmistakable but he could not place the second speaker other than a familiarity in the tone that left little doubt it must be Reichleiter Martin Bormann.

"Quite honestly Adolf, I don't give a damn about your stupid birthday party. Everything is in place for the day after tomorrow but I need your signature on several documents I've prepared. This will maintain the ruse long after you and Eva reach Patagonia."

"Give me the details, I'm intrigued."

"Well, we finally located a credible stooge for you, a doppelganger with passable acting skills who has been promised a huge sum of money to adopt your schedule for the next week. I told him you needed minor surgery on your arm and did not want to alarm the people by your absence.

"The same deal has been accepted by a local actress who bears a striking likeness to Eva. Of course, neither has any clue they will be killed in a staged suicide before they have any chance of cashing out. Four of my most trusted senior officers will witness your brave and heroic demise, and will solemnly carry out your last wishes for a funeral pyre. Their charred remains will be conveniently discovered by the Soviets, and your last will and testament will designate that leadership of the Reich goes to Goebbels. The poor slob truly believes his golden tongue can persuade the Russians he is prepared to lead a communist state on their behalf after the formal surrender. However, if they don't buy it, Joseph and Magda are prepared to commit suicide with their entire family to lend credence to your suicide."

"Commendable. I have always been very fond of Magda. But how do *we* get out?"

"The Inner Circle has been carefully creating their own alibis over the past weeks. For example, Hermann Fegelein and Eva's sister, Gretl, were able to disappear successfully about a week ago—thanks to you ordering his execution. During tonight's birthday party, Linge will escort Eva to the Chancellery gardens for a smoke break, returning with the actress I told you about. Both ladies are currently wearing identical outfits. Fegelein will meet Eva in the garden and escort her to our designated, secure gathering place.

"Adolf, pay attention. From the moment of the switch, you are going to have to treat this actress exactly the same as you would Eva. It is critical to my plan that this façade be maintained until I am able to pull a similar stunt that allows your doppelganger to take your place. Subject to some kind of crisis, this will happen sometime tomorrow."

"As long as she doesn't try to touch me, you know I can't stand that. Just tell me how and when I get to disappear."

"Remember Hannah Reitsch?" The Führer mumbled affirmatively at the mention of Germany's most famous female test pilot. "She's been ordered to bring Ritter von Greim here to officially replace that fat rat, Goering, as head of the Luftwaffe. She's going to land as close to the bunker as possible, perhaps in the Grosser Tiergarten, but her only passenger on the return trip will be you. Her small plane will then fly you to Templhof Airport, assuming we still have it under our control. From there, a Junkers will get you to Obersalzberg to meet up with the rest of the Inner Circle. This damn group has now swelled to over twenty people so it is essential they travel to Austria in small groups using different routes. Otherwise none of us will make it."

The Spider had been suspending his entire body weight from the conduit above the ceiling for almost ten minutes but his concentration in retaining every detail of the amazing conversation from below shut out the screaming pain from his muscles. Some debris dislodged and landed on the ceiling panels. It was the faintest of sounds but sounded like a rattling drum to Chez. He held his breath but the men below disregarded the rattle with a cursory reference to the munitions exploding in the distance. It was only when he heard Martin Bormann suggest they both return to the party that he realized he was at the very brink of his physical capabilities.

The Reichleiter paused at the door to whisper one last reassurance before he opened it.

"We'll all rendezvous in Berchtesgarten, rest a couple of days and then travel by a neutral commercial airline to Barcelona where I've summoned a convoy of three U-boats. Six weeks traversing the Atlantic to Argentina and we'll be drinking fine Lowenbrau at your new home in Patagonia. All the key people and resources will be there to plan the rise of the Fourth Reich at our pleasure.

"Now, after you Adolf; we mustn't keep your guests waiting."

CHAPTER TWENTY TWO

Bormann's Ruse

Reichleiter Martin Bormann chose the morning of April 22 to orchestrate the critical substitution necessary to bring final closure to the Second World War in Europe. The upper echelon of the Third Reich realized the tattered remnants of the German army had scant hours remaining before they ran out of the men and ammunition essential to keep the Russian Bear from ripping them apart limb from limb. Berlin was surrounded by Soviet forces deranged with hatred from atrocities committed since the summer of 1942; soldiers who would give no mercy to any German they found alive.

No more than a handful of extremely loyal Nazis were privy to Bormann's ruse; Joseph Goebbels did not even tell his family, unsure of how his wife, Magda, would react. He was reasonably certain his nine-year-old son, Helmut, was the result of an 'affaire d'amour' between his wife and Adolph Hitler during 1933 but fanatical loyalty to his Führer transcended even that. If he could not prove his usefulness to the Soviets, he was fully committed to reinforcing the subterfuge of Hitler's escape by any means at his disposal.

Other uber-devoted confidants, Reichsjugendleiter Artur Axmann, SS-Hauptsturmführer Edwald Lindloff, SS-Sturmbannführer Otto Günsche, SS-Obersturm-führers Peter Högl, Heinz Linge and Rochus Misch all pledged to take their risks with the Russians, hoping their testaments, given under threat of death, would add credence to the outlandish yarn they were about to spin.

The mastermind, Reichsleiter Martin Bormann, told these men what they would be allowed to see and what their interpretation had to be. They should be able to resist any torture and even new-fangled lie detectors if they only saw what he allowed. The rest of the witnesses to the subsequent staged meeting in the Führerbunker's stark conference room had no inkling that a master magician was about to manipulate their minds.

Following the customary routine, five seconds after his valet appeared, the faithful rose to their feet in anticipation of the Führer striding into the room. The predictability set a comfort level and their leader looked strong and confident. All were sympathetic as they noticed the tunic button used to secure the pocket flap over his heart was missing.

Greta Christian whispered confidentially to her fellow secretary, Traudl Junge, "Look, Traudl, the Führer is suffering the same hardships as we are. He always takes such pride in his appearance, it must break his heart; I must offer to sew that button later. What a great man!"

Adolph Hitler reached the third step of his pulpit, returned the salute and launched into an immediate tirade, thumping his good hand up and down on the handrail for emphasis as he blamed the treachery of his generals for the current downward turn of events. In front of those assembled, the Reichskanzler proclaimed he would personally fight fiercely until the bitter end, pausing to ask his personal physician, Dr. Werner Haase, a direct question about the most reliable method of suicide.

"Cyanide followed by a gunshot to the head, Mein Führer," was the studied response from the doctor. It elicited gasps from the staff and left Frauleins Junge and Christian sobbing openly.

Hitler's brilliant stagecraft chose this dramatic moment to stride back to his office, leaving the small crowd mumbling in fear and disbelief at the content of his ferocious outburst. However, a mere thirty seconds later, they were shocked into silence as the

Führer reappeared to continue his torrent of expletives. The staff, several with tears in their eyes, mostly chose to avoid eye contact and few noticed the slight variations in the Führer's appearance; the ears were a little smaller; his height was almost two inches less and his gammy left arm was held at a slightly different angle.

But a good magician distracts with one hand as he hides the ball with the other, so the button, such an unusual occurrence on a man so proud of his sartorial elegance, was still glaringly noticeable by its absence.

The substitution was a complete and total success. Karl Gebhardt, Julius Schaub, Christa Schroeder, Johanna Wolf and the other loyal staff not part of Bormann's sub rosa group, were unknowingly in the presence of Hitler's doppelganger, Gustav Weler whilst Adolph Hitler was shaving off his trademark hair and toothbrush moustache in his private bathroom before donning a dark grey double-breasted suit.

Martin Bormann waited patiently in Hitler's study and when the bathroom door opened, he turned a critical eye at his protégé.

"Let me see you wear the spectacles, Adolf. Ya, zer gut. Keep your hat in your hand to give everyone a view of that magnificent bald head. Ah-ha, you would fool your mother!

"Follow me back the Reichskanzlei. Herr Weler is instructed to keep the meeting going for another ten minutes so we should be able to duck out through the bathrooms; Lindloff is guarding the door."

When the moment was right, the two men moved quickly from the small, private hallway and into the bunker's bathroom. The useless cretin who cleaned the toilets was the only person there and Bormann completely ignored him as he turned to the Führer.

"Our schedule has adjusted a little. Hannah Reitsch must wait for a lull in the bombardment before she flies Generaloberst Robert Ritter von Greim into Berlin to meet Weler—ahem, you—and receive his appointment as head of the Luftwaffe. Hannah will then..."

"Martin, Hannah is good but how can she possibly land a plane in the middle of Berlin?"

"She is completely confident she can land a Fieseler Storch on or around the Ministry Gardens near the Reich Chancellery; close enough to get von Greim into the bunker. At the right moment, Linge will escort you to the plane and Hanna will fly you out to ..." The voices faded from the bathroom but the Spider had heard enough.

Mission accomplished. Be a damn shame if I don't make it back to the Adlon to tell the lads. Tally ho, as Billy would say.

Chez now focused all his energy on escaping from the headquarters of the Third Reich without the Nazis being any the wiser.

He headed straight for his electrical closet and

hoisted himself into the ceiling cavity. Fifteen minutes later found him at the opposing end of the bunker and climbing inside the new ventilation shaft. He was guessing, correctly as it happened, that the top of this four-foot square vertical tunnel would terminate within the tower identified from the outside as capped by a conical roof. Acutely aware that this escape route could only be used once, Chez also suspected that he might have an unknown number of guards to contend with and there would be no way back.

Can't think of one good reason why I would need to come back. Got the proof we came for, but I'm the only person outside the Nazi Inner Circle that knows what Hitler and Bormann are planning. If nothing else, I have to pass along this knowledge to Paddy before I die, Chez thought as he climbed the air shaft.

I CAN DO THIS; NO ONE MUST STOP ME.

The open shaft extended above a circular space about 12 feet in diameter and hearing voices, Chez grabbed the top of the shaft and cautiously eased himself upward. Apparently two guards, charged with protecting the new fresh-air shaft, were seated below on their Wehrmacht helmets, totally absorbed in a variation of Bavarian Schafkopf. Both soldiers were vigilant in keeping themselves well below the four openings that ringed the room, their rifles stacked carelessly against the outside wall.

The Spider, his heart racing with adrenaline, gripped the lip and edged the balls of his feet up until he coiled like a spring just below the top of the shaft. Taking a deep breath, he dived upwards and forward in a tuck, somersaulting to land like a cat between the guards. Both made the mistake of reaching for their holstered pistols instead of protecting their heads. One took a swinging back heel to the temple, the other a piston-like vertical elbow onto the top of his head. They both slumped unconscious to the floor. It was over in seconds.

Chez could not risk any evidence that might indicate a witness had escaped from the bunker so he propped one of the guards against an opening. After over a minute of exposure, nothing happened so he shoved a rifle up the back of the second man's tunic and maneuvered this torso into another opening that faced a different direction. On this occasion, it took only seconds for a Russian sniper from the south to explode the man's head from long range.

Holy shit, that guy's pretty damn good. I'd better be careful when I leave here.

He then relocated the other unconscious guard to similar effect and after a cursory glance around the scene of the crime, he hurtled down the stairs of the tower and into the vacated gardens.

Grateful for his civilian garb, he ducked low to scuttle from bush to bush within the Chancellery Gardens, making his way towards the welcome cover of Wilhelmstrasse. Once there, he was able to head north for three blocks and was at the back door of the Hotel Adlon in less than ten minutes.

The Resistance had posted a different guard at the door of the basement hideout; a man who had not seen Chez before and certainly in no mood to chat with a janitor.

"You cannot come in here. There are men inside with typhoid and you will catch it."

Chez cracked a smile and replied, "Tell the really big man that he's too mean to catch typhoid and the Spider needs to have a quick word."

The puzzled guard closed the door but dutifully delivered the strange message. Less than sixty seconds later, the door swung open again and the giant with the strange accent pushed past the guard to sweep the janitor up in a bear hug.

"Put me down, Paddy, before you break all my ribs."

Over the next ten minutes, the group convened in the basement, still mystified at the Spider's amazing transformation into a bald janitor but noticeably relieved to see their friend unhurt and safely back within their alliance. After the jokes, nervous laughter and congratulations calmed down, Paddy walked over to the Spider, put both hands on his shoulders and stated with wonderful sincerity,

"Welcome back, wee man. I cannot believe I have ever been happier to see anyone when you walked through that door. You have the floor, my friend."

There was a ripple of applause, which an embarrassed Chez Orlowski cut short by raising his hand.

"Well my friends, about forty five minutes ago, I watched the heavily disguised Adolf Hitler spirit himself out of the bunker while his double was covertly subbed in to rule the Third Reich under Bormann's direction. This dimwit thinks he's just filling in for a week while the main man has some discrete surgery, but he will be sacrificed in a couple of days along with some stooge that looks like Eva Braun.

"A small group of loyal Nazi fanatics will murder these two doppelgangers in cold blood but the witnesses will either lie or truly believe it to be a suicide. Within minutes, the corpses will be toasted into unrecognizable ashes using hundreds of liters of petrol. In fact, the bastards have already stashed the fuel close-by for the event.

"The Russians will have no problem finding the grizzly evidence; more than enough validation for the world's press to bring closure to Adolph's war!"

Although the story matched the theories broached by Zumwalt in the Hotel Lutetia, this hard evidence from Chez started a reverberation through the basement. McBride held up his hand and the room quelled immediately. "Chez, so far, this script could have been written by Commander Jimmy Fleming. Any changes to the epilogue?"

"Not really, Paddy; MI6 nailed it. The entire top echelon of the Nazi Party is planning on flying to Spain within the next couple of weeks to pick up a U-boat to South America and freedom."

"Not if I have breath in my body," said Colonel Patrick Samuel McBride with an intimidating growl.

CHAPTER TWENTY THREE

Hitler's Escape

I n full dress uniform, Reichsleiter Bormann led the way out of the Führerbunker. Not one guard dared question his familiar imposing figure or by association, the diminutive, clean-shaven, bald and bespectacled businessman walking beside him. The two strode confidently on their upward route from Hitler's inner sanctum two levels below ground and through the guards' chambers in the Vorbunker. Finally, they reached a blast door protecting the main tunnel that led north to the gardens of the Foreign Ministry and Old Chancellery or south to the New Chancellery Building, now referred to as The Reichskanzlei.

Bormann waited for the guard to open the blast door but indicated authoritatively that he and his mysterious companion did not wish to be followed from this point. Under normal circumstances, this was strictly against protocol but in fairness, the usual adamant discipline of the elite squad charged with protecting the Führerbunker was somewhat distracted by Russian artillery shells that exploded closer by the minute.

Now alone, the two men pressed north for no more than twenty meters before stopping at another heavy steel door, this one recessed deeply into the west side of the main tunnel wall. The uniformed general fished into his breast pocket and gave Hitler a large key, keeping a nervous watch for unwanted traffic as the Führer worked the mechanism. Both lock and hinges were well oiled and within seconds, the operation was reversed by securing the door behind them.

After negotiating a short, dimly lit corridor, they emerged into a secret air-raid shelter constructed under the Reception Hall of the Old Chancellery. Built as an integral part of the Vorbunker they had just left, Adolf Hitler had insisted the architect, Leonard Gall, remove evidence of its construction on all recorded plans as it contained a secret stair-case linking it directly to the Führer's apartment in the Old Chancellery. He felt it incongruous with his image as a fearless leader.

The Reception Hall, also known as the Festsaal mit Wintergarten, was a magnificent facility that could entertain almost 200 people in happier times. The northern façade was reputed to contain several exclusive guest apartments for the use of visiting dignitaries before the war; however all personnel had abandoned the building in November the previous year under executive order from Reichleiter Bormann.

There were two stairs leading upwards from the air-raid shelter and the men chose the alternative to ending up in the Führer's former apartment. The top revealed yet another severe concrete corridor, this one fed by rear doors from the guest apartments of the Reception Hall. Bormann strode to the third door and knocked loudly with the butt of his Walther pistol; four quick taps followed by two long ones. There was cautious movement heard from within before a female voice whispered, "Martin, is that you?"

"Ja, Eva, it is safe to open the door."

The bolts rasped back and a very scared, disheveled blonde woman peeked cautiously through the narrow crack. She stared past Bormann in puzzlement at the strange looking civilian until gradual recognition flickered in her eyes. "Adolf?"

Without a trace of emotion, the smaller man aggressively pushed past both Bormann and the woman to enter the space within.

"For Got's sake, shut that damn door; the air I have been breathing in that rat trap of a tunnel stinks like a sewer."

The Führer strode straight to the bathroom and did not emerge for almost ten minutes. The dissonance of his violent vomiting caused the other guests to glance at each other in embarrassment until Bormann broke the silence.

"Well, I do believe we've pulled it off. The strain might have killed lesser men but I think we did it without anyone outside our sub rosa group realizing the switch."

All the windows of the apartment had heavy blackout curtains installed so Bormann's eyesight had to adjust to an eerie flickering artificial light before he could identify the three fugitives gathered within. The 'Inner Circle' was expanding exponentially and each addition made Martin Bormann exceedingly nervous. He had been developing this contingency plan for years but only broached it to the Führer after the Barbarossa debacle. From the very outset, a couple of confidants were added to improve operational necessity but from that moment, the clandestine group had grown rapidly. There had been an increasing chain of dependency, each link insisting that they would refuse to escape without a loved one's inclusion.

What a fucking comedy! It is perhaps understandable that Adolf would not leave without Eva but then she insisted that her sister be given a chance to escape and that meant accommodating her recent husband, Hermann Fegelein. This shit has got to stop or I will be charged with spiriting the whole of Berlin from under Stalin's nose, Bormann thought furiously.

The situation was not improved by Bormann's suspicion that General Fegelein's marriage to Gretl Braun was one of convenience to advance his career by increased proximity to Hitler. However, the Reichleiter needed the full cooperation of the Führer in this critical phase and so he committed to at least the pretense of abducting all his charges out of harm's way.

The bathroom door finally opened and Adolf Hitler emerged smiling through his new countenance and held out a hand for Eva to join him.

"Well my darling, the most difficult part is behind us. Martin, surely you have something hidden away within this expansive apartment that we can drink to celebrate?"

"Of course, Adolf. I would caution that we still have some critical hurdles to negotiate but no doubt, this occasion certainly warrants the finest French champagne; quite possibly the only worthwhile thing we got from that miserable nation."

He disappeared to the kitchens of the Reception Hall and reappeared five minutes later with an impressive magnum of vintage Dom Perignon and five flutes. Ice was out of the question but beggars can't be choosers so he popped the cork with a flourish and delivered a toast.

"In a few short weeks, we shall be reading about

our heroic deaths; a signal to the world that the Third Reich has ended but went down fighting for our principles to the bitter end. Those goons in Britain, Russia and America are overly eager to announce victory and they have no clue what we have been planning for the past eighteen months." When everyone had a full glass in hand, Martin Ludwig Bormann clicked his heels and offered a shallow bow to Adolf Hitler.

"Mein Führer—the Fourth Reich!"

"The Fourth Reich!" echoed General Fegelein and the Braun sisters.

In the basement of the Hotel Adlon, Paddy McBride and his team grilled the Spider relentlessly about his two days inside the bunker. Chez expected and welcomed this, knowing his friends were probing to elicit any small facts that might prove important.

"So Chez, we know that all but four or five of Hitler's closest confidants were exposed to an elaborate ruse to replace the bastard-in-chief with a double—or as you call him—a doppelganger. We also know that Hitler has shaved off his hair and moustache to adopt the guise of a German businessman. The doppelganger remains in the bunker, unaware of what is in store for him as unseen, Bormann escorted Hitler out the back door, you suspect to a hideout somewhere in the Old Chancellery. Am I right so far?"

Chez nodded but elaborated. "I overheard that the hideout is some kind of secret room—whatever that means—and a group of important Nazis would be gathering there before they're all spirited out of Berlin to Austria."

"They are leaving as a group?" an incredulous Günter Hoenicke butted in. "That's insane!"

"Maybe not," Hans interjected. "It's fairly common knowledge that Hitler's architect, Albrecht Speer, incorporated hundreds of meters of interlinked tunnels in his rebuild of Berlin. Almost every public building is connected and most Berliners believe that the top brass could get from the Reichskanzlei to Templehof Airport without being seen if they needed to. They might even have vehicles down there for all we know; the tunnels have always been kept under wraps and heavily guarded." By now, the men had accepted Hans Dorff into their group as a trusted friend and nobody doubted his knowledge of his home turf.

"If I was in charge, I would not do that," interposed Paddy. "With all this shelling, those tunnels are most likely tombs to nowhere. I'm now firmly convinced that Bormann is the mastermind behind all of this and I'm starting to believe the Allies have seriously underestimated him since the get-go. He will use Hitler as a figurehead to unite the Nazi cause in his next iteration of evil, knowing this one has run its course. He will try to get Hitler and himself out of Berlin by the safest means possible; the others in the group will just have to take their chances, most likely as disposable diversions to cover the real mission." The big man paused to stroke his chin. "Come to think of it, he might want to hedge his bets and toss Adolf to the wolves if he can end up in Buenos Aires with all the money for himself. You can always buy another figurehead if things go wrong!"

"I agree with that, Paddy. I caught a snippet about Hermann Göring being fired as head of the Luftwaffe for conspiring to take over leadership of the country. Hitler ordered Göring arrested and announced the appointment of Ritter von Greim as the new commander in chief of the Luftwaffe; Hermann the German has not been seen since.

"This ties in with the other conversation I eavesdropped from the ceiling above Hitler's office. It was all about getting some woman called Hannah Rice to fly through the Russian bullets and land near the bunker. Apparently, Generaloberst Greim is her mentor and Bormann is using this prestigious appointment for no other reason than to get a small plane to land outside their back door…"

"You know what, lads; Göring's convenient disappearance from the front lines might also mean he has his bags packed for Argentina. Anyone ever heard of this Rice woman and whether she is that good a pilot?" Paddy looked directly at Billy Fagan as he asked this question and all eyes in the room turned to the pilot.

"Actually, Paddy, its Hannah REITSCH and she might be the best natural flyer the world has ever seen. If anyone can land a plane under these conditions, it would be her. Any scoop on what type of plane, Chez?"

"Sounded like… Stork? Does that make any sense, Billy?"

"Aha, more likely Storch—the Fieseler Fi-156C Storch would be perfect—and pretty easy to operate for a pilot who made her reputation flying a single seat rocket!

"Ah yes, flying a Storch would be a piece of cake for Miss Reitsch. By the way, the Fiesler Storch is only a two-seater; one passenger plus the pilot and luggage, so full marks to Paddy. The Führer is the only one who can escape by this route; given what I understand, Reichleiter Bormann carries a few extra pounds. Bormann has to have another escape route planned."

"I need the points and accept them," laughed Paddy. "Tell me more about this intriguing woman. The Nazis have never been a group that recognized the fair sex for anything but child bearing."

"Must be in her early thirties by now; she's

supposed to have coveted a career as a flying doctor in Africa but with the war looming and that, she gave up medical school to become an experimental glider test pilot at the German Research Institute for Sailplane Flight in Darmstadt. One of the first Germans to fly a glider over the Alps, this young lady owns a world long-distance record and won the National Soaring Contest.

"With the outbreak of war, Reitsch became a test pilot for the new Stuka bomber and around 1938 was awarded the Military Flying Medal—for flying a bloody helicopter inside a building!"

Günter interrupted. "Sounds like she could give you a run for your money, Billy." When the laughter died down the wing commander continued with a perfectly straight face, "Lads, I repeat, she could easily be the best natural pilot, male or female, in the history of aviation. Having said that, I heard she barely survived a horrendous crash whilst testing the Me-163B—the Komet—the single-seat rocket I mentioned earlier. There were severe injuries involved, borne out by Reichsmarshall Göring awarding Reitsch a special diamond-encrusted version of the Gold Medal for Military Flying along with an Iron Cross First Class. For the record, I have not heard of any other German woman getting an Iron Cross. So yes, gentlemen, the lady can fly."

"Chez, back to the conversation you overheard.

Think back; do you agree with me that the whole Göring scandal and calling Greim in as a replacement was nothing more than a ploy to excuse a small plane landing at the bunker?"

"It makes total sense and within the context of everything else I heard, I cannot see it any other way," Chez mused. "In fact, Martin Bormann should henceforth be treated as an evil genius. Everything he's doing is part of a calm and calculated plan for the rats to leave the sewer, himself being the King Rat. Remember, Bryan Zumwalt inferred MI6 intelligence believes he has been working on this for the past eighteen months."

"You're damn right I do. Glad those clever fuckers are on our side."

"Paddy, I've no clue if Hermann the German even cares that he's been fired from the Luftwaffe but Bormann used exactly the same stage craft when Heinrich Himmler was found trying to cut a deal with the Ruskis. Apparently, Hitler stormed into the bunker's central briefing area in a massive rage to order the immediate execution of General Fegelein, one of Himmler's staff. Not Himmler's execution, mind you, but pretty-boy Fegelein. Makes even less sense when you figure in that Fegelein might end up as Hitler's brother-in-law! I'm fairly sure that Fegelein's announced execution last week never took place because both Bormann and Hitler continue to talk about him in the present tense when they are alone.

"I'm willing to wager that Himmler, Göring and Fegelein are all in on the escape plot; card carrying members of the Inner Circle and most likely hiding out with Adolf and Bormann as we sit here." There was a lot of nodding, eyebrow lifting and murmuring which all indicated a consensus with Chez's conclusion.

"Oh, and one last thing I almost forgot. If Fraulein Reitsch pulls off the airmail delivery of Greim to the Führerbunker, she will stay with the plane, engine running. If the opportunity presents itself, Heinz Linge, Hitler's faithful valet, will escort the newly revised version of the Führer and Bormann to the Storch for a fast turnaround. After Paddy's analysis, don't bet the farm on Martin having a ticket."

The group was astounded at the wealth of intelligence the Spider had gleaned whilst hanging upside-down from pipes above Hitler's private office but Edmund Smolenski blurted out the obvious question.

"Holy shit, Chez, I thought I was as fit as any man in Special Forces but to move around silently and hang motionless by my fingernails for ten minutes in the pitch black of a ceiling cavity is weird ridiculous—even for you."

The Spider was not insulted, as no insult was intended, but to make a point, he smiled and slid into a low squat before exploding upwards to grab an overhead beam a full ten feet above the floor. Fluid motion from rock-hard stomach muscles elevated his body into a horizontal position that allowed him to jamb his toes against another, parallel beam.

"This is a lot better than that damn conduit; I could sleep up here if you want, Edmund," he laughed.

Paddy just shook his head. "If I find any fuckin' bat guano on the floor in the morning...."

"Okay, back on the floor, Chez. We have to work with what we've got and I turn to you, Hans. My team will concentrate on the Storch landing—assuming it takes place. My gut tells me Bormann is likely to choose that option to get Hitler out. If it works; brilliant. If it fails, and it is an extremely dangerous stunt, it gives Bormann incredible cover to disappear by other means.

"Trusting Billy's assessment, a small plane might be the best bet of getting Adolph through Russian lines, so we'll use all our resources to monitor Hannah Reitsch's planned visit. You and your resistance fighters need to keep tabs on any and all tunnels out of the Reichskanzlei and watch for unusual activity."

"Paddy, with respect, there is a myriad of ways these animals can escape and we will be in constant danger from the advancing Russians...."

"Welcome to my world, Hans."

CHAPTER TWENTY FOUR

Berlin Burns

M artin Bormann drained his glass after the toast and then smashed the beautiful, cut-crystal flute into the fireplace. There was a shocked silence.

"Don't worry; they have plenty of glasses and champagne where we are going." The others laughed and followed suit. "Now, if you will excuse me, I must return to the Führerbunker to make sure our 'stand-in Führer' does not renege on his pledge to our cause.

"Several critical details demand my attention but I expect to be back here within 48 hours. Adolph, I will be sending Linge for you if Plan A looks promising; otherwise, we will need to think of a Plan B. However, I feel supremely confident at this time."

Robert Greim was a genuine ace. Based upon his twenty-eight kills as a fighter pilot in the First World War, he'd been rewarded with the honorary title 'Ritter,' allowing him to continue his glittering career through the Second World War as Generaloberst Robert Ritter von Greim. Now, in the spring of 1945, Adolf Hitler made a field decision to promote the fifty-two–year-old to the rank of Generalfeld-marschall, inviting him to Berlin to assume the head of the Luftwaffe and replace the disgraced Hermann Göring. With the ulterior motive of 'Plan A,' the Führer personally requested that Hannah Reitsch fly the fledgling field marshal to Berlin immediately to receive the honor.

Reichleiter Bormann subsequently contacted Reitsch by telephone with the sub-plot, relying on the fact she was a devout Nazi who worshipped the Führer.

"Flugkapitan Reitsch, I have been instructed by our beloved Führer to ask your cooperation in a matter of the utmost national importance. Can I have your assurance that our conversation will be privileged?"

"Absolutely, Reichleiter, you are doubtless aware my life is dedicated to our cause."

"The Führer is humbled by your lifetime of devotion and has a special place in his heart for you. You have been made aware that at the earliest possible opportunity you will be flying Generaloberst Greim to take over as head of the Luftwaffe?"

"Jawohl, Mein Reichleiter, I am scheduled to meet him in thirty minutes at the Luftwaffe Test Center in Rechlin. We'll be airborne as soon as we can."

"Zer gut. Well, there is a top-secret mission attached to your trip that not even Greim is privy to—and it must remain that way. Although we are under siege, it is critical your plane land safely in the Ministry Gardens to the north of the Reichskanzlei. A detachment of elite guards will secure the plane for you to stay and supervise re-fuelling whilst the soon-to-be Generalfeldmarschall Robert Ritter von Greim meets with our Führer. Greim will remain at The Chancellery to supervise his Luftwaffe but you will be taking off immediately with a distinguished civilian passenger, a man critical to the future of Third Reich. Get this man safely out of Berlin and thence to a secret destination, only he can reveal to you. Any questions?"

"No sir, you can count on me but I will need to know the weight of this civilian; the payload of the plane I plan on using is quite limited."

"He is about 75 kilos; it shouldn't be a problem."

Within the hour, Hannah took off from Rechlin in an FW 190, transporting von Greim to Gatow in southwestern Berlin. Once there, they transferred to the much more maneuverable Storch for their final leg to the Chancellery Gardens. Unfortunately, for Reitsch, the future field marshal pulled rank on her and insisted in taking the pilot's seat, no doubt believing that his reputation demanded a spectacular statement in front of his Führer.

There was an intermittent blanket of cloud covering northern Germany and the Storch was able to fly the short journey mostly unobserved from the ground. The veteran pilot used the dome of the magnificent Reichstadt as a visual marker before dipping to one thousand feet for final approach. However, once venturing beneath the clouds, the noise of the swastika-emblazoned engine became a tempting target. Russian soldiers in the streets of Berlin treated the small plane like a plump duck flying across a meadow.

The situation rapidly escalated to one of extreme danger and the slow plane had to maneuver from side to side to avoid the increase in ground fire as more young Russians joined in the sport. Despite the evasive tactics, the Storch was hit several times and

Greim badly wounded in the foot, so Hannah Reitsch took over the controls and used her superior skills to land the Fieseler Storch without further damage on the improvised strip in the Ministry Gardens.

Jurek Podolski was taking his turn monitoring the powerful radio the SAS had set up in the basement of the Hotel Adlon. There was a dedicated frequency for telegram transmission from their base at Braunschweig Airfield and suddenly it began to spit out a short stream of paper:

"REPORT FOM ZUMWALT – STOP – GREIM AND WOMAN SEEN LEAVING RECHLIN IN FW190 – STOP – SSMJ – STOP"

Jurek glued the message strips onto a letter-size sheet of paper and rushed to wake Paddy. The big man shook himself with a yawn before swinging upright to sit on the edge of his inadequate cot. There he calmly studied the telegram several times before passing it around. After everyone had a chance to read the message, he turned to Billy Fagan.

"Ideas, lads! You especially, Billy. Any clues?"

"Assuming SSMJ is my favorite staff sergeant, the rest is perfectly clear. Even Hannah cannot land a Folke Wulf in a garden but Chez heard mention of a Storch, a plane she most certainly can. They are en route to land safely somewhere close to Berlin. Once there, they will be switching aircraft.

"Saddle up boys, Miss Reitsch will be at The Chancellery within the hour."

A determined line of six men left the basement of the Adlon in single file and turned left onto Wilhelm-strasse. Three were dressed in hospital scrubs, one very tall, a second, rotund with a magnificent moustache and a third blessed with no defining characteristics. They had ropes around their ankles and wrists that seemed to limit their movements severely whilst being escorted in the general direction of the New Chan-cellery by three smart Wehrmacht guards carrying Schmeisser machine guns. Just before they reached the Ministry of Propaganda Building, the guards pushed their prisoners across the street and into a narrow, east/west alley that led directly to the Ministry Gardens. At the far end, a guard post had been set up to control access and two seated SS guards officiously demanded they show papers.

"Absolutely," stated Jurek and turned to Günter Hoenicke with a theatrical gesture to produce. The eyes of the two shutzstaffel followed Jurek's languid wrist as if hypnotized and never noticed as Paddy and Chez looped ropes over their heads from behind. Though not as subtle as a piano-wire garrote, the ropes instilled the same final effect by crushing both guards' trachea.

Colonel McBride peered cautiously around the corner to assess the Ministry Gardens for clues before he turned back to his men.

"Bad news, I'm afraid. The reception committee is wearing similar black uniforms to these clowns. That means they are crack ShutzStaffel who will have zero inclination to entertain any crap from lowly Wehrmacht soldiers. They seem to be staged in a greenhouse to the south of the open space and I count ten."

The Black Widows started when a volley of small arms suddenly erupted from behind them to the north. Within the fracas, Billy Fagan's keen ear picked up a faint noise.

"I can hear a light plane and it sounds like it's attracting a fair amount of unwanted attention. I'm betting it's the Storch and those bullets are Russian soldiers using it to practice skeet shooting. From the wind direction, Hannah should be coming in right over our heads from the east."

"Billy, do you have to bet on everything?"

A few seconds later, the light plane zoomed low over their heads as Billy predicted but made such a shaky touchdown that Fagan expressed doubts the famous Hannah Reitsch could possibly be at the controls. However, with plenty of room to spare before running onto Hermann Göring Strasse, the single-engine aircraft carrying the fat man's imminent replacement swung around and taxied towards the squad of soldiers, now snapped to attention outside the greenhouse.

Paddy, Chez and Billy watched passively as the ShutzStaffel scurried to guard the flanks and rear of the small plane. A petite woman with dark blonde hair clambered out onto the right wing and gestured to the SS, four of whom ran around to assist an injured, high-ranking Luftwaffe officer emerge from of the pilot's door.

In a stroke of relatively good luck, only three SS guards stayed with the woman and the plane, as the rest were conscripted to carry the wounded pilot by stretcher into the New Chancellery.

Chez had navigated this piece of real estate relatively recently and he gestured towards the Old Chancellery at the opposite extreme of their vision and explained.

"Before he retreated to the Wolf's Lair in Rastenburg, Adolph Hitler had his office right over there. Can you make out that long, low building in front of the Old Chancellery? That's a reception hall called the Festsaal mit Wintergarten, where diplomats used to be honored by an audience with Hitler. I heard he had a grand staircase built to connect his office directly to the Reception Hall so he could make his patented grand entrance."

"How do you know all this shit? Have you been inside?"

"No, but my father's family lived in Berlin so I've got many relatives who saw the rise of the Third Reich; I was a very inquisitive kid at Christmas time. Not to mention, I've been a recent guest in the Führerbunker. It's about twenty or thirty feet below the ground to the right of that reception hall, right beneath those two small turrets. The round one on the right doubles as a guard tower and ventilation shaft; I left two very dead guards in it after I sneaked out yesterday.

"By the way, this reminds me that the Russians have a damn good sniper in the spire of a church in the Tiergarten. He can see those turrets but I'm fairly certain he's unable to get a bead on anything below the second storey."

"Hey Paddy, why don't we drop some gas bombs into the ventilation tower and kill all the rats at one fell swoop?"

"Because, Günter, I want to be certain of Hitler's death and don't want to jeopardize our mission with a side show. For all we know, that Greim character needs enough medical attention to cause the fake Hitler to hold his inauguration in the Reichskanzlei and everyone we'd end up killing in the bunker would be underlings."

"Good point," added the Spider. "There is a direct underground tunnel from the Reichskanzlei to the Führerbunker and those rodents can scurry back and forth all day and night without being seen."

"Let's stay focused, Chez. The best present we can give Mr. Churchill is to have Billy land you on Horse Guards' Parade and see you frog march that piece of shit into Number Ten for a tête à tête with the Old Bulldog himself."

Jurek and Edmund stripped off and changed into black uniforms removed from the dead SS guards.

"Günter, stay here with Billy and await my signal. Jurek and Edmund are going to arrest us again and we'll attempt the same stunt with the ropes. Let's go."

The three Waffen-SS storm troopers were so entranced at meeting the famous aviatrix, the two newcomers and their prisoners were within twenty paces before they noticed the movement.

"Alt! Do not come any closer. This is a restricted area."

"No problem. We found these two hospital patients sleeping in the bushes over there. We can either let them go or lock them up." Jurek punctuated his statement with a stiff right arm and smart, "Heil Hitler."

"We could also just shoot them right here. With your permission, sir," added Edmund.

"Wait a god-damn minute," Chez interjected with an exaggerated Berlin accent. "I am a good German citizen who fought bravely for the Fatherland. I

271

damage my lungs breathing gas and Germany rewards me with a bullet?"

The guards looked at each other in confusion over this development and caucused. When they reverted, their combined gaze was horrified to be looking straight into the barrels of four 7.65mm Walther PPK's.

"Lay down your weapons and walk slowly into the greenhouse. You too, Fraulein Reitsch. We are a special detachment assigned to the safety of the Führer and charged with checking security. You men just failed miserably." Chez spoke with the confidence of someone in authority; in addition, how else could he possibly know who Hannah Reitsch was?

She found the whole situation amusing but the three SS guards felt unfairly done by, fearing a black mark that would tarnish their records. But they obliged without further resistance. Their day took a quantum turn for the worse when they were bound and gagged. Jurek and Edmund cloistered them beneath a low planting table to the rear of the greenhouse. On the other hand, a perplexed Hannah Reitsch began tossing a barrage of aggressive questions at Chez so Paddy intervened by rendering her unconscious with chloroform.

Jurek signaled back to the alley and Billy and Günter joined them in the greenhouse. They sat and waited, feeling terribly exposed; six Black Widows, an unconscious German heroine and three trussed

SS guards. The SAS squad felt extremely exposed in a glass house in the center of Berlin with several of the most evil men in the world somewhere below their feet in a concrete bunker.

"Paddy, listen up. There are two men approaching from the direction of that Wintergarden building," Edmund pointed out. "One is an SS officer, the other's a rather dodgy-looking bloke wearing civilian garb and carrying a briefcase. They're zigzagging from tree to tree like they don't want to be seen. Do you want Günter and me to go get them?"

"No, Edmund, let the flies visit the web."

Chez got off the floor and stared over Edmund's shoulder for several seconds before announcing in a matter-of-fact voice. "Well, well, it's Hitler, Paddy and the uniformed officer is his valet, Heinz Linge; surprise, surprise, no Bormann. Everybody get down below the window line and remain perfectly still. Günter, on my signal, take out the valet, I'll look after Adolph."

The well-dressed, bald businessman ducked hurriedly into the greenhouse after a final surreptitious glance over his left shoulder satisfied him the outside world had not seen his furtive scurrying over the fifty meters from the Reception Hall. Linge dutifully followed his boss and closed the door behind them. Both exhaled in relief, but when their eyes adjusted to the gloomy interior, they could barely reconcile the unexpected shock of seeing five men squatting on the floor. Even more horrific, the men were staring menacingly at them from just beyond the prone body of Flugkapitan Hannah Reitsch.

Harsh reality materialized and Obersturmbannführer Heinz Linge lunged for his pistol; Günter Hoenicke's throwing knife appeared in the center of the loyal valet's chest before his hand even touched the butt.

The cold steel of a Walther pressed against the businessman's ear and a calm voice whispered in impeccable German,

"Wilkommen, Herr Hitler."

CHAPTER TWENTY FIVE

Friendly Fire

Without ceremony, Colonel Paddy McBride reached once again for the dark-brown glass bottle that Hans Dorff had filched from the Adlon pharmacy. He emptied a liberal quantity onto a folded handkerchief and held it firmly over the mouth and nose of the bald businessman identified as chancellor of the Third Reich.

"Hold your breath and step outside for a minute, lads, this chloroform is fuckin' potent."

Paddy joined them and after several deep gulps of outside air and a few moments waiting for the inside to clear, the six re-entered the greenhouse and checked their charges' pulses. Hannah had a smile on her face and even the three SS Gefreiters, tied up under the planter were swimming in La-La Land.

"Okay, Edmund, check our guest of honor for the cyanide capsules Chez warned us about, then bundle him into the cargo space behind the seats in the Storch. Billy, will the combined weights of Hitler, Chez and your good self be okay for a take-off?"

"With an extremely healthy man like myself at the wheel, it'll be close, but I don't see a lot of choices, old sport."

"Get ready to crank her up. And, Billy, good luck.

"Chez, we're going to take Adolf's briefcase and beetle it back to the Adlon. I need to get some intelligence from Mike Johnston on the battle for Berlin before we attempt to sneak through the Russian lines. Probably too late to reuse the ambulance so we might have to fight our way back on foot, but plan on meeting us at Braunschweig Air Base in a couple. Good luck to you too, wee man."

Chez nodded, "All the prisoners are sleeping like babies so you should be able to get a head start, Paddy."

The colonel then turned to Billy and watched incredulously as the veteran flyer peeled off his hospital scrubs. Underneath, he was wearing Royal Air Force blues replete with medal bars.

"For King and Country, Paddy," he smiled as he doffed the flying cap he pulled out of a pocket.

"Un-fuckin-believable! God speed, both of you. Now, let's get Mrs. Hitler's little boy stashed behind the seats in the Storch."

Squadron Leader William Wallace Fagan gave Chez a thumbs up and watched the young Pole put all his force into spinning the propeller. It did not quite catch on the first three attempts, but on the fourth, the engine coughed and the Storch spat out smoke as it roared into life. The Spider scrambled up onto the starboard wing and squeezed into the cockpit. By now, some security guards catching a smoke break at the rear of the Reichskanzlei, began to take initiative by shouting for them to stop. Fagan inched the Fi 156 Storch into motion, heading towards them by necessity to gain advantage from the wind. He waved with a smile as he passed within twenty meters of the guards before turning onto the temporary runway and gunning the engine to maximum revolutions. A bullet from behind screamed between them before smashing through the windshield.

"Maybe wearing your RAF uniform was not your smartest move of the day, Billy!"

Full throttle and fifty meters later, the plane and its heavy cargo were still struggling to win the battle against gravity. Chez was certain they were going to ram straight into the rear of the buildings on the west side of Wilhelmstrasse and he swore they clipped a roof just after they rotated and soared towards the low clouds.

Below, four non-descript men paused on the street to look up at the commotion before continuing their purposeful walk towards the Hotel Adlon.

Chez noted Billy Fagan was chortling and whistling throughout the whole adventure. That did not unduly concern him because men react to stress in different and peculiar ways but, after five minutes, when Fagan brought the plane around in a 180 to make a perfect landing on top of the flat roof of a large government building, he was certain the Brit had flipped his lid.

"What the hell, Billy, we're going to Braunschweig. Don't tell me we only had enough fuel to fly ten blocks!"

"We will not make it out over Russian or British lines with these swastikas on our wings, old boy." He reached into his tunic and passed Chez a bottle of Booth's gin to hold before locating a small package. "Ah, here we go. Give us a hand, Sport." The two men jumped out, engine still running, and helped each other tape sheets of white writing paper from the Adlon onto the underside of the Storch's wings. Back in the cockpit, both men took healthy slugs from the gin bottle.

"Let's give it the old college try. Tally ho!"

There were no real incidents as they crossed the Russian lines and little sign of any fierce fighting but Chez noted from above that the Soviet armies were clearly positioning to tighten their noose and deny General Wilhelm Mohnke, the unlucky man charged with defending the government center of Berlin, any chance of retreat.

The center of the bull's-eye is clearly the Reichstadt, Chez mused, *the Adlon's next door neighbor. It'll take a bloody miracle for Paddy and the lads to break out.*

After just over forty minutes, the Russian lines far behind them, the little Fieseler Storch passed over the River Elbe, signaling the forward holding positions of both the British and American forces. Billy banked onto a final heading for Braunschweig and was offering Chez a celebratory chug of Booth's when an unexpected hail of bullets ripped through the fuselage. An astute British patrol had noticed the paper masks coming adrift leaving the swastikas back in plain sight. Chez turned around to check Hitler and was relieved that he appeared to be okay and still unconscious from the chloroform but as his gaze returned to Billy, the news was not so good. Fagan's face was covered in blood and his right arm dangled uselessly beside him.

"I'm afraid I can't see a damn thing, Chez. You are going to have to fly us home or at least put this crate down somewhere we can hitch a ride."

"Holy shit, Billy. I don't know how to fly a bloody plane!"

"I will do the flying—I can do that by feel—but you, my friend, will have to be my eyes."

The former joviality was now totally absent.

Fagan, completely blind and having lost a considerable amount of blood from his partially severed right arm, was starting to lose consciousness. The entire side of his proud light blue tunic had turned a deep purple and Chez suspected the arm and head were not the only injuries. The veteran reclined in the pilot's seat and controlled the plane with his feet and by joystick as he gasped to instruct Chez to read the dials periodically,—instantly if an anomaly occurred. They were now over flat farmland at three thousand feet and Chez was politely asked to look for an open, level grass area.

Amazing how many damn hedges there are in this part of the world, he thought.

At long last, he was able to tell Billy about an open, reasonably flat meadow to port.

"Can you figure out the wind direction, Chez?" and after hearing no reply, "Try looking at the trees or the grass."

"I am guessing from two o'clock, Billy." Fagan

made some adjustments to the rudder and the plane responded by sliding into the wind. "I can sense we have the wind where we want it. Now where's that bloody field you like?"

"Dead ahead; maybe half a mile. We might get a bit of luck for a change. Looks like some Brits are camped right in the middle of where we're headed."

"Do I have more chance to the left or the right?"

"I'd say right."

"Confirm our altitude and speed. I'm thinking 500 feet and 80 knots?"

"Pretty good, Billy. We are at 500 feet on the button but our speed is only 75 knots." Chez marveled at how the plane and the man had somehow become one.

"Thanks, Chez, now I know our wind speed and direction, I am going to set us down right beside those Brits. Good luck to you son, no matter what happens."

The indefatigable William Wallace Fagan put the plane down without so much as a bump about 50 yards from a startled British army patrol. When he felt the forward motion cease, he killed the engine—and died where he would have wanted—in the pilot's seat.

Chez jumped onto the wing, ripped off his green hospital shirt and waved it frantically at the patrol.

"Medical emergency. Medical emergency." The British soldiers swarmed over the plane and removed the two prone passengers, placing Chez under immediate arrest. The plane was a Luftwaffe Storch, two men were unconscious, although one was starting to mumble unintelligibly in German and this lunatic on the wing, his English heavily accented, was clearly not British, in fact, he sounded like a damn Kraut too.

Messrs. Hitler and Orlowski were unceremoniously tied up and then frog marched to a nearby tent where they sat on the floor under guard. After about an hour, the platoon commander, Captain Nigel Pakenham-Smythe, stepped through the flap to question them but the Spider interrupted impatiently.

"Captain, this is a matter of urgent national security and I must insist you call Brigadier Zumwalt of the Special Air Services immediately. He can be located at the Hotel Lutetia in Paris.

"How are my travelling companions?"

"Well, old boy, let's get something absolutely clear at the outset. You will shut up and not tell me what to do. The pilot is dead but we found papers on him indicating he was a Squadron Leader in the RAF—the least likely person you might find flying a small Nazi plane. I must suspect you killed him before landing the plane with the intention of convincing His Majesty's Armed Forces that you are not who you are. Along with your companion, who is now babbling hysterically in German, I believe you both to be spies. Therefore, you will be shot.

"Take them outside, Corporal, and dispose of their bodies as far from our camp as possible."

Two enlisted men grabbed the Spider's arms and forced him, facedown into the dirt floor of the tent. As the back of Pakenham-Smythe's Saville Row tailored uniform strutted towards the flap of the tent to make his exit, Chez raised his head and called after him in a frighteningly calm voice.

"The Hotel Lutetia is the designated SAS headquarters for my operation, if you refuse to call Brigadier Zumwalt, so be it. But you will never be able to hide my death from Colonel Paddy McBride, of that; I can assure you with my last breath."

Captain Pakenham-Smythe froze. After almost half a minute of inward contemplation, he turned slowly to confront his prisoner. "How well do you know McBride? Apparently not very, because he is a major, not a colonel. Take them away, Corporal."

As the Spider correctly gambled, everyone in the entire British army had heard of Paddy McBride; he was a bona fide legend as one of the most decorated soldiers, not just in this war but also the long military history of the country. This in itself created a quandary; the men guarding Chez Orlowski became noticeably reluctant to treat their prisoner without newfound respect but Pakenham-Smythe rationalized that any good spy would be dropping names at will in an attempt create credibility and thereby save his own skin. However, in prudence, he decided to hedge his bets.

"We will make a concerted effort to find out the truth here. If nothing turns up in one hour, you and your companion will be shot as promised; executed for the murder of a Royal Air Force officer. Sergeant Burton, have Sparks get hold of someone at HQ and see if we can verify this nincompoop's story about the SAS.

"Dismissed."

To all present, the captain was visibly shaken but his boyhood days at Eton taught him that an English officer did not have to pay undue attention to dirty little wogs with foreign accents.

CHAPTER TWENTY SIX

The Fight to Get Home

P addy, Jurek, Edmund and Günter barely made it back alive to the basement of the Hotel Adlon, not because of the Russian army but because it was raining concrete. The Russian bombardment of Berlin increased in intensity by the hour; long-range guns now lobbing huge shells indiscriminately into the central government district. Falling masonry from once-grandiose buildings was crashing down everywhere and Hans Dorff was visibly relieved to see the four men, covered with dust, bursting through the back door. He looked around and immediately asked, "Chez and Billy?"

"Hopefully headed safely for Allied air space," replied Jurek before adding the canned version of events that Paddy insisted he use to maintain the secrecy of the kidnapping. "We got control of the plane okay but Hitler was a no-show. As it could only carry Billy and one passenger, we voted for Chez,—easy choice. As for Hitler, we know we foiled his primary escape plan. If you and your men keep a close eye on things, I think the Russians are going to find the real Hitler will be unable to escape his fate in the bunker. Good riddance to him and mission accomplished, now we have to find a way to get the hell out of here. Any suggestions, Hans?"

"Well, as you might have noticed, things are getting progressively worse. Your best bet might be to try the U-Bahn. The U-2 line goes west to Ruhleben; no trains are running and the tunnels are full of refugees but it is only a six-mile hike. With any luck, you'll come out behind the rear of the Russian lines as most of their forces are massing to the east and south of Berlin."

"Jurek, ask him what the downside is. Maybe the Russians are planning to use the U-Bahn as an uber-convenient way to penetrate German defenses—I certainly would—and if that's the case, the four of us could walk slap bang into a thousand Ruskis. We would have nowhere to run, nowhere to hide if we get trapped underground in a tunnel."

Hans' response to Jurek was even more frightening than that chilling scenario. "I'm afraid it's common knowledge the Führer will order the U-Bahn flooded if word comes down the Russians are using it. You would not die from bullets; you would drown."

"Wait a minute, those tunnels are full of refugees, innocent Berlin citizens sheltering from the battle. Won't they all drown, too?"

Hans shrugged despondently and muttered, "There's no bastard quite like a Nazi bastard!"

Hans agreed to ferry the men by ambulance from behind the Adlon to the Zoologischer Garten station on the U-2 line. Potsdamer Platz would have been closer to the hotel but the zoo gave them more cover and a much less chance of bumping into the Waffen SS. All four carried small arms of course, but they would be no match for a heavily armed German patrol.

"Tell Hans he's welcome to come with us. If he decides not to, he can keep our radio transmitter," instructed Paddy.

"Danke, but I prefer to die in Germany and right here in Berlin would suit me fine. I will kill as many of these traitors as I can before they get me. Viel Glück, meine freunde."

There was no mistaking the Banhof Zoo Station. The iconic, grand old building was commissioned in 1882 and had been an important part of the U-Bahn system since 1902.

"We need to get out of this ambulance and walk the last part to blend in with the locals."

Edmund passed on the request from Paddy and responded, "Hans is going to drop us on the far side. We'll enter the station from Jebensstrasse, a street well known in western Berlin for prostitutes and drugs. Hans figures the best intelligence about current Russian positions will come from, uh, ladies of the night. They are probably already practicing their Russian for the upcoming change in clientele."

The four remaining Black Widows then reluctantly bade farewell to Hans Dorff, their eyes unable to disguise the high probability that they would never meet again.

Five packs of cigarettes and a few deutschmarks consolidated a consistent story that Jurek, Edmund and Günter shared with Paddy. Most importantly, their gained knowledge concluded no more than a mile separated them from the advancing front line of the Soviet infantry.

"Let's get into the U-Bahn as fast as we can and

head west. It's about five miles and seven stations to the end of the line at Ruhleben. That should put us safely behind their rear guard and maybe we can talk them out of a truck for the ride back to Magdeburg. After all, we are supposed to be on the same side in this damn stupid war!"

"Paddy, I'm not sure what side the Ruskis are on—never have been."

As soon as the Black Widows descended the stairs to the platforms, they encountered a terrifying mass of humanity; frightened Berliners, mostly women, children and the elderly were trying to deny the futility of avoiding inevitable death. Families huddled under threadbare blankets, around candles or makeshift fires, the youngest crying as they sensed vibes of fear emanating from their elders.

Stepping as carefully as they could around these scared people, it took over an hour to negotiate the long mile from the Bahnhof Zoo to the next station, Deutsches Oper. A frustrated Colonel McBride was about to move his squad back up to the fresh air on Bismarkstrasse when he noticed the crowd stirring to its feet and moving in their direction. Jurek stopped a middle-aged woman and asked the obvious.

"Paddy, they're coming. Now only about 500

meters away and apparently singing Russian battle songs to scare the shit out of these poor people. We've gotta get outa here; it's a coffin."

"They're most likely coordinating with a front line above on Bismarkstrasse so they can tighten a coordinated loop. What is behind that door to the right of the stair over there?"

The door, constructed of vertical planks, was secured to the frame by a padlocked, horizontal bolt. Günter Hoenicke pressed his Browning flat against the wall and used his Sheffield steel blade to lever the bolt's iron receiving loop from the frame. This left the padlocked bolt untouched on the door. Paddy flicked his Zippo lighter to reveal a storage room filled with shovels and bags of gravel. The singing was much closer and they could hear the crunch of the advancing marchers on the loose stone of the tracks.

"This'll have to do. Günter, stick that loop in your pocket and rub some dirt on the splintered frame. Quiet as you can, boys."

The Russian infantry sang their way past the hiding place but a couple of soldiers, charged with checking such locations, peeled off. The four SAS soldiers held their breath as they heard footsteps approaching the door. Paddy moved silently forward and grabbed the interior handle with one of his huge hands, bracing the other against the inside frame.

Please don't look too closely at the bolt, he prayed as he felt one of the soldiers pull on the door.

"Jammed solid, Sergeant; feels like it hasn't been opened in years. Let's catch up with our comrades." The footsteps receded to join the cadence of their squad.

From a rough estimate, the ten minutes it took for the last crunch to pass the door meant they had avoided approximately 1,000 soldiers, about the right number for a complete battalion. McBride, Hoenicke, Podolski and Smolenski waited cautiously for a further five minutes until they were certain the Russians were well away from the storage room. Paddy McBride cracked the door open very slowly to be greeted by silence and darkness from both directions of the tunnel.

"We'll proceed west with vigilance, though I doubt another battalion will choose this route. They've probably sent most of their forces up top, with groups such as the one we just avoided, sent to mop up and secure the U-Bahn."

With ears pricked for any sounds, the four solders walked in single file down the center of the tunnel. After ten minutes, the glow of artificial light signified the next station, Sophie Charlotte Platz. It was completely deserted, as were the next two. Then, after another thirty minutes, they got a shock; the track began to rise noticeably and natural daylight seeped into the tunnel.

"Bloody Hell, Hans might have warned us about

this; I think we're about to cease being an underground track!" Sure enough, they were given no options other than reversing themselves all the way back to the Zoobahnhof—and they positively did not want to do that. It seemed the track swept up onto grade in a gentle right hand curve. Furthermore, they could hear birds chirping and the air smelled a lot cleaner.

No fuckin' way we could have walked all the way out of a major city to the country. Something is just not right here, they all thought collectively as they waited.

"Okay, Edmund, you probably speak the best Russian. Remember, we are all in civilian clothes so technically, we could be executed as spies. Leave your gun with me and poke your nose outside. If we get caught, surrender immediately; our story will be we are non-combatant observers for Britain at the request of Russian forces. Not sure that will fly but it's all I've got."

Edmund Smolenski was one of those rare humans who had never been scared, not even as a five-year-old. He actually savored the adrenalin rush as he turned towards the daylight and advanced up the track. Twenty minutes later, he returned to his friends with a big grin on his face.

"You lads want some coffee and black bread?"

The three followed in trepidation as he confidently strolled out of the mouth of the tunnel for a second time. He led his three friends towards a large tent erected in the middle of an enormous paved plaza, large enough to play soccer on, maybe even several games at once. This tent had a number of vehicles parked around it, every one emblazoned with the Russian star but most extraordinary of all, towering above the encampment was the famous Berlin Olympic Stadium where in 1936, the United States introduced Adolf Hitler to Jesse Owens. The Führer had planned to humiliate the world with the athletic dominance of his blond master race. Jesse taught him lessons he would have been wise not to ignore—but of course, he did.

As they caught up with Edmund and walked together towards the tent, Paddy whispered urgently, "WHISKY TANGO FOXTROT, Eddy, could I have a few details of what the hell you're up to before I get shot?"

"Don't worry, Paddy, this was the mess tent for that battalion we missed in the tunnel. Of course the men inside don't know that. I told them we bumped into their comrades who told us to buy the entire mess crew a round of vodka. Just follow my lead.

"Here we are, Vladimir. Let me introduce the rest of my squad; Colonel McBride, Jurek Podolski and Günter Hoenicke. The colonel doesn't speak Russian but the rest of us do. We're most appreciative of your hospitality."

"You are the famous Paddy McBride?" Paddy could translate what Vladimir had said just by the body language and nodded pleasantly in the affirmative.

"Wow, I heard you were three meters tall but I'd put you closer to two and a half. Regardless, you are one big motherfucker! It is an honor to meet you.

"Sit down boys, we are de-camping to follow our regiment into Berlin but I have some good Russian bread and sausage I can share with you." The large and jolly Russian sergeant had an enormous white chef's apron wrapped around him and a giant smile on his face. "Looks like we'll get this war over in a couple of weeks and we can all get back to being with our families."

After joking and laughing with their new comrades for almost half-an-hour, Edmund pushed the envelope of friendship a little further.

"Vladimir, our base at Braunschweig will probably be relieved we've made it back to Allied lines, do you have a radio we could use for a quick transmission?"

"Da, conyeshna. Alex Stefanovich, help our British friends get a message to their base."

Sergeant Gareth Burton reported back to his captain just as the hour of grace was about to expire.

"Sir, with regard to our German prisoners from the plane, we managed to get hold of the SAS, supposedly based at an airfield in Braunschweig. A Staff Sergeant Johnston vouched for the foreign chappie in a theatrical Scottish accent bordering on the unintelligible. He insisted we await for a direct transmission from '*Colonel*' McBride. Sounds awfully suspicious to me, sir. They're informing me that McBride's transmission will take a while to set up."

"Good work, Sergeant. Load of codswallup if you ask me. Bloody German S.O.P. You catch the bastards, then they loop you round in a circle to get verified as authentic by some bloody poof in the Reichstadt. I must admit I could use a little entertainment, so patch through that call from the bogus bloody McBride as soon as it comes in.

"You know what, Sergeant, I might want to shoot those two silly buggers myself!"

After a further thirty minutes, Sergeant Burton re-appeared, this time holding a field telephone. With an unconcealed grin, he handed the handset to his stuffy captain.

"I have '*Colonel McBride*' on the radio for you, sir. By the way, we have triangulated his signal as emanating from the Olympic Stadium in Berlin!"

"Really? That is too bloody ridiculous for words."

There was considerable static before a distant voice materialized over the airwaves.

"This is Colonel Samuel Patrick McBride, Special Raiding Squadron of His Majesty's Special Air Services. Please excuse the reception, there are several Russians within earshot, I must keep my voice down and the length of this transmission to a minimum. To whom do I have the pleasure of talking with? Over."

The syrupy upper-crust voice of Captain Nigel Pakenham-Smythe did not buy the ruse for one second.

"So you are Colonel Paddy McBride? My arse is Colonel Paddy McBride. I have two of your under-cover agents in my custody and I am going to execute them as soon as I hang up this phone. You and your bastards are going to get what's coming to you and I am just the man to do it." His voice started to crack with false bravado and five seconds of deafening silence followed.

The politeness left McBride's voice and although Gareth Burton could not hear the other end of the call, there was no doubting the captain's change in pallor as the fierce man from Belfast blistered him.

"Listen very carefully, you stupid English turd. There were three men on the plane we sent out of Berlin. I am assuming the deceased pilot is Wing Commander Billy Fagan and I will be personally investigating his death. The second man is German and my prisoner—not to be touched under any circumstances; he catches a cold and you are fucked. The third man is a young Pole called Chez Orlowski; that is all you need to know. Orlowski works for me and on this mission, I work directly for a man who smokes cigars, drinks brandy and lives at Number Ten Downing Street. Do you understand me, old sport?"

Pakenham-Smythe started to sweat profusely. Sergeant Burton noticed his voice taking on an affected lisp and stammer as he tried to compose a response to save face in front of his men.

"Whoever you are, you are certainly not an officer or a gentleman and I suspect you are in cahoots with the German high command and attempting to pl…"

"One more time, dickhead. I am not a gentleman but outrank you by fuckin' miles. I will get your exact coordinates from HQ and be there within twenty-four hours. I want my prisoner, Billy Fagan's body and Chez Orlowski ready for my team to do a hot extraction back to England. Get in my way and I will personally pull your heart out through your throat. *Over and fuckin' out.*"

The connection reverted to dead static and Captain Nigel Pakenham-Smythe immediately bent over, dry heaved and then without much ado, threw up onto the floor of the tent.

Paddy reverted to the frequency on which he had talked to Mike Johnston just ten minutes before. The man from Glasgow knew this call was coming and was on the microphone immediately.

"Get on well with the captain did we, Paddy? Over."

"Mike, as you might imagine, I am in no mood to be fucked with. Call Bryan Zumwalt immediately. I want you, Scotty, Gino and Mitch to get to that arse-hole's encampment with orders for his immediate arrest. Give me coordinates and we'll meet you there as soon as possible. Out."

Then turning to Edmund, he pulled off his special issue SAS wristwatch. "Give this to Vladimir if he can find us transportation to these coordinates."

"Already asked him, Boss. Vladimir is a big fan and says the look on your face can only mean that you have a family emergency. Keep your watch, he has two pilots and Tupolev ANT-9 that can be ready for take-off in ten minutes."

For over an hour, Pakenham-Smythe attempted to reconcile if he was being duped by a German spy ring or bullied by a rogue SAS major. Discretion delayed the planned execution of the two Germans but he tripled the guard nonetheless.

"Sergeant, full alert tonight; no-one approaches our encampment without being fully challenged. I must seriously consider the possibility this camp might come under attack. One thing of which I am completely certain; those two Germans are extremely valuable to either the SAS or a group pretending to be the SAS. After the twenty-four hour period is up, they are to be executed on schedule. Clear?"

"Sir, are you su.........Yes, sir."

Burton's troubled eyes looked into the soul of his panicked commander but instead saw Captain Bligh on the Bounty.

Guess that makes me Fletcher Christian!

CHAPTER TWENTY SEVEN

Conundrum

S ince his felicitous avoidance of assassination at Wolfschanze the previous July, Adolf Hitler maintained a strict regimen of daily medications to counteract his injuries, all prescribed by his personal physician, Ludwig Stumpfegger. However, the once-powerful leader of the Third Reich was trembling uncontrollably, not so much from fear but from drug withdrawal.

A quandary now faced the Führer; he was sitting in a corner of a British army tent with the mysterious young German who had helped kidnap him from the Chancellery Gardens and a rosy-cheeked young private who guarded them both with transparent disdain for anything remotely German. *My only chance will be to befriend this confounded German youth; play upon his devotion to me and the Fatherland,* he concluded.

"What is your name, son and where do you call home in Germany?"

Chez felt the magnetic power of Hitler's intellect within the syrupy tone of the questions.

Here we go! The sonofabitch is trying to play me. Well, it is the only entertainment in the room....

"Mein Führer, I was born Czeslaw Wah. My father should have won a gold medal for the Fatherland at the Antwerp Olympics in 1920 and I grew up in Weimar with my mother, Josepha. Like my famous father, she was also a gymnast."

"May I call you Czeslaw? That is a Polish name, is it not?"

"Ja, Mein Führer. I have family in Western Silesia; although geographically a part of Germany, most of the population has Polish heritage."

"But you do consider yourself German?"

"Oh yes, and very proud to be so, sir," lied the Spider.

Suddenly, there was uncommon activity outside the tent and Chez chose to drop the charade until he determined the cause.

The flap opened and three older non-comms replaced the ruddy-faced private.

Uh oh, this beef-up in security does not bode well. I

suspect that asshole captain is going to top us both in the morning just as he promised. I need some clues to what's going on.

"Excuse me gentlemen, to what do we owe the pleasure of this added attention?"

"The captain just wanted to make sure you're tucked in safely, sweetheart. Then me and my chinas (mates) are going to read you a Jack A Nory (bedtime story,) aren't we?" laughed one of the corporals through his heavy cockney accent. This was apparently highly amusing to his two friends and a spirited though unintelligible repartee ensued.

I don't sense any immediate danger. They're settling down for a game of cards so maybe I am going to see the sun rise tomorrow. What if they all fall asleep? I have to be patient; have to bide my time and watch for an opportunity to escape.

The problem's going to be schlepping this Nazi bastard with me. Do I really need to be risking my life so Mr. Churchill can check his ID before executing him? Chez thought sourly.

Hitler eventually dozed off and was snoring loudly in the corner. Chez feigned the same but kept his senses razor sharp. The chance took over two hours to arise but come it did. And the Spider was ready.

"Oy, Jimmy, I 'ave to piss like a racehorse. You lads be okay for a couple?"

"I'll come with you, Fred. Popeye can 'andle the

sleepin' beauties 'til we get back. Alright wiv you, Popeye?"

"No problem, lads, the old one looks sick as a dog and I doubt the young scrawny one could burst a wet paper bag. Bring me a cup–a-Rosie (tea) would ya? Milk and two sugars?"

Chez waited until the voices of Fred and Jimmy completely receded into the night and then watched Popeye through hooded eyelids for even the slimmest of chances, knowing his window of opportunity could close at any moment.

Corporal Popeye Brown took a long drag on his Woodbine cigarette and its unfiltered inch of grey ash finally succumbed to gravity. Popeye jumped up to avoid the mess spoiling his uniform, nevertheless, it splattered onto the tent's folding table. Squinting through smoke from a cigarette now clamped firmly between his teeth, he reached to brush his consequence onto the dirt floor and failed to notice a small lively tobacco ember within the ash. Popeye morphed into Charlie Chaplin as he swept the burning residual onto his tunic.

"Shite!" he muttered as he focused his concentration on slapping at the smoldering cloth.

The Spider's strong left arm closed swiftly around the corporal's throat; his right hand clamping over his mouth. Within forty seconds, Popeye's world began to spin from a lack of oxygen and he surrendered all consciousness. Chez held the grip for a full ten seconds more before releasing Popeye's limp body into a heap on the floor.

After turning down the kerosene light on the desk he took the knife from Popeye's belt and poked a small slit through the rear wall of the tent—nothing but blackness outside. He carefully enlarged the slit until he could stick his head through the hole and waited for his eyesight to adjust to the night.

Seems to me that we are on the perimeter of the camp; perhaps a hundred meters of flat grass and then a tree line, Chez calculated. *Pretty obvious what to do but on the other hand, that is exactly the direction where they would search for me so I might have to rethink. Time to wake Adolf up.*

"Mein Führer," he whispered urgently, as he patted him rapidly on the cheek. "Wake up, you have to follow me or we face a firing squad in the morning."

Adolf Hitler seemed very confused but took one look at Popeye's inert body and immediately decided his best bet was still to trust this newfound friend. The knife enlarged the slit again until it was large enough to allow both men to step through into the darkness.

"Be very quiet and follow me. Grab my shirt-tail and step in my footprints."

With the ageing, shaking Reichchancellor in tow, Chez walked twenty paces east towards the tree line before stopping to listen for any warning noises from the camp. Hitler's night vision was close to zero under the starless sky so he did not see the Spider rip the sleeve off his shirt, but he heard it.

"What are you doing?" Hitler panted in mounting panic.

"Just leaving a stimulating clue for our friends," Chez explained as he made a shallow cut on the forearm of his right arm, squeezing it to coax blood onto the torn cloth. He left the torn and bloody evidence on the ground before reversing their course to the camp, warning Hitler to follow in silence by holding his finger up to pursed lips.

Suddenly they picked up the faint sounds of Jimmy and Fred on their way back to the tent. Chez jerked his companion to the left, speeding up to circle the perimeter of the camp before heading west.

Yells of alarm and lights erupted from the camp but thankfully not specifically directed at them—yet.

Less than ten minutes elapsed before a completely distraught Captain Nigel Pakenham-Smythe burst into the damaged tent and demanded a briefing.

"Well, sir, Jones and Walcott went to the latrines leaving Brown to guard the two sleeping prisoners. Next thing, one of them got him in a sleeper hold. Looks like he'll be fine but the prisoners took his knife and cut their way out of the tent. Footprints show them heading east towards those trees."

"You three are up on charges and busted down to private immediately," he screamed. "I want this entire camp roused to find those two spies within the hour. Shoot them on sight; they have revealed themselves to be exactly what I suspected—German spies."

Just then, an excited soldier burst in holding a piece of green cotton in his outstretched hand. The evidence had not been exposed to the morning dew and everyone agreed it seemed to match what they remembered as the shirt the younger prisoner was wearing. "Found it over there, sir. Look, it's got blood on it."

"So we know they are headed east and the younger one is injured. Tempus fugit, Sergeant, assemble the men at the double."

Dawn broke and all the multiple patrols Captain Pakenham-Smythe had sent out returned empty handed. So convincing was the spoor that sent them east, it was three to four hours before they tried other points of the compass out of desperation. Regardless, they returned exhausted with nothing to show.

As if he had not had enough misfortune, Pakenham-Smythe's worst dream, as if scripted, deteriorated rapidly into a nightmare when a small truck carrying four Special Forces soldiers caromed noisily into the camp just ahead of its self-generated cloud of dust. The two British sentries bravely demanded the battle-hardened warriors to halt and get out of their vehicle. They got their wish. Specialists Mitch Arnold and Gino Blando vaulted out of the truck, disarmed the two nervous soldiers, swept away their legs and knelt on their backs. Staff Sergeant Mike Johnston pulled out his nine millimeter Browning and chambered a round. To the ears of both sentries, the slide ratcheting back sounded like a death knell as the crusty Glaswegian spat.

"Where the fuck is Pakenham-Smythe? Immediate response required!"

The faint sound of a single-engine plane grew apparent and then came into view as it floated in to land in the meadow. Four, non-uniformed men got out and the pilot turned his Tupolev around to take off as soon as they cleared.

Johnston recognized the arrivals instantly and shifted his attention from the prone sentries to walk over and greet his comrades.

"Just got here ourselves, Paddy, haven't had the honor of meeting your good friend the captain yet. Shall we?"

Yet another private with a Lee Enfield rifle confronted them as they entered the inner sanctums of the camp and demanded they stop and produce identification. The chiseled giant in civvies gently pushed aside the rifle and bent over to confront the shaking youngster. When their faces were no more than twelve inches apart he softly whispered, "Son, I am Colonel Paddy McBride, in command of His Majesty's Special Raiding Squadron and these are my men. I am here to speak with Captain Pakenham-Smythe, your commanding officer."

"I will suh...suh...see if he is available, sir," choked the young man within gulps of saliva.

"That won't be necessary, Private," interjected Sergeant Gareth Burton as he approached the visitors. "Please, follow me, gentlemen."

As the motley group of warriors meandered purposefully through the camp in 'V' formation, their reputation preceded them.

"Holy shit, you mean that's Paddy McBride himself! Big motherfucker, isn't he?"

"Jesus, I'm glad those lads are on our side!"

"Bloody hell, I'm not sure what side the Captain thinks he's on right now. McBride and his men look pissed off."

Just before the group entered through the flap of the captain's tent, Mike Johnston stepped in front of Sergeant Burton and put a firm open hand on his chest.

"You'll be way better off staying out here with us,

Sergeant." Burton held both his hands palm up, grinned and winked, "No problem, Sarge. Nooo problem at all."

Paddy barged straight in, put both his fists on the captain's desk and glowered in silence. The blustered captain kept his head down, maintaining the pretext of important paperwork but his hands were shaking so badly, his pen spun wildly onto the floor.

"Luh…luh…look here, you you…you cannot just march in here luh…luh…like……"

"Shut the fuck up! Where are my three men?"

Nigel Pakenham-Smythe could not talk; he held his head in his hands and blubbered, "The dead RAF chap is in a body bag but I don't know where the two Germans are. They just disappeared last night."

Again, the hapless captain probably thought it could not possibly get any worse—but it did.

A helicopter landed in the meadow and shortly thereafter, two smart be-medaled officers strode into the tent to see the SAS colonel holding the very distressed captain by the lapels, Pakenham-Smythe's legs dangling two feet off the ground.

"Please put him down, Paddy."

Then, turning his attention to the disheveled Pakenham-Smythe, he cut to the chase. "Captain, I am Brigadier Bryan Zumwalt and this is Colonel Timothy Geary, your replacement. You are removed from your post henceforth and will return to England with my men.…

"B-b-b-but, sir, it was not my fau…."

"Oh shut the fuck up, you sniveling idiot!" commanded the brigadier. "Colonel Geary, please give us a moment. Inform the men that you are their new commander and to rest easy. Then, send a couple of soldiers to put this piece of garbage in the brig. We will be using his tent for a while.

"Paddy, what the bloody hell has this dickhead done to Chez and our guest?

Chez and Hitler covered almost ten miles on foot before the dawn light started to streak the sky at their backs. As they walked down a web of narrow country lanes, the leader of the Third Reich had difficulty keeping up with his travelling companion so they talked little—but both thought to themselves a lot.

If I can get into this young man's confidence, I can use his remarkable survival skills to get me to a neutral country, maybe Sweden or Switzerland. Somehow, I've got to find a way to rendezvous with Martin and Eva in Barcelona before our U-boat leaves for Argentina, Hitler plotted.

That bastard behind me has murdered half the world. Why am I even thinking about saving his ass? I should slit his throat right now as revenge for the life of Jadwiga's brother, Czeslaw and my friend, Jan Kowalski. I really don't owe Churchill a damn thing;

as far as I'm concerned we can call it even; screwing with the V-2 rockets in Blizna for my family's safety. So why am I risking my life to get the most hated man in the world to England? Might have to rethink this one, Chez considered.

However, something within the Spider's essence rose to the challenge. He could see the logic in bringing closure to the demise of the Third Reich. Closure that demanded he do everything within his power to deliver the snake to justice before the head was cut off. It was at this point, Chez's attention snapped back into reality when he noticed an old black bicycle leaning against a fence post.

With Adolf Hitler balanced precariously on the crossbar, Chez pedaled hard to put even more distance between them and the insane British captain. Hitler took this respite to resume their courtship.

"Czeslaw, that was very impressive, the way you killed that soldier in the tent...."

"I didn't kill him, Mein Führer but he will have the prince of all headaches when he wakes up. Technically, we have committed no crime against the British, so if they catch us we might still escape a firing squad. *That might be a sketchy claim for you, ty lajdaku, but I'm now a British citizen and have absolutely no intention of shitting in my own mess kit,* Chez thought.

"Very smart, I wish I had brave young men like you instead of the traitorous generals who betrayed me.

"You know, I remember meeting your father, Albrecht. He personified everything good about the Aryan race. I hope we can become friends, Czeslaw."

"Yes, Mein Führer, it would be an honor. "*Good God, I want to top this bastard before I throw up. Maybe I'll just pull over and do the world a big favor—and leave his body in a ditch. Or, I could slice him up and leave him in multiple ditches…*" The last thought brought a wry smile to Spider's lips.

"I have quite a few deutschmark in my pocket, Czeslaw. Can we find a village to buy some food?"

"Of course, Mein Führer." *What if the bastard gets recognized and persuades some nut job to shoot me? Better get a little more skin in the game. What was that scheme I heard Bormann talking about? Something about U-boats in Barcelona?*

"If we can get to my brother's place in Hamburg, Wlodek has a boat that could smuggle us all the way across the Baltic."

Hitler could hardly disguise his excitement at Chez's revelation. "Excellent, my young friend." *This is going to work. Let me sweeten the deal over breakfast.*

With heads shaved hairless from their recent disguises, the two bald men could easily be mistaken for brothers, perhaps father and son, as they rolled up to a small village grocery store. The owner was starting his day by putting some tables and chairs outside and while sitting in the crisp morning air eating fresh bread, cheese, cold cuts and drinking coffee, the conversation and sparring continued.

"Czeslaw, tell me more about your brother in Hamburg. Wlodek, was it? Could his boat really reach Sweden?"

"No problem at all, Mein Führer, but where would we go from there?"

"I choose not to tell you everything but I do have the codes for some numbered Swiss bank accounts sewn into the lining of my jacket. I will designate one of those accounts, worth many millions, to you and Wlodek if you help me. There is a catch however." Hitler was giddy with how easy this mind game was developing.

Dangle the bait and the little fish will take the hook.

And for his part, the Spider danced the dance.

All the more reason for me to slit your bloody throat and take all the codes, you dumb Nazi piece of shit. Why the hell did I make that commitment to Paddy? I want to kill this bastard sooooo fuckin' badly right now.

"I do not need money to help you Mein Führer. But what is the catch you refer to?" the Spider lied smoothly.

"I will give you the account number but both of you must accompany me to Sweden. From there, you and I will travel to another location, where we will part. Swiss account numbers are worthless without a pass-code but you will receive them once I am at my final location and you can take them back to Wlodek and receive the funds. This way we both win; I escape to safety, you and your brother become very, very rich.

You stupid little boy, Heinrich Himmler will personally slice you into a thousand pieces before feeding you to the cats and dogs of Barcelona.

"It will be a great honor to serve you, Mein Führer and I understand your need for security, but there are a couple of things that worry me, on behalf of my brother." He looked at Hitler expectantly and did not proceed until the Führer nodded his assent. "When the British forced me at gunpoint to assist in your abduction from the Chancellery Gardens—I was plucked off the street because I speak German—the kidnapping must have created extreme panic within the High Command of the Third Reich. Surely, there must be a nation-wide manhunt for you, even as we sit here?

Come on, Adolf, spill the beans.

Notwithstanding his plans to eradicate this worthless peasant within the next few days, Hitler was so proud of the Bormann Ruse, he leant forward to confide in the young man.

"Nobody, except you and a privileged few are aware that I have actually left the bunker. Several days ago, Reichleiter Bormann substituted doppelgangers for most of the High Command. The Third Reich is essentially over due to incompetent generals who refused to follow my orders. The Fourth Reich will arise from a secret location.

"As we speak, the upper echelon is headed there by independent routes to reunite and rebuild."

Nothing I don't already know. Let's see if we can't push the envelope.

"Mein Führer that is pure genius. However, I would be honored to travel with you for the entire journey if I might eventually serve in the Fourth Reich."

Hitler pondered this new twist for a few seconds before confiding,

"That can be arranged, Czeslaw. Can you speak Spanish by any chance?"

"Si senor, I speak several languages, including Spanish." *Well, I'm sure I will be able to pick it up pretty quickly if I have to. Can't be as tough as English!"* Tell me more stories about the doppelgangers."

Chez projected a fawning devotion and enthusiasm towards the older man; under any other circumstance, he would have been physically sick.

"Well, I see no harm in that, after all, you are now part of my team so you deserve to know how masterful we have been in planning my ... ehr, our future.

"Herr Bormann is the puppet master and will be the last to leave the bunker. He controls every word uttered by Gustav Weler, my doppelganger. The devoted staff will attend a touching wedding ceremony between Weler and some street-floosie Martin found—don't believe I was ever told her name—believing it to be the last official act by our brave Führer before he and his new bride unselfishly commit suicide to save the German people from further conflict. Before you ask, both the bodies will be cremated into unidentifiable ashes in front of loyal witnesses. The most evil triumvirate the world has ever known, Churchill, Truman and Stalin, will jump at any chance to bring closure to their victory and our witnesses will swear to their deathbeds about the veracity of their Führer's last brave and heroic act.

"There will be no search for me; funding is in place; the Fourth Reich is already in existence. Seig Heil!"

Chez jumped to his feet. "Seig Heil!"

As the proprietor of the grocery store glanced around nervously to ensure no one saw this overt display of Nazism, a Russian transport plane was noticed climbing out of an adjacent valley to head east. Five minutes later, a British helicopter flew over them and descended into the same approximate location. Hitler looked concerned with this flurry of aerial activity.

"Could they be looking for us, Czeslaw?"

"Ja, but apparently still focusing attention to the east; I believe we are safe. Excuse me, I need to take a piss before we move on."

With all that activity, I'm willing to bet the Black Widows have somehow made it to the camp. Time to stop this sickening charade and head back to reality. He had already completely dismissed any fortune and nonsense he had just been offered from his mind.

Hitler resumed both a shit-eating grin and his perch on the crossbar and they headed down the valley.

Major problem. It's just a matter of time before he realizes we are headed back to the British camp. Better think of something quick. "Watch out for that tree branch, Mein Führer!" Chez swerved the bike violently, grabbed on to the Nazis chest as if to save him and slammed the heel of his right hand behind Hitler's ear. Both bodies tumbled onto the road. The stunned German Chancellor was not fully conscious, so could not possibly appreciate the body control of the Spider as he rolled on top of his prey, holding him in a sleeper hold until the ageing Führer floated into a deep sleep.

It took every ounce of the young Pole's strength to carry the prone body in a fireman's lift as he righted the bike, mounted the saddle and pushed the vehicle into motion.

"Bryan, that idiot captain apparently tripled the guard on Chez and Hitler. I figure Chez took the initiative and escaped in case numb-nuts had thoughts of a morning firing squad."

"You're telling me that one man can fool an entire battalion and just disappear! At the same time, he is protecting the most hated man in the world; a man with a gimpy arm who can hardly walk!? I am having a little trouble comprehending this. It defies logic, Paddy."

The big man smiled and shook his head. "Remember that insane incident last year? The Spider walking around the V-2 assembly plant in Blizna for an entire night, booby-trapping rockets under the very noses of a crack SS squad. A squad that had no clue he was there—even to this day!"

"How does he do it? Can he really make himself invisible? Moreover, why would he not just kill Hitler, especially after all the Polish people have suffered? How in hell will we ever find him?"

"That's a lot of questions, Bryan. There is no magic or logic, the Spider is just a phenomenal natural athlete and gifted with amazing clarity of thought. He has a very keen sense of duty and my guess is he will try his level best to deliver Hitler to you unharmed.

"As for us finding him—not a fuckin' chance! He will find us."

Staff Sergeant Mike Johnston was playing cards with the rest of the SAS squad on a makeshift table beside Brigadier Zumwalt's helicopter. A body bag within the aircraft contained their late good friend, Billy Fagan and they wanted to honor his spirit by playing gin rummy.

"As long as I don't hear a zipper opening that bag from the inside, I might have a chance of winning this game!"

In sadness, an Armstrong Whitworth Ensign AW.27 was already en route to transport Billy and the team home to England.

A bald man carrying what looked like a very heavy sack over his shoulder rode towards them unsteadily on an old bicycle. Johnston was suspicious and spun away from his cards and into a firing crouch, the Browning as steady as a rock. Jurek restrained the crusty sergeant and called out in recognition.

"Chez, nice day for a bike ride, my friend!" The last time Johnston had seen the Spider was in Braunschweig and his appearance was now completely different.

"Help me get the esteemed Führer off this bike, he must weigh a bloody ton and is getting heavier by the second. Had to knock him unconscious a couple of miles back as I didn't think I could get all the way to the camp before he twigged I was circling back. Hated to have to do that, we were having such a great conversation."

Chez waited for the warriors to stop laughing before he nodded at the helicopter and continued. "I rode by you twice before I was positive you guys had made it. I take it the brigadier wanted to stick his nose in as well?"

"Don't know who is having the worse day, Adolf or Nigel. Bryan and Paddy flew in to give their regards to the good captain but I'm not sure he's having a good time." Mike Johnston gave Chez an enormous wink as the rest of the squad started to laugh. "The lads will look after Mrs. Hitler's little boy, so come with me, Chez."

As he left with Mike, the Spider called back over his shoulder before he left earshot. "Still got that chloroform? Keep him unconscious—and the two of us separated if you can. There might be advantages in him continuing to believe I am his friend.

"Oh, and please let me have me his jacket."

Mike was wearing what could only be described as a shit-eating grin when he strode into the former captain's tent.

"Bryan, Paddy, look what the cat just dragged in."

EPILOGUE

Two Men; A Pole Apart

I t took quite a while for Hitler's eyes to adjust to the darkness of the dank room after he finally regained consciousness from his drugged state. The only source of light came from three slits high in the stone walls. The leader of the Third Reich wore ill-fitting pajamas and found himself tied securely to a bentwood chair. Ten feet in front of him, that big bastard who kidnapped him in Berlin—McBride was the name he recalled—stood menacingly over the young German, Czeslaw Orlowski, whom he noted was dressed in similar fashion to himself and in the same predicament.

So we didn't escape. Somehow, the Brits captured both of us. Maybe I can use the bait of the Swiss Bank

Accounts to bribe this gorilla, Hitler thought. Then, in a panic, he realized his jacket was nowhere to be seen.

McBride was slapping the young German about and yelling at him in a language he couldn't understand at all.

Where am I? Where could this nightmare be taking place? Seems like a dungeon and smells incredibly moldy. I have no doubts the ape-man will turn his attentions to me after he finishes with Czeslaw. Hitler tried not to show his fear as he sought to remember the sequence of events that led to this disaster.

Dammit, the last thing I remember was being on a bike in Germany—then we crashed into a tree branch. I am lucky to be alive—I guess.

Orlowski slumped in his chair and sure enough, McBride swung his attention from the unconscious young man to the Führer. "Where the hell is all the gold you stole?"

Hitler could not understand a word of English and desperately needed Czeslaw as a translator. McBride started to roll up his sleeves, an indication that he was going to inflict pain whether his questions were answered or not. Then the panic-filled Führer caught a glimpse of movement behind the towering colonel.

That amazing young man was bluffing. I think he is going to get out of his bindings if I can buy him a little time, he thought with a surge of hope.

"Ich bin trauriger Oberst, ich kann nichts verstehen, was du sagst," he pleaded dramatically to the colonel and despite his bindings, he performed ridiculously animated attempts at distraction, yelling that he could not understand a word of English.

In response, McBride flew into a spittle-enhanced rage. He was gearing up a fearsome punch when Czeslaw came from behind and smashed a chair into his back. The colonel sank to his knees, eyes rolling upwards before he fell with a crash onto the stone floor. Hitler was further surprised to see the young man dart forward, grab the Ulsterman's sidearm and empty two loud shots into his back. McBride's body, face down on the stone floor, jerked three times then went motionless except for an expanding pool of dark liquid that began to seep out from under his body.

Chez tossed aside the shattered remains of the chair and sucked air into his lungs to counter his efforts.

"Czeslaw, that's the second time you have saved my life. Quickly, get me out of these ropes…"

"Not so fast, Mein Führer, I need a little time to think about this. I have just killed a man so my own death sentence is guaranteed. You, on the other hand, are tied up so they will know you could not have had anything to do with this murder, in which case, they might let you live. Not to mention, I have a much better chance of escaping without you. Remember the last time? I would have been long gone through the forests if I hadn't felt obligated to transport the two of us on a bike—right into a British patrol.

"I believe we are in England and now held prisoners in the Tower of London, so I might be able to get out through Traitors' Gate, swim across the Thames, find the docks and bluff my way onto a supply ship back to Germany.

"I wish you well, Mein Führer. Auf wiedersehen…"

"Remember who I am, you stupid boy. They will kill me anyway, trussed up or not. However, if you are correct and we are in London, I have a close trusted friend here. A friend extremely high up in the British government who has been secretly loyal to Germany throughout this war. He will be able to help us."

"That is ridiculous and I don't believe you. Last time you tempted me, you were going to abandon me with false promises of a pass code to a Swiss account. You really must think I'm a total moron." Then the Spider paused before resuming pensively.

"However, if we were to leave here together, I insist we go to wherever you are planning the Fourth Reich. I must have money, your protection and a job for life. But before we can do any of that, you must tell me where we are going and how the hell your friend can get us out of London."

The Führer relaxed, now convinced he had conquered the young man's mind, so his tone softened as he responded.

"We have purchased 250,000 acres around the town of Bariloche in Patagonia. General Juan Peron and the Argentine government have guaranteed our secrecy and security for generations to come—in return for half the art treasures of Europe. Your golden future is assured, my loyal friend."

Chez pondered the deal before responding, "Okay... Mein Führer, I will get you out of this place or die trying. Assuming we can escape this dungeon, who is this friend we can count on to get out of England?"

Despite being alone in the Tower, save for Chez and a dead colonel, Adolph Hitler glanced furtively around the stone cell before whispering conspiratorially, "The clandestine head of our London operation is Lord Sowood; I know his direct telephone number. Now, get these damn ropes off me."

"You must forgive me, sir, but you are wearing pajamas. Are you saying that you know this man so well you have committed his phone number to memory?"

"Whitehall Two Zero Eight Six," the Reich Chancellor stated in a monotone whilst staring unblinkingly into the young Pole's grey eyes.

Chez made no move towards the Führer of the Third Reich, instead he turned towards the heavy, English-oak door of the cell and thumped it with the heel of his fist. Three bolts were heard to clatter back from the opposite side and the only entrance to the dungeon slowly creaked open. The erstwhile dictator froze in horror as a small, rather rotund man with a walking stick entered the cell, preceded by a cloud of cigar smoke and followed by two, high-ranking men in Royal Navy blues.

The slightly lisping speech of Winston Spencer Churchill was harshened by the hard stone surfaces. "Ah-ha, Adolphus the Hun in person. Please, don't get up on my account." Hitler's jaw dropped in shock that transformed into puzzlement when the two navy men, by insignia an admiral and a commander, both carried chairs into the cell.

"Mr. Orlowski, I would be very much obliged if you would immediately recount, in English, your most recent conversation with Mr. Hitler—but only after you make sure our good friend from Belfast is okay." At this prompt from his Prime Minister, Paddy rolled away from the pool of theatrical blood, sat on the floor and rubbed his head. He then looked across and grinned at the Spider.

"Chez, you could've loosened those chair legs a little more before crowning me but the reality aspect seemed to work, even though that damn Stephens red ink ruined a perfectly good shirt! Did you get everything you needed?"

"I am reasonably sure he told the truth, Paddy. Mr. Churchill, is it okay for me to give you the English version in front of everyone here?"

"Absolutely, I believe you met Admiral Godfrey

and Commander Fleming in Paris. They are both with MI6 and just need confirmation of our mole. No notes will be taken and we will deny this whole incident ever having took place." Chez nodded and reaffirmed all the beans Hitler had spilled.

At the conclusion of the Spider's recount, Churchill turned to both navy men with a satisfied smile. "Sowood! Can't say I'm surprised. It had to be someone close to Halifax."

"Disappointing, Mr. Prime Minister, I know he was your colleague but he was the top of our list of finalists. May we take him into immediate custody?" Churchill gave an affirmative nod and the two spy catchers hurried out, closing the door behind them. The Prime Minister then pulled his chair to within five feet of the Reich Chancellor and sat down.

"Mr. Orlowski, Colonel McBride, please stay. I intend to thank you both personally for fulfilling this magic moment for me." With that, the British and German antagonists faced each other, a historic moment that begged a camera but because of circumstance had to be forever disavowed as having occurred.

"Over the past six years, you have spent a great deal of time and energy trying to visit us here in London. I am sorry if the accommodations are not all you might have expected but this particular building is very well located should you wish to take a stroll over Tower Bridge to the East End. However, as you are responsible for killing hundreds of men, women and children when you blitzed that neighborhood, I strongly recommend that you stay inside during the balance of your very brief stay." His impish intellect relished the moment as he continued after the Spider's translation paused. "This is a very historic building, you know. Been prime riverfront property for almost a thousand years and its Kentish rag-stone proved more than a match for your bombs. Why, Queen Elizabeth the First's Mum, Anne Boleyn, stayed in this very room whilst awaiting her unfortunate beheading over four hundred years ago!"

The jocular tone suddenly vanished and if Adolph Hitler harbored any illusions that he matched Churchill as the greatest orator of the twentieth century, this encounter shattered them beyond reconstruction.

"For the second time this century, Germany has attempted to conquer my country. It is wearisome and, I am sure you will now agree—ill-advised."

Hitler started to sweat profusely despite the cold air prevalent within the Tower of London; Chez dutifully translated Churchill's words with undisguised disgust. The Austrian corporal's coal-black eyes widened in despair as Churchill persisted in driving the reality home.

"Herr Hitler, you have promulgated an unfortunate career out of manipulating the minds of the German people. It is therefore fitting in your last hour that you stand before a German-born Polish man with ethics above corruption. Czeslaw Orlowski could have killed you on many occasions and disappeared with the millions of Swiss Francs with which you tried to bribe him. God knows no sane person would have called foul. Instead, he delivered you and the numbered bank accounts to me as trustee. These funds will not approach recompense for the loss and suffering you have caused to uncountable human beings, but their heirs are the rightful owners of this money."

With unabashed sarcasm dripping from his tongue, he added, "The local rabbi here in London will no doubt be one of the first to write you a thank you note for the share I plan to repatriate with the Jewish people."

"You will never get me to reveal the pass codes. NEVER." Hitler went into a rant, spittle spraying like foam from his mouth, a technique that had rattled his most Teutonic generals. Winston however, sucked slowly on his cigar, smiled softly and responded after Chez translated.

"No need, old chap, Swiss bankers compete ferociously to send their sons and daughters to Adcote, Tudor Hall, Eton and Harrow, not to mention Oxford and Cambridge. His Majesty's government—represented most humbly by myself—can make that opportunity either very easy or impossible for these financiers. No Adolf, I do not believe pass codes will be necessary to the process of repatriating these funds with the peoples you and your Nazi gangsters stole them from."

This frank statement sunk deep into the brain of the former dictator and he came to the realization that he was now left with nothing. Nothing, except perhaps the hope he could argue his legacy in front of the world's press at his War Trials. However, even that forlorn chance was dashed when Churchill performed the coup de grace.

"I really must thank you and Herr Bormann for the elaborate demise you have orchestrated for yourself. As history will recall, in a few short days the Russians will find that petrol flames consumed your body after you blew your own brains out in your concrete palace beneath Berlin. In short, Adolph, in the eyes of the world you never made it out of Berlin; the man I see before me does not exist!

"Our nation will accept much-needed closure and I shall not attempt to rewrite this history. These two gentlemen are going to close the book by assisting you in enjoying a delicious cyanide pill for your last meal. His Majesty's Royal Navy will then transport your body in a weighted sack to an undocumented location somewhere in the North Sea.

"I have no doubt you will rot in hell, since that's where you came from, you filthy bastard!"

Adolph Hitler was numbed into complete silence.

As Churchill was leaving the cell, the Bulldog turned to the Spider and gave him a wonderfully sincere smile that travelled all the way to the corners of his eyes.

"An enormous personal pleasure to finally meet you, Mr. Orlowski. I am extremely aware of your contributions to our war effort." He added with a grin, "And most grateful that you used your enormous talents to combat evil. Should you ever need anything, Chez, you must contact me directly. The British people will always be grateful.

"By the way, does Hitler know who you really are? Only fair you give him one of your infamous business cards, I would think.

"Now, I believe you have Malcolm and Margery McClain's wedding to attend in Blackpool. My very best wishes to them both and, of course, my personal regards to Jadwiga and your extended family."

The ancient oak door closed and the temperature within the stone cell dropped significantly. It could have been from the vacuum caused by the great man's departure but more likely from the cold presence of the Spider. Paddy had seen the look many times before but it still chilled the big Ulsterman to the core.

"You can put this bloody pill back in your pocket, Paddy. It's much too easy a death for him."

"For Poland, Chez," Paddy whispered and turned to face his friend.

"No, not just Poland, for the millions, *millions* of innocents whose lives have been lost or ruined by this bastard," spat the Spider as he pulled a square of paper from his pocket and held it a foot in front of the sad wreck of a man.

Adolf Hitler focused his pleading eyes and puzzled over the crude drawing of an oval with eight legs. Then his brain put it all together and his face contorted in terror.

"You are the Spider? Of course, now it all makes sense. I should never have believed a simple German man could possess your skills...... But you are a lot smaller than I was told!"

His mouth opened wide but the fierce, maniacal scream that had petrified half the world was reduced to a gurgle as the Spider slipped behind him, and holding his forehead firmly, sliced his throat from ear to ear.

"I dare say a lot of people would have liked to do that. I must say, it felt—underwhelming—so I'll have no trouble sleeping tonight."

The two men turned their backs on the empty husk of the most evil man in the world, and walked out of the cell together.

"Paddy, I have to get to a telephone and let a certain young lady know I will be home for dinner."

Then, his mind digressed from the calm, peaceful life of married bliss that awaited him. "Do you think the lads would be up for a trip to South America? I hear they have great wine, steaks, music...and Martin Bormann. Maybe we should talk about this after Malcolm's wedding?"

"Ah well, there y'are now."

The End

AUTHOR'S NOTES

A t the risk of being branded a conspiracy truth-seeker, I have hidden behind this fictional novel as a means of exploring the mystery of Adolf Hitler's suicide. Almost every World War II buff will have come across these theories but for those readers interested in forming their own opinion, I offer the following sources for your entertainment:

Grey Wolf: The Escape of Adolf Hitler, Simon Dunstan and Gerrard Williams, Sterling Publishing, 2011.

Hitler's Escape, Ron T. Hansig, Athena Press, 2005.

Escape from the Bunker, Harry Cooper, Sharkhunters International, 2010.

And a couple of videos, which record the official historic version:

> ***The Bunker*** starring Sir Anthony Hopkins, Time-Life Productions

> ***Downfall***, starring Bruno Gantz, Momentum Pictures

READ A SAMPLE OF

BALLS
OF LEATHER AND STEEL

THE FIRST BOOK IN THE SPIDER TRILOGY

CHAPTER NINETEEN

1943 – Revenge is Sweet

L eft alone with Malcolm in the Brodnik living room, Chez calmly summarized their predicament.

"The Germans will be here shortly, my friend. You must hide in the passage and wait for Savo and his men. They'll get you to Semic and freedom by tomorrow."

"Sounds like you're not coming with me," Malcolm said, frowning.

"If we both leave now, the Nazis will be suspicious of an empty house and might search and find the passage. There might not be enough time for Savo to get back here and rescue us. I'll keep them occupied here for a while before I..."

He broke off abruptly, swinging to squint into

the blaze of headlights that suddenly flooded the interior of the house.

"...join you in the tunnel," Chez finished calmly.

"Shit! Time to scramble!" Malcolm said.

He followed the back of the Spider as it bounded upstairs to get a better view from the front bedroom.

"You sure you want to play the hero?" McClain said uneasily. But then, he had never looked into the eyes of a close combat adversary. Flying Officer McClain had been used to killing his enemy from 20,000 feet.

The odds were not insurmountable as far as Chez was concerned. Outside, on the flat forecourt only two Krupp troop transporters had drawn up, joined by the two motorcyclists; a patrol of fourteen soldiers in all.

"Hardly a full magazine load," Chez judged coldly. He had been up against worse odds, and 'The Spider' had always managed to survive.

Then suddenly, the odds against them lengthened as another pair of headlights materialized behind the Krupps. One of the bikes revved up and turned back towards the new arrival, its headlight clearly illuminating a staff car with an SS major in the front passenger seat.

"Well, well, well," Chez mused softly. "It looks like our favorite Sturmbahnfuhrer has decided to follow this lead himself. That makes it personal for all of us... and in turn, leaves me rather looking forward to the next few minutes."

The soldier who had remained to observe the house was reporting to SS Major von Keller who remained seated, ramrod straight, in his Mercedes.

"Herr Major, two elderly people and two younger men headed up the valley in a small bread truck about twenty minutes ago. I judge that at least two other men remain inside the house."

Von Keller then stepped from the staff car with careful deliberation.

"Corporal, take the other motorcyclist and one troop carrier. Catch that damn bread truck! If it remains headed up the valley, they must be climbing over the top of the mountain to Rogia and then back down into the Drava Valley and Maribor. They have a twenty-minute start but there's only one road. In the meantime, I'll radio for troops from Maribor to block that road at the river. They have no escape. SCHNELL!"

While the pursuers sped off up the valley, von Keller turned sharply to address the remainder of his patrol.

"Until I can determine whether our prime suspects have remained here or taken flight in the bread truck, we will stay to interrogate the two inside. I rather suspect that McClain will be trying to escape in the truck—but he will find himself back here for a little chat regardless."

"In your dreams, Sturmbahnfuhrer," Chez grinned.

"The chances of them finding—let alone catching—Savo in those mountains are somewhere between slim and zero."

Then it was time to focus on the immaculate bastard in the polished black boots and jodhpurs. The major raised a megaphone and addressed the house. Simultaneously five Wehrmacht soldiers trained their headlights and machine pistols on the windows, a sixth staffing the MG-42 light machine gun mounted on the troop carrier.

"I know there are at least two of you in the house. You have five minutes to surrender and step outside."

The surrounding facets of the old marble quarry gave von Keller's already amplified voice an added quality of menace. Malcolm reflected back to the movies he had watched at the Arcadian on Albert Street, goggle-eyed as a kid in Belfast. No money needed from those who had none; two empty jam jars had been enough to get a front row seat. A smile flickered across his face. "Seems this is another fine mess you've got me into, Ollie," he said quietly.

Chez looked blank: going to the cinema had never been part of his childhood prison camp experience but he thought, "Damn, this Irish guy has ice in his veins.—I kinda like that!"

Regardless, their survival time was shortening by the second.

Malcolm blinked, as without warning, his

companion suddenly ripped a sheet from the Brod-niks' bed then pulled up the casement and proceeded to hang the linen outside. McClain was about to blink even harder when the Spider's shout in German took on a most uncharacteristic whine.

"I have Flying Officer McClain here. He is very badly wounded and the occupants of the house were sent to get medical help. We surrender! Allow me a minute to get him downstairs ... but please don't shoot."

Malcolm spoke no German but the meaning was easy to follow. "What the hell ...?" McClain began to blurt before Chez whirled urgently.

"Shut up an' follow me to the Wine Vat in the barn."

Without waiting, the Spider turned and led the way downstairs, navigating each flight in one effort-less jump. On reaching the ground floor, he darted left into the kitchen where a rear door went directly into the barn. By the time Malcolm caught up with him, the young Pole was already holding open the Wine Vat's secret access to the passage. He gestured for Malcolm to enter. With the Irishman inside the void, Chez started to close the secret door from the outside.

"You go ahead, Malcolm. There is one small detail I need to take care of before I catch up."

Sturmbahnfuhrer Abelard Hans von Keller was exceedingly pleased with himself. Although he had not expected it to be this easy, he had the two bastards he wanted and could leave it to others to apprehend the Partizani bit-players in the bread truck.

There was no hurry, which afforded him time to savor his coming rehabilitation in the eyes of his superiors. With the knowledge that McClain was virtually back in the bag with no harm done to his career, von Keller pleasured on being able to exact retribution on that still-mysterious traitor to his Fuhrer's beloved Third Reich; the man with the Berliner accent who had almost pulled off the successful kidnapping of his prize.

Walking briskly back to his staff car, he could already feel the adrenaline coursing through his body. He vividly imagined himself placing his gleaming jackboot between the bastard's shoulder blades before shooting him in front of McClain.

Sliding into his car seat, von Keller reached into the glove compartment, retrieving a short, black ebony cigarette holder into which he carefully pushed a Balkan Black Sobranie. He had never permitted himself to become an inveterate smoker—the Fuhrer would have disapproved—but there were occasions when one could justify a brief, discreet deviation from the SS model of perfection. He thumbed the flint of his silver, monogrammed lighter and pulled the rich, satisfying smoke deep into his lungs. He smiled a cold smile and murmured out loud, "As you stagger through that door, you treasonous cretin, appreciate your last few moments on this earth ..."

The major felt a slight pinprick, the irritation of a mosquito biting his neck. It was a curious sensation in itself. As he swatted it, a dark spray splattered the inside of the windshield in front of him. Puzzled, Hans von Keller slowly raised his warm, wet left hand until he could see the sticky glint of what could only be his own blood. While he was still frowning in confusion, a strong hand clamped across his sagging jaw and he heard a soft Berlin accent from the back seat.

"I am not a treasonous cretin, Herr Major, because I do not consider myself a German. I am Czeslaw Orlowski, a proud Pole and one of those resistance fighters you hold in such contempt. You might know me better as 'The Spider'?"

As von Keller's carotid artery continued to pump out warm blood, his body involuntarily began to shut down. With a supreme effort, he compelled his brain to focus on analyzing the facts: *Unmistakably, he had just heard this same voice from the upstairs window: He had detected neither movement from the house nor the slightest sound since returning to his car: He had not even felt the blade slice his throat.*

He still felt little pain; it made no sense and, for the analytical mind of Sturmbahnfuhrer Abelard Hans von Keller, that came as a terrible revelation.

"Spider, Spinne ...? But you're a myth. You don't exist outside the pipe dreams of your filthy Partisa ..."

Nevertheless, before he slipped down to the eternal flames of Hell, von Keller heard the voice softly utter the last earthly words he would ever hear.

"With fond remembrance of Goran ... and Biba!"

Chez slid silently out of the car and dissolved into the shadows. But his luck finally ran out as he returned to the barn and was climbing to negotiate his way through the roof trusses towards the wine vat. Suddenly, a powerful flashlight snapped a fix on him. He had little option but to freeze.

"Come down right now, whichever one you are, or you'll be shot," demanded Corporal Manfred Gimmstadt, one of three grey-uniformed Wehrmacht troopers in the barn.

Then, a most unexpected event occurred.

"I believe you may be looking for me as well?" Flying Officer Malcolm McClain called almost conversationally from behind them.

Without understanding his English, the three soldiers whirled in shock. Gimmstadt re-directed his torch towards the new challenge. When, the confused corporal directed the beam of his flashlight back into the rafters, he found them empty.

"Verdammt!" he snarled, quickly returning his torch to illuminate McClain. This caused a second furious soldier to train his Schmeisser on the seemingly nonchalant British flyer. The third slung his machine pistol across his chest and motioned for McClain to step forward, hands above his head, to be searched.

Commendable standard practice, only Gimmstadt did not realize he was dealing with a man from Belfast. McClain's demeanor transformed into a whirl of action as he took one step forward to grab both lapels of the German's uniform. In a crisp motion, he pulled the soldier towards him, simultaneously smashing his forehead into the bridge of the trooper's nose. A brutally unsophisticated but extremely effective tactic known colloquially as giving '*a stitch*' by those fighting for survival around the Springfield Road.

Allowing his victim's semi-conscious body to slump to the floor, Malcolm swung on the second soldier and in a continuous, flowing movement, stabbed the ball of his right foot straight into the man's crotch. With this leg still airborne and the unfortunate soldier already doubling in agony, Malcolm completed the scissor kick with a roundhouse left foot to the soldier's right temple.

When kicking a leather ball, a professional

football player's boot can travel at over 75 miles per hour, and McClain had perhaps the most lethal left foot in the game. The second guard was brain-dead before his body hit the floor. Two down in as many seconds, McClain was already pivoting to dispatch the last captor when he stopped in his tracks.

Before his eyes, the beam of light that had started the debacle began to rise steadily towards the rafters. Then the torch dropped with a clatter to the accompaniment of a strangled gasp. McClain could just make out Gimmstadt's frantically flailing jackboots as the corporal swung higher and higher. Malcolm recovered the lamp to illuminate the elevated soldier dangling helplessly, his neck pinioned in the vice-like grip of the Spider's thighs. Hanging effortlessly from the rafters, Chez rotated his hips savagely, first to the left and then right. There came a snap and Corporal Manfred Gimmstadt's corpse joined his inert comrades on the floor of the barn.

"Well done, Chez," Malcolm announced almost matter-of-factly as the Spider landed like a cat in front of him. The young Pole's respect for his foreign charge had tripled in the last few seconds.

"Now for the rest of those bastards!" McClain said but Chez restrained him with a hand.

"Enough, Malcolm. Remember, my prime mission is to get you safely out of here. Though, I'm starting to think that you are looking after me!"

Just as they were ready to close the secret passage door, they heard urgent shouting from the courtyard.

"Hold on here for now, Malcolm," Chez grinned as he caught the gist of the guttural conversation. "If they've found what I suspect they've found, then we might not need to negotiate that long damp passage."

Apparently, the three Wehrmacht soldiers remaining outside in the yard with von Keller's increasingly nervous SS driver, had become restless while awaiting Chez's promised surrender. Even more unsettlingly, Corporal Gimmstadt's party who had entered the barn to prevent any back door escape had not reappeared. Nor had they heard the reassuring sound of shots from within. Direction was needed ... *but where the hell was Major von Keller when the arrogant bastard was needed?*

They soon found out. The panicked shouting Malcolm and Chez had heard provided evidence enough. To compound their disarray, the soldiers then ran back to the barn to locate their missing men and tripped over three bodies, only one of which retained any signs of life.

The decimated squad's sergeant, a grizzled veteran of the Russian front, stared at the seemingly vacant farmhouse and made a battlefield decision.

"Load the bodies into the Krupp, leave the staff car for now and we'll return to Maribor for orders!"

Only while they were carrying the dead major to

the troop carrier did one of them see the salutation, pinned to Sturmbahnfuhrer von Keller's chest by the Thiers Issard cutthroat razor Chez had commandeered from the Brodniks' bathroom.

The square of paper showed the infamously feared caricature of a spider. Beneath the oval with eight legs was a terse message in German.

"To The Fuhrer. With the compliments of the Spider!"

ABOUT THE AUTHOR

G uy Butler was born in Blackpool where his
father, Malcolm Butler, did in fact play for
the famous Blackpool Football Club. When his Dad
retired, the family moved back to Belfast, Northern
Ireland, where its roots go back to the 17th century.
Guy spent his youth playing soccer all day and bass
guitar in a band called 'Johnny and the Teenbeats' all
night. The other group in town was Van Morrison and
Them, who went on to much bigger and greater things.

Despite the resultant horrific grades, he managed
to get accepted into Queens University's College of
Architecture, where he played soccer for the Northern
Ireland national colleges' team against Wales, Scotland
and England.

Guy currently owns a boutique architectural firm that specializes in golf resort design all over the world. While *Balls of Leather and Steel* was mainly written at 35,000 feet en route to China, Nigeria and the Far East, Guy chiseled time away from his busy architecture office and home life to craft *A Gordian Web*.

The Butler family lives in Orlando, Florida. Learn more about Guy Butler and his architecture and design firm by visiting www.guybutlerarchitect.com.

Made in the USA
Columbia, SC
16 February 2021